FOREVER OURS

FOREVER SERIES
BOOK 3

JENNIFER J WILLIAMS

Copyright © 2022 by Jennifer J Williams
All rights reserved.

This book is a work of fiction. Any similarity to real people, places, or events is completely coincidental. No part of this book may be reproduced in any form or by any electronic or mechanical means, including information storage and retrieval systems, without written permission from the author, except for the use of brief quotations in a book review.

This book is intended for audiences over the age of 18. It contains mature subject matter. If you do not like steamy sex scenes, adult content, and all the smut, this book is not for you. Trigger warning: pregnancy complications

Cover designed by Wanderlust Ink and Tome

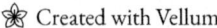 Created with Vellum

For my amazing arc team who deal with my chaos and shenanigans while sending me all the times I mess up the character names.

CHAPTER ONE

Harper

God dammit.

This is not how today was supposed to go.

I had grand plans for the day.

Finish work early.

Order my favorite takeout.

Get in my comfy clothes and watch an episode of Gilmore Girls for the umpteenth time while I enjoy a glass (or bottle) of wine.

Spend an hour with my favorite BOB: battery-operated boyfriend. Cuz your girl is in a fucking dry spell with men. Well, except for two nights. So we won't talk about that major indiscretion.

Instead, I'm frantically packing up my apartment because my landlord just evicted me from work and home. See, I live in an apartment above my salon. I'm a hair stylist, and I love it.

And frankly, I love my one-minute commute to work. I've been living above the salon for three years, and suddenly my landlord decided to almost double my lease on both places.

When I said I couldn't afford that, he evicted me from the apartment. He offered to let me pay in other services, which, *duh*, I said no. Because my landlord is about sixty-five years old, he always looks like a greasy pimp and smells weirdly of sauerkraut and salmon. It's not a good look, and it's definitely not an appealing smell.

My girlfriends don't know. Em just had babies. Liv is about to marry Liam. I don't want to stress them out. My parents live in Florida, and I don't have any other family here. And even if they did live here, they've been 'hands off' in their parenting style since I was a tween. I basically raised myself. I only talk to them a couple of times a year. Once I hit the legal age of adulthood, they were long gone. And frankly, I wasn't sad to see them leave.

I've never been the type to have a massive group of friends. I'm perfectly content with my small circle of ride-or-die girls. Seeing how they're slowly pairing off with men, I should probably start branching out and finding some new singletons to bond with. It's hard, though. I know I'm a lot to take on. My filter is...well, it can be nonexistent. I'm also always rocking a resting bitch face that can scare small children. Once you've scared one small child, you learn to avoid them, which is why I always try to avoid the little crotch goblins. Em's kids are adorable, though, and the only two that I'm willing to hold. Well, only for a few minutes. I'm not dealing with poop.

I only employ one other stylist in my salon, and she has her own family. So I don't have a plan other than moving everything into a storage facility and then maybe living in my car. There's literally no one I can ask right now. Well, almost no one. But do I really want to go there?

I'm so fucking stressed, and the only person I can think of who might help me is Owen. But our history is ... complicated.

I've known of Owen for most of my life. He's sort of always been in the background of my mind since I was a teenager. Once Liv and I became close, Owen was always there because of his friendship with Nathan, Liv's brother. I've always harbored a crush on Owen, and he's known about it for almost as long as I have. Maybe a crush is too strong of a word. I've always found him attractive. Which is why he pesters me all the fucking time. He knows it infuriates me to no end.

Owen is gorgeous. He is too good-looking for his own good, and he knows it. He's a self-proclaimed man-whore. Owen is a little on the shorter side for guys, just under six feet tall, but he makes up for it with washboard abs, luscious chocolate brown hair, and the darkest eyes I've ever seen. When he smiles, I basically have an orgasm. Every fucking time. Don't even get me started on how he dresses: the man rocks a suit like no one else.

I'm so incredibly attracted to him until he opens his mouth. Then, the man just won't stop arguing with me. He will fight about anything. I can say the moon is out, and he'll squabble about the time of day, and that clearly, I must be wrong. Sometimes he does it out of spite because no one can make me blow my top faster than him. Other times he argues just to argue. His ability to find fault in anything I say and then argue about it is why he makes a good lawyer.

In some ways, maybe we'd make a good connection. I've got a fiery personality to go with my natural auburn curls that have a mind of their own and generally stick out in every direction. I don't back down from a fight with him. It's a weird kind of foreplay with Owen. All that arguing leads to mind-blowing sex. Ask me how I know that.

Twice now, he's shut me up by kissing me and making me

forget how to breathe. What that mouth can do ... holy hell. The man is gifted with his tongue. Best sex of my life.

And both times? Owen slipped out in the darkness of night and never mentioned it again. It is like it never happened. A figment of my imagination. But I know it happened. My body reacts to his every time we're in the same space. I can feel every molecule pulling me toward him, begging me to let us find that bliss again. The most excruciating pleasure I've ever experienced.

All I can afford right now is the doubled rent for the salon space. I don't care about living in my car or storage facility. But I care about my salon and the other stylist with a family to support. I'll make do. But as I look around at the years of memories I've made here, I dissolve into a puddle of emotion and drunkenness.

So here I sit, in a pile of my belongings and haphazard trash bags full of clothes, hiccuping into my second bottle of wine. And the only person I can call is the one man who bugs the shit out of me. And the one person I know has the power to absolutely destroy me.

In a moment of sheer weakness, I tap his contact and hold the phone up to my ear.

"Hello, Harper. Fancy you calling me on a Friday night," Owen drawls into the phone. I can hear lots of noise in the background, so I know he's out trolling for pussy.

"Owen," I hiccup.

I hear a commotion and then a door slamming. Suddenly the phone is quiet.

"What happened, Harp? What do you need?" he asks.

"I need your help, Owen," I say quietly.

"I'll be there in thirty minutes."

CHAPTER TWO

Owen

Fuck my life.

Seriously, just fucking *fuck* my life.

I'm generally a happy-go-lucky dude. I mean, what do I have as reasons to be unhappy? I'm single, have great friends, am good-looking, and have a great job that pays well.

But at this fucking moment? Fuck my life.

I'm out trolling for pussy. Not even gonna sugarcoat it. I haven't had good sex in ... well. In awhile. Don't even want to admit who that was with because she'd never let me live it down if she knew she was the best I've ever had.

In any case, I'm at a bar on the far east side of Colorado Springs. It's a good hour or more from home in Mountain Springs. I come all the way to places like this to meet a woman and hopefully never see her again. I don't lead women on. I let them know right from the beginning that this is a one-night thing. They'll get theirs multiple times if I'm on my game and feeling super generous, and I'll get mine.

So, why ... *why* is fucking Amelia McCallister at this bar.

This woman is bat-shit crazy.

She's been after Nate, Liam, and me since high school. The worst part is that she's married and doesn't even try to hide it. She's got her ring on right now. Just another prime example of why I'll never be in a relationship.

My small-town law firm is essentially a general practice firm. I handle all kinds of things thrown my way, from estate planning to personal injury or bankruptcy. But what I do most is in family law. Nothing makes a person more adverse to relationships than handling divorce and custody battles. And trust me, I watched my parents battle it out for *years* over stupid shit. Why bother focusing on your kids when you can fight over a mint-condition Nolan Ryan baseball card from 1974? It literally goes for two hundred bucks online, but back in the day, my parents fought over it. They fought over everything.

My sister Danielle and I were pawns in their relationship. Dani is five years younger than me. An 'unexpected surprise,' as my mom said. One night after a bottle of whisky, my dad told me oh so eloquently that Dani was a 'drunken mistake.' I've never told Dani that, but she's never had a close relationship with our father.

After their incredibly tempestuous and exhausting divorce, my father moved to California. He promptly found an upgraded wife much closer to my age than his. Their marriage only lasted a few years. Wife number three didn't even last an entire year, and wives four and five were back-to-back over eighteen months. He's currently engaged, and my new potential stepmother is twenty-eight. Ten years *younger* than me.

My mother never remarried. Instead, she spends all her

time spewing vitriol about my father and stalking his whereabouts on social media. She, thankfully, moved to Denver, so I don't have to see her as often as she expects. I can only handle so much complaining about the past.

My sister decided to get the hell out of Colorado and moved to the east coast. We try to FaceTime every month, but it doesn't always happen. We aren't exactly close, but we don't have a bad relationship either.

So how did I end up thinking fuck my life?

Well, as Amelia McCallister stalks toward me with determination in her eyes as I'm talking up the cute blonde to my right, I know my night isn't going to end up with my face between the blonde's legs. Because I really need to buck this dry spell and put Harper behind me. If I can't get behind her, I need to be able to get behind someone else. And fuck them hard.

But I know Amelia will do something to mess up my night.

Ever since both Nathan and Liam settled down, Amelia has been on a tear. Her husband doesn't even care. He's a defense attorney, so we run in the same circles. Because he covers the county, he keeps an apartment in Colorado Springs. I assume he's got side pieces, too. Amelia graduated the year before I did, but due to the amount of plastic surgery she's had, she actually looks much older.

"Owen," Amelia coos as she sidles up next to me and has the nerve to put her hand on my inner thigh, almost touching my dick. "I've been looking for you!"

The blonde looks nervously between us and then sends me a questioning look. Before I can say a word, Amelia turns and snarls at the blonde. Becky? Bailey? Shit. I already forgot her name.

"You can go now. I'm with him," Amelia says triumphantly.

"The fuck you are!" I yell as I push her away. "I swear, Beth, I don't know her. She's not with me."

"Oh, please. We went to high school together. His name is Owen Taylor. He's an attorney. I know where he lives," Amelia says with glee.

"Jesus, you know where I live? Are you stalking me?" I ask Amelia before looking at Barb. Fuck, that's not her name. What is her damn name?

"I'll leave you two alone, Owen. And by the way, if you hadn't been staring at my breasts the entire time we were talking, you might remember my name is Britney," she says with disdain as she jumps down from her bar stool and flounces away.

Oh, yeah. That's why I kept talking to Britney. Dumb as a box of rocks, but girls named Britney are almost always wild in the sack.

I attempt to turn away from Amelia to walk in the other direction, but she grabs my arm.

"Take your fucking paws off me, Amelia," I snarl.

"You sure you don't want to have my paws on you elsewhere?" she says as she slides her hand to grab my junk through my suit pants.

"Are you fucking serious?" I yell as I jump back. "Did you really just do that?"

She shrugs.

"Come on, Owen. We could have some fun. I know you don't want a relationship, and neither do I. Just want to have some no-strings sex. I have a fantasy about doing it in a club restroom ..." she trails off and waggles her brows suggestively. I can't hide the sheer revulsion that covers my face.

"I don't know how many people need to tell you this, Amelia. It's never going to happen. Never. Gonna. Happen. Get that through your botox-ridden filler-full face. Did you follow me here? I have no problem getting a restraining order.

You *do* know a good defense attorney, so I'm sure you'll have no problem explaining this," I tell her. Her eyes narrow in anger.

"You really want to play that card, Owen? You think I don't know how you fucked your way through the public defender's office?" she says.

"Main difference here is I'm single. Not married. Unattached. And every single one of those women knew that. But, of course, I also made sure none of them were married because I may be a man whore, but I'm not a home wrecker," I tell her pointedly.

Amelia's eyes flash with anger as she turns like she's going to lash out and strike me, but I grab her arm as it's airborne.

"I wouldn't do that if I were you," I whisper menacingly. "Just like your husband, I'm an attorney. And I have no problem pressing charges."

Amelia seethes and then cries out as she attempts to remove her arm from my grasp.

"Someone help! He's hurting me!" she shouts, and people turn our way. I release her arm and attempt to step back before a guy grabs me by both arms.

"You put your hands on a woman?" he says coldly.

"Just to stop her from hitting me," I reply, trying to keep my composure. Again, I say, *fuck my life*.

"Ma'am, you okay?" the guy says to Amelia, who is excellently playing the victim. Damn, she can even cry on command.

"I think so," she stammers, and I can't help but roll my eyes.

"Let's take this guy out back and show him what we think of abuse," the guy says to his friend, who enthusiastically nods.

Great. All I wanted was a quick lay, and now I'm going to get the shit kicked out of me.

I try to explain to the guys that they have it wrong, but

they're not listening. Amelia is trailing behind them gleefully, obviously wanting to see the torture.

Once out behind the bar, I've barely turned around before pain swipes across my cheek, and then I'm doubled over after being sucker punched in the gut. Then I'm unceremoniously pushed to the ground before I feel a heel of a work boot stand on the side of my head.

"Any last words, abuser?" the guy taunts me.

"Yeah. Ask her why I grabbed her arm," I force out, the pressure of his foot on my face leaving hardly any room for my mouth to move.

"He was gonna hit me!" Amelia cries out.

"Fucking liar," I snarl.

"I am not a liar," she says.

"You gonna tell your husband about tonight? How about when you tried to proposition Liam in his squad car? Or how you tried to get Nathan's wife fired because you were pissed he was with her?" I say as the guy finally removes his boot from my head. I scramble up and step away from the three of them. "You followed me here, you convinced the girl I was with that you were with me, and then *you* tried to hit *me*. I grabbed your arm to stop you. I've never hit a woman, Amelia."

The guy turns to me with a look of confusion on his face. He then turns to Amelia.

"Ma'am, is this true?" Amelia's stunned expression answers him right as the bar door swings open, and a breathless bartender emerges.

"He's telling the truth. I watched them all night. She's not a victim," the bartender says. Amelia screeches and turns to run away, tripping twice. None of us attempt to help her. Once she's out of sight, the guy turns to me.

"Um, damn, man. I'm sorry for that," he says sheepishly. I shrug.

"It's okay. She's a viper. Known her for over twenty years,

and she's never gotten any better," I tell him. I turn to walk back into the bar so I can get my coat and leave.

"Uh, are we cool, man? You gonna call the cops?" the guy stammers nervously.

"Nah. I really don't want to deal with that tonight. We're cool."

He sighs in relief and slaps me on the back. We trudge back into the bar, and I grab my coat. I sweep my eyes over the parking lot to see if I can find Amelia or her Lexus. We all know her damn car because she's a fucking nut job who stalks all of us. I hope she's tucked tail and will lick her wounds elsewhere.

As I'm about to walk out into the parking lot, my phone rings. I'm surprised to see Harper's name and even more surprised that it's relatively late on a Friday night. Is this a booty call?

"Well, hello, Harper. Fancy you calling me on a Friday night," I drawl, expecting her to seethe and spout something back at me. Instead, I hear a sniff and the unmistakable sounds of crying.

"Owen."

My heart rate immediately accelerates as I can hear the pain in her voice. I walk quickly out of the bar, the door slamming behind me. I need quiet to better listen to her. Something is wrong. She wouldn't call me otherwise.

Harper is one of the strongest people I know. Not even the strongest woman: one of the strongest people. She doesn't take shit from anyone. For her to call me crying? Something bad definitely happened.

"What happened, Harp? What do you need?" I say urgently.

"I need your help, Owen," she whispers.

"I'll be there in thirty minutes," I respond.

I gingerly slide into the front seat of my Infiniti QX60. It's not an incredibly flashy SUV, but it does the job. I wanted an SUV for the crappy roads every winter, and Infiniti fits the 'I'm a lawyer' code. Some attorneys might drive Bentleys or Jaguars, but us small-town lawyers have more sense. And less budget.

I'm about to attempt an hour's drive in thirty minutes. Fortunately, the roads are mostly empty this late on a Friday night. I have many connections with the sheriff's office and the CSPD should I get pulled over.

But I need to get to Harper. I have this insane need to get to her, to protect her from whatever has happened. My mind is sliding through all the possibilities. She's not close to her parents. She wouldn't be calling me if something happened to Liv. Their wives would call me if anything happened to Nathan or Liam. She said she needed 'help.' This has to be about her landlord. That's the only acceptable conclusion.

The only 'help' I've ever given her was to shut her up a few times when we were arguing, and the only thing I could think of was kissing her into silence. Which led to the best sex of my entire fucking life. Because, apparently, hate sex is really amazing. And while I absolutely think Harper hates me, I don't hate her at all. I find her intoxicating and alluring. If I thought I could get away with just fucking her without a commitment, I'd sign up for that in a millisecond. But Harper deserves more than that. Someone will come along and snatch her up. It'll suck watching her get her happy, but I'm not cut out for the relationship bullshit. Owen Taylor is single as a pringle and definitely gonna stay that way.

But, man. The sex? The sex was life-changing.

CHAPTER THREE

Harper

Twelve months ago

It's a rare night when I have an opportunity to hang out with Liv and her new friend Emily, who works with Liv. I really like Em. She's got this sweet southern personality. And Liv's already told me Nathan and Em have crazy chemistry.

Using liquid courage, I goad Em into giving me details on her run-ins with Nathan. I may be in a self-imposed sexual moratorium, but I'm all for forcing others to get out there. Gonna live vicariously through friends. Too many recent ghostings and bullshit 'what's your favorite color' questions on dating apps have made me take a step back.

Besides, in the back of my mind, I compare anyone to Owen. Which, in all honesty, pisses me off. I get that it's a subconscious thing. But I don't *want* to want Owen. I really don't. He's just so delicious. If he could not speak at all, he'd be perfect. But, once he opens his mouth, I'm reminded why I don't want to want him.

In any case, as I see Nathan, Liam, and Owen walk into Peaks Bar, our favorite local joint in town, I simultaneously try to hide from Owen and watch how Nathan interacts with Emily.

"What's going on with Harper here? Has she already reached her limit for the evening?" Emily teases with her southern twang, which I can already tell comes out more when she's drinking.

"Nope. She's got a thing for Nathan's buddy, Owen, and she doesn't want him to see her," Olivia laughs. I slap her arm.

"Shut up! That is privileged information, dammit!" I seethe. Em immediately asks why I'm hiding. I explain that I overheard Owen recently talking about the women in our town. Specifically, why he won't date anyone here. According to Owen, there's no one here worthwhile to fuck, let alone anyone to date.

The fact that I live here was not lost on me. Broke my little teenage heart that had a crush on my best friend's brother's best friend. Whew, that's a mouthful.

It again solidified, however, that Owen is much more attractive when he keeps his damn mouth shut.

I manage to redirect the conversation back to Emily and watch with avid interest as Nathan sits next to her. As soon as he sat down, sexual tension exploded in the room. I swear, if they don't end up together, I have no faith in love. I could feel their auras pulling toward one another. I'm not typically one to go for all that natural energy mumbo-jumbo, leaving that to my stylist Tori at the salon, but I think we all could feel their connection.

When Em decides to leave and Nathan trails after her, I'm saying goodbye to Liv when Owen comes back to our table.

He and Liam had roamed around talking to different people for the last hour, so I relaxed and enjoyed a few drinks. As Owen approaches, my spine stiffens as I ready myself for battle. Because Owen lulls you into a false sense of security and then attacks at the most unexpected times.

"Either of you ladies need a ride?" he asks casually.

"No," I blurt out. Owen's eyes widen.

"Jesus, Harper. Pull the gigantic stick out of your ass and relax for once," he mutters with a chuckle.

"Excuse me?" I half-yell. "Just because I don't want a ride from you, I have a stick up my ass?"

"Yeah, you really do," he says, staring me down. "I was just being nice."

"Why were you being nice, though? I thought no one here was worth it," I say viciously. I don't even notice Liv has slipped between us and quietly left the bar. Owen and I are just staring each other down. In hindsight, I'll see this as insane sexual tension, the same tension I saw between Em and Nate. But right now, I'm just pissed.

"What the fuck are you talking about?" Owen asks.

"Forget it," I tell him, huffing. I grab my purse and walk to the door. My apartment is only two blocks away. I intended to walk home anyway. Owen follows me out the door.

"No, I'm not going to forget it. Tell me what you meant," he says.

"It doesn't matter," I mumble, picking up my pace as I cross the street. I'm speed walking at this point, trying to get away from Owen.

"It does matter. I want to know why you said that," Owen says. I refuse to answer. I cross another street and reach the entrance to my apartment, hoping once I unlock the door to the stairs, Owen will take that as an undeniable sign to leave.

He doesn't.

As I pull open the door, his hand reaches out and grabs the door next to my head.

"What did you mean, Harper?" he says quietly. The feel of his hot breath wafting over the skin of my neck gives me goosebumps, which somehow pisses me off even more. He's not allowed to make me feel good.

I whip around to face him but falter when I see how close he is to me. Our faces are only a few inches apart, our chests almost touching. With my heels on, I'm not too much shorter than him. But, God, he's so fucking gorgeous. And that infuriates me.

"You want to know what I'm talking about?" I ask him, malice dripping from my tone. He nods. "I heard you, Owen. I heard you tell Liam that there was no one in Mountain Springs you'd even fuck, let alone date. That's why you go to Colorado Springs looking for women."

Owen noticeably pales.

"How did you hear that?" he asks quietly.

I laugh with derision.

"Jesus, Owen. Sometimes you are so oblivious. I was right behind you at the diner when you told Liam. Liam knew I was there. Blows my mind that you didn't," I comment.

"Why do you care where I find women, Harper?" he asks, cocking his head to one side with a smirk slowly growing.

"I don't *care*, Owen. It was just a comment that was incredibly disrespectful to all the women who live here," I say defensively.

"Including you, obviously," he comments.

"Well, I do live here, so ..." I trail off.

The smirk grows.

"Aww, that's so sweet, Harp. Love knowing you're still pining for me after all these years," Owen comments with a smile, but his tone has dropped significantly. His pupils are dilated, and his breathing appears to have quickened. What the hell? Is this conversation turning him on? It sure as hell is turning me on. I need to get a handle on things.

"Whatever, Owen. You'd be lucky to get with someone like me," I mutter.

"Oh yeah? You think you'd rock my world?"

"I know I would, asshole," I retort.

"Damn, baby, that's amazing pillow talk," Owen drawls. My eyes widen when he uses the term of endearment. Him calling me baby? Holy shit. That went straight to my core. Can't let him know it affected me so much. I step closer to him, our noses touching.

"Yeah, *baby*, I know I'd rock your world. You'd be surprised by what I can do with my tongue," I whisper against his lips.

I really shouldn't have been so surprised when his lips smash against mine, and my body is yanked to his.

I shouldn't have been surprised when we stumbled up the stairs together into my apartment or when he took me the first time against the door. Or when he pulled me into the shower and fucked me with his tongue, making me come so many times I blacked out. Or when he fucked me from behind, against my headboard, where I had the best orgasm of my life.

But I really shouldn't have been surprised when he snuck out in the middle of the night. And the next time I saw him, he acted like I didn't exist. Like that night never happened.

No, I really shouldn't have been surprised. That is Owen's M.O., after all. Dine and dash. Just never thought I would be the meal or that it would be the best meal of my entire life. If I had difficulty comparing men to Owen before this, it would be essentially impossible after.

CHAPTER FOUR

Owen

I know I shouldn't have snuck out.

But...

It's *Harper*. I was not prepared for that. For the chemistry. For the connection. What the fuck was that??

Listen. There's always been a little bit of tension between us. I get that. But for it to explode like a bomb of pleasure? Nope. I don't know how to handle that. And my typical reflexes took over, thank fuck. Got the hell out of there in the darkness of night like a damn criminal. I feel guilty as hell for leaving her like that, but also incredibly relieved. Laying in her bed, listening to her breathe, I was spiraling. Everything I thought I knew about Harper was up in the air.

I took one last look at her striking naked silhouette as I snuck out. Jesus. The curves that I now know intimately will permanently be embedded in my mind. That hourglass figure is what wet dreams are made of. I've never been crazy about stick figures. I prefer women with some meat on their bones ... but I also don't discriminate when I need a quick fuck. If you're unattached, I find you attractive, and you're willing, let's fucking go.

But I've never ... and I literally mean *never* ... taken a woman multiple times in one night. I don't know what came over me. It was like I had to erase every memory she had of any other man. Lost track of the number of times she came. I was completely possessed.

I'm all for giving a woman pleasure. A woman comes first, in my opinion. And hopefully, more than once. But I don't necessarily go out of my way to continue her pleasure. One-night stands are a get-in and get-out situation. I don't stay over. Once she falls asleep, I'm out. It's why I've never brought a woman back to my house. My space, my sanctuary.

But with Harper ... I wanted to stay. I wanted to wake up next to her and get her on my tongue again. I wanted to have breakfast with her, maybe fuck her again before lunch. And I've *never* wanted that before. It fucked me up. So I tore out of there.

I'm just about to turn thirty-nine. I've got a great life, one that I'm comfortable in. So feeling what I felt with Harper is putting a massive kink in my grand plan of living a bachelor lifestyle. And I don't know how to process that.

So, for now, I'll do what I do best. Live in denial that it ever happened. Stay as far away from Harper as possible. And not tell a soul that she was the best sex of my life.

I MANAGED to go two months before running into Harper again. And if looks could kill, I'd be dead immediately. The hostility came off her in waves. Not that I blame her. I'm a dick. I know it, and she knows it. I never try to get with the same woman twice, which is why I've avoided Harper like the plague. Didn't trust myself around her.

In the last two months, I've struck out more times than I'd care to admit. And it's never on the girl's end. It's always me. I can't stop thinking about Harper. This is the longest I've ever gone without sex since I was a teenager. I'm becoming an incredibly surly bastard because of it.

So when Harper glares at me, I glare right back. Of course, this is all her fault.

"Satan," Harper seethes as she stares daggers at me.

"Oh, aren't you hilarious, Daenarys," I growl. Her eyes narrow.

"Really? That's what you're going with?" she says, rolling her eyes.

"Hey, if the bat-shit crazy shoe fits ..." I counter, shrugging.

"You are such an asshole," Harper mutters.

"And you are ..." I trail off.

"What? What am I, Owen? Go ahead, finish your sentence."

I sigh, suddenly acutely frustrated, turned on, and pissed off, all at the same time. I don't know which emotion to focus on.

"Forget it. Not worth the time," I mumble.

"Oh, I'm well aware of how you feel about women here, Owen. So why are you even here? We're all beneath you, remember? No one you'd date, let alone fuck," Harper says as her voice floats across the bar. Great. Now everyone is looking at me.

"Jesus, Harp. Did everyone need to hear that?" I ask. I wasn't sure which emotion to focus on before, but I damn sure know which one I'm letting lead the way now. Fucking *pissed*.

"Worried you won't be able to catch any tail here, Owen? Poor little Owen. I'm sure you're gonna be so sad," she whines with a fake sad face.

"For fuck's sake, Harper. Let's talk about *your* sex life. When was the last time you got some action? You could use it. Loosen you up a bit," I say as I dramatically wave my hand up and down her body, suggesting she's tightly wound. She can't know that I think she looks fucking phenomenal, and I'd love to lick every damn inch of her skin.

"Last week, actually."

Hold up.

Wait ... what?

I stare at Harper incredulously, shock evident on my face. She had sex last week? No. There's no fucking way. I've been unable to get it up for anyone else, but she has?

"Seriously?" I stammer.

Her eyes don't leave mine as she slowly nods, but I notice a slight hesitation. I step closer to her.

"Someone else has been in your pussy in the last seven days, Harper? Someone else tasted you? Someone else knows how you sound when you come?" I say quietly. Her breathing quickens, but she doesn't answer. "Tell me the truth, Harper."

She sighs.

"No."

I unclench my fists and shake out my hands. I didn't even realize I'd dug my nails into my palms. I'm relieved Harper hasn't been with anyone else, and at the same time, I'm furious with myself for having this reaction.

"I should take you over my fucking knee for lying to me," I mutter.

She inhales quickly.

"You wouldn't dare," she whispers.

"Just try me, Red," I whisper back.

My cock is straining so hard against my pants that I think

it will break through and pull itself toward Harper. I'm so fucking hard that I'm surprised I'm still standing, with all the blood going straight to my groin.

I'm about two seconds away from dragging Harper out of the bar when Liam walks up, and our eye contact breaks. Harper steps back, and I can see the exact moment she regrets our entire interaction.

"I have to go," she says as she turns and stumbles toward the door.

"What did you do?" Liam asks me, his eyebrow cocked in question.

"Nothing."

"Fucking liar. Seriously, what is going on with you two?" he asks again.

"Nothing."

"Yeah, none of us believe that."

"Well, believe it. Nothing going on with Harper and me."

Liam shrugs, but I can tell he doesn't believe me. In all honestly, I don't even really believe me. There's something there. Something I need to discover. Just really don't know how to do that.

CHAPTER FIVE

Harper

Owen and I have only been in the same vicinity a couple of times over the past few months. We, of course, were at the hospital after Emily got shot by her sister. Owen refused to look at me. He seemed much grumpier than I'd ever seen him. He's typically a happy-go-lucky guy, so I'm confused about his attitude.

I know I shouldn't have teased him when I saw him at the bar over the summer. He just gets under my skin so damn easily! Honestly, I haven't been with anyone. Haven't even had a date. I'm consumed with work and trying to keep my landlord off my back. He's begun to hint that he'd be willing to lower my rent if I spend time with him outside of work. Hard pass. Eww.

It's now Thanksgiving, and I'm headed to Liv and Nate's mom's house with reinforcements. I'm not showing up there without some kind of buffer for myself. An old friend is visiting his cousin, and I invited them both to come as 'dates' for Olivia and me. I know Liv and Liam have their own secret issues, so I figure it'll also benefit her.

Declan and Logan are great guys, but Liv and I aren't interested in them at all. In fact, I didn't even tell Liv I was bringing the guys. She was as surprised as everyone else. To see the look on Liam's face when we walked in was priceless. But other than a slight jaw clench, Owen didn't react. God, I was so pissed.

Dinner is slightly awkward and uncomfortable. Nathan and Emily leave early, and we all know he's taking her home to propose. Owen snuck out at some point and didn't even say goodbye. Declan and Logan excused themselves when they realized it was a lost cause. I hung out briefly with Kathryn, Liv's mom, and Jack, Nathan's son because I just didn't want to go home.

I'm typically okay with my life. I get it. I'm a thirty-something singleton, and I rock that shit. I have no problem being a ball-buster. But the holiday season always depresses me. Especially when seeing happy little couples like Em and Nate. Don't get me wrong, I love that they found each other. They deserve happiness. But that doesn't mean I don't get to be down in the dumps about my lack of social life. I'd like someone to cuddle up with this winter. Someone to buy presents for. To celebrate Christmas and New Year. So it just sucks when I'm doing it all alone all the time.

When I finally go home, it's beginning to snow. I hope Nathan's proposal went okay. Liv told me he intended to propose outside watching the sunset. But, unfortunately, the weather here can change so quickly. Can't even tell you the number of times I've been in a torrential downpour with my sunglasses on because the sun was blaring into the car from one angle, and the rain was coming from the opposite direction.

As I park my car around the back of my building and trudge through the snow, I sigh. I'm suddenly so damn sad with my lot in life.

Once I get to my door, I stop and tilt my head up, closing my eyes so I can feel the snowflakes coat my face. It's so quiet and serene when it snows. Ironically, I'm so focused on the feeling of the flakes on my skin that I don't hear footsteps smooshing into the snow.

"Did you bring him to try and make me jealous?"

I whip around to see Owen, his hands deep in his coat pockets, looking so calm and collected. He's wearing another gorgeous suit that makes me salivate. All evening I watched him out of the corner of my eye. I rarely see Owen in anything but a suit, and he fills them out so well. I mean, I know his chiseled physique on an intimate level, but even his tailored suits showcase his body. He's just too suave and pretty. He looks calm and collected right now, but one look in his eyes tells me he's absolutely furious.

I don't answer him.

Owen steps closer to me.

"Answer the question, Harper. Did you bring him to make me jealous?"

"Does it matter?" I ask. His eyes bore into mine as he searches for a response.

"Yes."

"No, it doesn't matter, Owen. It doesn't. Why are you even here? You're being ridiculous. You barely spoke to me all night," I mutter as I turn to unlock my door. I don't see him reach out and grab my arm as he spins me to face him.

"It does fucking matter, Harper. It matters that you tried to make me jealous. It matters that I had to watch him fawn over you the entire night. It matters that I can't fucking get you out of my head," Owen blurts out. My eyes widen, and my mouth drops open.

"What?" I breathe.

"Fuck. Forget I said all of that. God dammit!" he stammers, sliding his hand through his hair in distress. It's hard to tell with the snow falling, but I think he's got a couple of gray hairs coming in. For some reason, this makes me secretly pleased. I hope I'm the one responsible for rupturing his perfect appearance. I hope I gave him every last fucking gray hair.

He steps away from me and turns, then stops before turning back to me. "I don't want to think about you. I don't want to be with you. I don't fucking know what is going on in my head. I hate this."

He gives me a miserable look.

"Jesus, Owen. You really suck at this," I comment as his words sting my heart. He doesn't want to be with me. He doesn't want to think about me. "You really should work on your pickup skills. That's not the way to compliment a woman."

I turn back to my door because I can feel tears filling my eyes, and I don't want him to see it.

"Shit, I'm sorry, Harp. I don't know what I'm doing."

I snort.

"That's obvious," I say quietly. I hear Owen sigh behind me, and I know I can't look at him again. "Please leave. Just ... please, Owen. Please leave me alone."

My voice trembles on the last sentence, and I know Owen can hear the sadness. I don't wait for a response. Instead, I step inside the door and immediately close and lock it, effectively locking Owen out. If only it was easy to lock up my heart like this.

I'M able to avoid Owen for quite a few months, only seeing him in passing a couple of times. It helped that whatever was going on with Liam and Liv seemed to have stalled, so she was as willing as me to steer clear of any typical hangouts and avoid any friend gatherings.

After Liv was assaulted at her townhouse, Owen and I were at the hospital together briefly. The tension was palpable.

"How are you, Harp?" he asked quietly.

"I'm fine. You?" I respond.

"Good, I guess."

"You guess?"

"Yeah, I guess. I don't know. Everything is weird. I miss you, and I don't know what to do with that," Owen blurts out.

I turn to look at him, and he's staring at me with a vulnerable look. For some reason, that look really pisses me off.

"Oh? You wanna be with me, Owen? Want to be my man? Make it official?" I taunt him. "Come on, let's do this. All or nothing, O. All or nothing."

A look of sheer panic crosses his face as he stammers to respond.

"Wait, Harp, well, umm, that's not what I meant," he says, refusing to look me in the eye.

"Oh, I fucking know that isn't what you meant. You want your cake, and you want to eat it too. Well, guess what, asshole? I'm off the fucking menu. Tell Liv I'll be back later. I can't be near you right now," I growl as I stomp away. I don't look back. I'm furious.

I get in my car and find myself driving to Em and Nate's house. I know she'll be there. She's super pregnant with the twins and basically incapable of doing much of anything. I text her first to let her know I'm here, and she responds to come inside.

Grabbing the door handle, I find the door unlocked.

"That's totally safe, Mrs. Riggs," I call out as I enter.

"It takes me too fucking long to get to the door," she shouts back, and I laugh. When I round the corner into the family room, I find her reclined back on the couch with a bowl of ice cream balanced on her extremely large baby bump.

"How's Liv?" she asks with a mouthful of ice cream.

"Physically or mentally?" I ask.

"Both."

"Physically, pretty beat up, but better than she might have been. Mentally, she's destroyed. Liam broke up with her on the phone this morning while I was there. I think Nate went to Liam's," I tell her. She nods.

"Big brother has to save his sister," she muses.

"Owen was there," I say casually, and Em straightens as much as she can in her position.

"Oh yeah? What did he say?"

"Good stuff. How he misses me, but he doesn't want to miss me. How he doesn't want to think about me or be with me," I tell Emily bluntly.

"Are you shitting me?" she yells out.

"Nope. It was quite poetic how he stumbled over himself and muttered it all out like it's really my fault," I say.

"God, he's such a dumbass."

"Yep. It's not my fault he kissed me, and we …" I trail off, realizing I've given out way too much information that no one knows.

"What the fuck!" Em shouts. "When did he kiss you?"

Shit.

"Umm, a while ago. Last summer."

Her mouth drops open as she stares at me.

"Harper. You've held onto that information for this long? What else happened? You slept with him, didn't you?"

My refusal to answer is all the answer she needs.

"Oh, Jesus."

"Yeah."

"He was good, wasn't he." Emily isn't asking me a question. She's stating a fact.

"Yeah. Best I've ever been with. Hands down. Absolute best," I whisper.

"Oh, sweetie, I'm sorry. I can't believe you've held this in for months," Em says quietly.

"Well, you got shot, then knocked up, then married. Liv had all her drama with Liam. I just didn't think there was a good time to start talking about whatever nonsense this is with Owen," I tell her.

"It's not nonsense. It's your life. You've had a crush on this guy for years, and he finally reciprocates those feelings, and then I assume he bolted?" I nod. "Fucking Owen. God, he's predictable. I barely know him, and I figured he'd run for the hills. Jackass."

"Now I really don't want to be around him, so if you could hold off on having those babies for a while, I'd appreciate it," I tease her, and she rolls her eyes.

"No can do, my friend. I'm popping these girls out of here as soon as the OB lets me. You try having two girls playing soccer with your bladder. You'd want them out, too," she says with a half-smile. I get it. Pregnancy looks good on Emily, and she's absolutely glowing. But I can also see that she's uncomfortable and miserable.

"Honestly, I doubt I'll have kids, Em. I'm looking forward to being fun Aunt Harper to the Riggs minions, though," I say, smiling. I've never thought about having my own kids. Growing up as I did without a maternal figure in the house, I don't think I really have a motherly instinct. I don't even have a houseplant to take care of. I have enough difficulty taking care of myself.

"That might change when you meet the right man," she says quietly.

"If."

"Huh?"

"If I meet the right man."

"When."

"Emily."

"Harper," she mimics me. "I'm just going to say this once. I think you and Owen are destined to be together. He's just got his head up his ass right now. But I really feel you will be with him soon. Call it mother's intuition, but I see you as a mom and having babies with him," she tells me.

"You've been hanging around Jack too long," I tease her. Nate's son, Jack, seems to have a weird intuition about things. He predicted Em's twin pregnancy before doctors even found it and said they were both girls.

Em gives me a beaming smile. "That's an incredible compliment, and I'll take it."

I head out to give Em time to get cleaned up before Nate comes home. Once Olivia is released from the hospital, she'll stay at her mom's house for a few days and then live at my apartment while hers is getting remodeled. Whoever attacked her did quite a bit of damage to her home.

Upon getting home, I find a note tacked onto my apartment door.

Rent is going up $200 a month. Unless you want to work out a deal?

God dammit. This lecherous fool is trying to force me into some kind of messed up landlord-with-benefits relationship. I shudder at the thought. He's so disgusting.

I yank the note off the door and realize my door is actually unlocked. I peek my head into the apartment and see nothing has moved. I'm suddenly paranoid that the landlord has been in my space, messing with my things here. Oh, fuck, maybe he put a camera in here. I wouldn't put it past him. I'll have to ask Liam if he can look through the apartment to see if he notices anything. Then I can kick his ass for what he's done to my friend. Yay! Killing two birds with one stone. I'm all for multitasking.

I settle in for a quiet evening of Netflix and a frozen pizza. I'll look at my budget tomorrow when I have a night of sleep under my belt. I think I can still swing it. I'll just eat a lot of ramen noodles until I can increase my rates at the salon. No problem. I can handle this. No one needs to know I'm barely surviving.

CHAPTER SIX

Owen

After Harper left the hospital, I stayed until Nathan got back. I didn't want Liv to be alone if she woke up again. Once he arrived, I shot out of there like I was on fire. I needed fresh air. I swear the natural scent of Harper still hung around after she stomped out. Or maybe I just memorized the scent and can conjure it up, which is just fucking awesome.

I don't know what to do with myself. I'm so confused. Not only have I never felt this way about a woman, but I've never gone this long without sex. Haven't been with anyone since Harper. I used to only go a couple of weeks between partners, but this has been *months*. My own palm isn't even cutting it anymore. It's like my body knows what it could have and refuses to cooperate until I give in and give it Harper.

I know I don't want a long-term relationship. I don't think I can do a relationship. It's just not for me. And I don't want to lead Harper on. So I try to stay away from her. But then I see her, and my fucking dick starts talking instead of my brain, and I get myself into even more trouble.

I end up back at my office, going through some paperwork. I've basically lived at work for the last few months. I can drown myself in client files, motions, dismissals, and acquittals. I can't figure out my personal life, but at least I can shut that down and focus on work. I have a handle on my professional life, thank fuck.

After a few hours, I decided to give Liam a call. After what happened with Liv, I know he's not in a good headspace.

"Hey, O," Liam says as he answers.

"Hey, man. Just checking to see how you're doing," I tell Liam.

"Fine."

"Liar."

"Yep."

I snort. At least he's honest.

"What are you gonna do, man?" I ask.

"Nothing. Liv is better off without me. I'm a fuck-up, and no one needs to be around that," he mutters.

"Come on, man. That's ridiculous. No one thinks you're a fuck-up except for you. Liv's never once judged you or thought less of you because of your past."

Liam is quiet.

"I'm not sure I can get past it. I don't think I'll ever fully trust that anyone could love me despite my past," Liam says quietly. I'm unsure of how to respond. How do you try to convince someone that love is worth it when you yourself don't think it is?

"Listen, I haven't had dinner. Want to head into Colorado Springs and grab something? I've had a shit day, and I'd love some company," I tell him.

"Uh, sure. Sounds good."

We make plans for me to pick him up and head into the Springs. I get to his house thirty minutes later, and he's already out front. His face is rocking a grotesque black eye.

"Shit, man. You look awful," I comment.

"Yeah, I know. The guy at the Apple Store told me as much," he says.

"Nathan?"

"Yeah."

"Why'd you have to go to the Apple Store?"

"I threw my phone against the side of my house."

"All because of Liv?" I ask, and Liam nods.

"It's just too fucked up. Can we talk about anything else? Take my mind off my troubles, O. Give me something else to think about," Liam mutters.

"Okay. You mind if I make a quick stop? A suit I custom ordered is in, and I need to grab it."

"Jesus, man. You and your fucking suits. How many do you have?" Liam asks, chuckling.

Fuck if I know. I've never counted. They just keep accruing in the closet. What can I say? I'm a heterosexual man who loves women, but I also love looking good. And nothing looks better than a well-fitting three-piece suit. I'm a confident guy. I'm sure some would say I'm cocky, but I prefer to call it confidence. A tailored suit expresses confidence, success, reliability, and virility. I'll be the first to admit my suits have gotten their fair share of women over the years. If I'm wearing a suit in a bar full of guys in jeans or joggers, you bet your ass the women are flocking to me. As they fucking should.

After grabbing my suit, we hit a sports bar on the west side of Colorado Springs.

I'm half tempted to spill my guts about Harper. Tell him everything: how we slept together and how I haven't been with anyone since. Never gone this long without sex, and I honestly don't know how to feel about it.

"Tell me about whatever girl you're messing with. I don't want explicit details, but tell me all about your man-whorish ways," Liam says with a slight smile. I awkwardly chuckle.

"Well, umm, to be honest, I'm going through a bit of a dry spell," I admit. Liam's eyes widen comically.

"Seriously? Why?" he asks, and I shrug in response.

"Long story, my man. Not sure I'm ready to tell anyone what's going on in my head," I say. He nods.

"I can understand that. I wasn't ready to talk about Liv for years. Everyone knew I had a thing for her, but I thought I hid it well."

"Yeah, neither one of you hid it worth a damn. We all knew. We were just waiting for one of you to break," I tease him. He gives me a small smile.

"Yeah, that's what we all think about you," he tells me. I cock my head to the side, studying him.

"What do you mean?" I ask.

He gives me a pointed look.

"You know exactly who I'm talking about, O. Don't even try and act all surprised. We all know something is going on with Harper," he tells me at the exact moment I decide to take a drink of my beer. Of course, I immediately choke and spew it all over the table.

"What?" I chortle.

"Just proved me right, didn't you," Liam laughs.

"Nothing going on with Harper and me." Deny, deny, deny. Full denial mode over here. Owen Taylor, the Lawyer, has activated. "I really don't know what you're talking about. I'm not the relationship type."

"Never said anything about a relationship."

"Harper knows I'm not interested in a relationship. And she is. So that's the end of that," I tell him.

"Oh, so you admit you'd want to fuck her if she only wanted that?" Liam asks.

"That's not on the table, so it doesn't matter," I respond matter-of-factly.

"Oh. Well, in that case, you won't mind if I set Harper up with a co-worker, will you? Ran into a friend this week who I think would be a great match for Harper," Liam says, a wicked gleam in his eye.

"Umm, well, sure. Yeah. Whatever," I mumble. The thought of Harper with anyone else makes me want to throw everything across this restaurant, but I'm trying to remain calm. Collected. Unattached and unconcerned.

"Cool. Let me text him real quick …" Liam trails off as he brings up his phone and begins to text. "Think I got a pic of Harper on here, somewhere. Gotta make sure he's into redheads."

"Who the fuck isn't?" I retort, my anger beginning to rear its ugly head.

"You, obviously," Liam says quietly, still focused on his phone. I hear his phone vibrate and look at him expectantly. "Great, he's interested. Says she's hot."

"Great."

"Great."

"Already said that, Liam."

"You're full of shit, Owen."

I don't respond. I'm just trying to hold it together. I can't show Liam that the thought of Harper with someone else is grating on me. I don't have any right to have an opinion about this. We fucked once. That's it. End of discussion.

Liam sighs.

"It's getting late. I need to get home. You ready?" he asks, standing up. We each throw some bills on the table to cover our meals and head out to my car.

We are both silent on the drive back to Mountain Springs. My thoughts are a convoluted mess of emotion, denial, and fear. I have no doubt Liam is thinking about Liv.

I drop Liam off at his house and head back to mine. My home is typically my sanctuary. My job forces me to be go-go-go all the time, so when I come home, I want to relax and unwind. As I walk inside tonight, however, I'm suddenly aware of how empty it is. For the first time in my life, I'm second-guessing my decision to stay single.

CHAPTER SEVEN

Harper

Summer flew by.

Em had the babies. Liv and Liam worked it out and got engaged. I've been working nonstop to keep my head above water. Even increasing my rates a tiny bit hasn't helped much. My landlord has become increasingly belligerent and demanding I 'service' him. Not happening.

One Friday night at the end of August, Liv and I meet Em at Peaks Bar. Em hates leaving the twins, but we convinced her to meet us for a couple hours for girl time. Liv still hasn't picked out a dress, but she hasn't had time. The start of the school year was hectic. She's hoping to get married in October, so hopefully, she can find some time for dress shopping.

"Anything new with you, Harp?" Liv asks me as she finishes a long swig of her margarita.

"Nope." I'm not telling them anything. Not letting a

newly engaged woman and a mom with twin newborns know my life is going in the crapper. "Same old, same old."

"Has anyone seen Owen recently?" Em asks suddenly, and I snort.

"Lord Owen grace us with his presence? Doubtful," I chortle.

"Is that what you're calling him these days?" Em asks, giggling.

"Well, mostly, I refer to him as Satan," I say.

"And I refer to her as Daenerys. Queen of the dragons and bat-shit crazy," a deep voice startles from behind me. I whip around to see Owen with a smirk on his all-too-beautiful face. Dammit. I can't help but let my gaze drift quickly down. Owen is still dressed for work in a fitted suit, complete with a vest and tie. His tie is slightly loosened, and one button of his shirt is undone. Some men can rock suits in just typical bland colors. Not Owen. He seems to have a suit in every color possible. Today he's wearing a dark green suit. He looks positively sinful. "Eyes up here, Harp."

My eyes whip to his as he gives me a cocky smile. I growl in response, which makes him chuckle.

"Ladies' night?" he asks Liv and Em, and they both nod. I am seething furiously. How dare he interrupt the rare time I get with my besties.

"Yep, girls' night. Which means no boys. Take care, goodbye now!" I say loudly, motioning toward the door.

"Jesus, Harper, you don't have to be so rude," Olivia says admonishingly. "She hasn't had enough liquor yet, Owen. Sorry. I'll apologize for her."

"Nothing I'm not used to, Liv. I bring out the best in our girl here," Owen responds as someone bumps into him, and he's pushed into me. One hand grazes my inner thigh as his other lands on my lower back, and immediately I feel heat course up my spine. It's been over a year since we slept together. In that year, I've come one too many times with his name on my lips. No one else has touched me. Primarily due to the fact that I'm constantly working to make ends meet, but also because I haven't put myself out there. I know it will end in a letdown when whatever guy I take home doesn't make me feel like I know Owen can.

Owen's eyes don't leave mine as he straightens quickly, but I see a determined glimmer in his gaze as his hand slides between my thighs and pushes against my clit. I reflexively gasp, and Owen gives me a wolfish grin.

"Knew you'd like that, Red," he said quietly in my ear as he continued to straighten. He clears his throat and grabs the stool next to mine. "You know what? I'm gonna invade ladies' night. Just because it'll irritate my favorite ginger."

Emily giggles nervously while Liv studies both of us. I can feel my cheeks reddening under her gaze. Owen's left-hand lands on the back of my chair.

"So, how have you ladies been? Haven't seen any of you in a while. How are the girls, Em?" he asks as he slides one finger up my spine and twirls a piece of hair around it.

"They're great. Well, as good as newborns can be. A lot of eating, sleeping, and pooping," Emily says. "Want to see some pictures?"

"Of course," Owen says good-naturedly while still playing with my hair. My entire body is rigid with tension. No one on the planet manages to get me off-kilter like Owen. Typically I'd have something to say or do to get his hand off of me. Not only am I coming up blank, but I'm not sure I want him to stop. The way he makes me feel ... really *feel* ... is unlike anything I've ever experienced.

I remain silent, and Owen asks Liv and Em tons of questions. He carries on a conversation with them brilliantly while I'm slowly disappearing into a puddle of tension and need.

When he slides two fingers underneath my hair to lightly grab the back of my neck, I almost come.

"Excuse me, I need the restroom," I stammer with a small moan. Owen gives me a knowing smirk, a very victorious smirk, which does me in. This was all a game. He managed to humiliate me in front of my friends.

My face must show my emotions because his smirk falls.

"Harp ..." he starts, but I turn away and bolt for the bathroom. I bypass it and head out the back door, thankful I wore sandals today, so I can run home. I get to my front door as tears fall. I'm panting and crying, full of frustration and agonizing feelings. My hands shake as I unlock my door.

As I trudge up the stairs, I am startled by a pounding on the door behind me.

"Harper!" Owen yells.

Fuck. I didn't think he'd follow me.

"Go away, Owen," I call back. My voice clearly trembling. I don't want him to see me this way. I'm humiliated enough for the day.

"Let me in, Red," he responds. God dammit. I both hate and love when he calls me Red. "I'm not leaving until we talk. Until I apologize."

I sigh. Trying to school my features, I quickly wipe my face to remove any wetness and rub under my eyes to ensure no evidence of mascara. Walking back down the stairs, I take a moment before opening the door.

Owen's face is full of remorse.

"I'm sorry, Harp. I didn't mean to upset you," he says quietly.

"Okay."

He frowns, looking at me.

"That's it?" he asks.

"What do you want me to say, Owen?"

"I was hoping you'd forgive me," he responds.

"I'll think about it. You can leave now, okay? I'm fine. Just go back to the bar," I tell him. I can feel the emotion bubbling in my throat, just threatening to boil over.

"No. I'm not leaving until we talk more."

I grind my teeth, and he smiles.

"There's my girl," he says softly, "the girl who doesn't take shit from me. Come on. Can I come upstairs and talk to you for a few minutes?"

I nod, momentarily taken aback by him calling me 'his.' I turn and walk up the stairs and begin to unlock the door when his hand slams out to the side of my head.

"What the fuck is this?" he roars, holding a piece of paper. Oh, shit. I don't need to read it to know it's another notice from my landlord.

"Let me see what he said this time," I say, trying to pull the paper from Owen's hands, but he won't let me.

"Who the fuck does this guy think he is? Another $200? How much is your rent? And what services is he asking for?" he demands.

My mouth opens, but no words come out. Owen takes the keys from my hand and unlocks the door, ushering me inside. He leads me to the couch and sits.

"Harper, you need to tell me what's going on. I can't help you unless I know everything," he says quietly, his eyes boring into mine. I steel my spine. He can't see my weakness. I'll never live it down.

"It's nothing I can't handle, Owen. Everything is fine. I forgive you. You can go now," I tell him as I attempt to walk away. He yanks my arm hard, and I fall into his lap.

"Why don't you trust me?" he asks softly as both hands find my hair. I can't even stop the moan as he massages my scalp. "Let me in, Red."

"My landlord keeps raising my rent. I don't know what to do. I can't afford it," I admit.

"How much is the rent?" he asks, continuing to massage my scalp.

"Twenty-five hundred."

"That's not too bad, I guess..." he trails off.

"Each."

"Wait, what?"

"Twenty-five hundred each. So five thousand a month total," I whisper. I suddenly feel incredibly humiliated. His hands on my scalp stall as he takes in the information.

I subconsciously shift my weight in his lap and feel his hardened length. His dark brown eyes are almost black as he stares at me. I'm not sure who moved first, but suddenly we are in the throes of a passionate kiss.

We're a flurry of movement as we both struggle to remove clothing. I've got my shorts off within moments, and Owen has undone his belt to pull his cock out. I slam myself down on him, impaling myself fully and letting out a guttural moan.

"God damn, you feel so good," Owen mutters as his hands latch onto my hips and his fingers dig into my skin. I'll probably have marks tomorrow with how hard he's gripping me, but I don't care. This is the best I've felt in a year. I needed this.

"Shut up and move," I retort. I don't need Owen to be any sexier. He needs to fuck me. I need to come. Give me at least one moment of blissful pleasure in the shitshow that has become my life.

"Jesus, woman. I got you," he mutters as he forcefully slams me down. I throw my head back as heat courses throughout my body. Yes. God, I needed this.

The only sounds in my apartment are grunts, moans, pants, and skin slapping against skin as we both chase our orgasms. I begin to whimper as I get closer, a layer of sweat covering my body as Owen pummels into me from below.

Owen reaches between us, presses his thumb to my clit,

and I immediately soar. He's right behind me as he thrusts up into me, once, twice, and then roars out his release. My head falls to his shoulder in exhaustion. My entire body finally feels relaxed.

Owen's cell phone rings, jarring my moment of peace. I launch out of his lap, suddenly embarrassed.

"Oh, shit," he murmurs, looking down at my pussy. I look down and see his cum running down my leg. "I forgot a condom, Red. I can't believe it. I never forget one."

"Oh. I'm on the pill. It's okay. I'm clean, too," I tell him as I make a beeline for my bathroom.

"I'm clean, too," he calls out. "It's been a while for me anyway."

I snort as I clean myself up.

"What's 'a while' to you? More than a week?" I tease him.

"Something like that," he mutters.

When I come out of the bathroom, Owen is standing and composed. If it weren't for the fantastic ache between my legs, I wouldn't think anything had happened.

"So, umm," I stammer. He gives me a lopsided grin. "Do you need to go?"

"No. Not until you tell me what's going on with your landlord," he tells me earnestly.

"No."

"Yes."

"I'm not involving you, Owen."

"I'm already involved, Harper."

He moves toward me slowly until he's standing in front of me. His hand reaches out and tucks a piece of wayward curls behind my ear.

"Why won't you let me in? Let me help you," he whispers as his eyes implore me to answer.

"I don't need anyone to help me," I blurt out. Owen studies me for a moment.

"Do you think it makes you weaker to let people help you?" he asks.

"Yes," I answer him honestly. "I've been on my own for this long. I can do anything myself."

"It doesn't make you weaker, baby. It just means you have support. I want to be your support. Let me in, Red. Let me help," he whispers as he leans in and tenderly kisses me.

I whimper as my arms slide around his neck and the kiss turns passionate in seconds. Owen pushes me against the wall, and I pull one leg up to wrap around his waist. I love his height. I know he hates being 'short' by society's standards, but he's perfect for me. I can stand on my tiptoes with only four inches separating us and feel him right against my core.

"Help me come. That's what you can do," I whisper against his lips. He chuckles.

"That I definitely can do," he responds, grabbing my thighs and lifting me up, so my legs are wrapped around his waist. He walks me into the bedroom before launching us both onto my bed. I come twice more before falling into a deep sleep.

And in a weird déjàvu, Owen is gone when I wake up. Again, I shouldn't be surprised. But I honestly felt like something had changed. His desire to 'help' was evidently only to get into my pants again. I should have known better. He's a man-whore and always will be.

CHAPTER EIGHT

Owen

Yeah, I did it again. I know.

I shouldn't have snuck out, especially after everything. Knowing Harper needs help but won't admit it to me. In some ways, the fact that she *won't* tell me what she needs help with is why I left. I don't like that she won't open up to me. But my relationship with Harper has always been tumultuous. So, I'm honestly not surprised that she's hesitant to trust me.

Fortunately, I'm an attorney. I have connections. So it takes me less than an hour to find out who her landlord is and what her rent is for. Michael Jensen is close to sixty-five and has ten properties across the county. He's had multiple citations for inappropriate behavior and has two current restraining orders.

Harper has been leasing her salon and apartment from him

for three years, and in that time, he's raised her rent ten times. I'm able to find the lease agreement online, and I see that he's written a stipulation in there that allows him to raise the rent whenever, as well as enter her salon or apartment without warning. I'm not too familiar with rental laws in the state of Colorado, so I need to research if he's allowed to raise her rent that often. Makes my blood boil thinking he could sneak in there when she's sleeping.

At first, he raised her rent because of increasing repair costs. Then it was raised due to a roof repair. He did it so slowly, at only twenty-five or fifty dollars an increase, that I'm sure Harper didn't object. But then it began jumping a hundred bucks. And from the note he left on her door last night, it appears the rent increase is now at two hundred a month. I'm just assuming the 'services' he expected of her were of a sexual nature.

I'm even more furious with Harper for signing this lease without an attorney reading it first. Jesus, she had me at her disposal and didn't use me! I would have immediately let her know to not sign. Or, at least, force this jackass to change some wording. He owns her.

But I don't know how to help her without coming across as an arrogant asshole. Harper and I already have a tempestuous relationship, and she's not taken my help multiple times. Logical me would step away and rethink the problem. Consult with someone. Take steps to legally silence the landlord.

But logical me has left the fucking building. I can still smell Harper on me. I can still taste her. This new Owen, the possessive and controlling Owen, doesn't do logic. The new me finds the address for the jackass landlord and gets there within a few minutes.

I'm still in my suit from yesterday, but I've taken off the tie. I know I look every bit like a well-established lawyer. I hope to threaten my way over this sleaze ball and make him leave Harper alone.

Slamming my fist against the door, I hear a man muttering on the other side. The door flies open, and I see a guy with a pot belly, a dirty tank top, and a comb-over hairdo.

"What the fuck do you want?" he snarls, taking a swig of a beer. Jesus, it's nine o'clock in the morning.

"I want you to leave Harper Williams alone," I blurt out. His eyes widen almost imperceptibly, then narrow as he grins vindictively.

"Oh yeah? What's it to you?" he leers.

"Considering I'm the attorney she's retained, it's a lot," I tell him. "I've seen your lease agreement. Stop raising her rent, and I won't be forced to press charges."

"That agreement is completely legal. I have an attorney also, you know. And she signed it. She's agreed to every single raise," he says.

"But now you're requesting 'services,'" I say, with air quotes, "and we both know that's completely illegal."

He shrugs.

"What she does in her spare time is none of your business," he says.

"Leave her the fuck alone, or you'll regret it," I warn. He cocks his head back and laughs.

"You can't do anything. So don't come back here."

He slams the door in my face.

Shit. That didn't go as I expected it to.

I decide to go home and do a little more research, see if I can find any legal reasons why their lease is invalid.

IN HINDSIGHT, I suppose sneaking out in the middle of the night and then not calling Harper after our dalliance is a big deal. But, in my defense, I got swept up in researching the lease with her landlord, and then one of my clients in the throes of a difficult divorce and fighting her soon-to-be ex-husband over parenting responsibilities needed help. Colorado no longer uses the term 'custody' in divorce and refers to it as parental responsibilities with sole decision-making authority and parenting time. Her ex-husband is fighting every concession we make just out of spite. It's been incredibly difficult to contain evidence to show the State that it is in their child's best interest to remain in the care of his mother.

I've spent countless hours reviewing this case and preparing for our next court date. I've slept at the office more than once this week. By the weekend, I'm relieved I can take a day off and spend some time with Nathan and Liam.

Liv finally found time to go wedding dress shopping, so the guys and I are having a pseudo-bachelor party for Liam. We're all not the biggest partiers ... well, at least they aren't. I've had my fair share of shenanigans in recent years. But the two of them, now settling down, have found peace in staying close to home and steering clear of bars or clubs.

We decide to grill out at Nathan's house and enjoy some beers. September in Colorado can be a mixed bag of weather, but today is beautiful. There's a crispness to the air that allows me to look forward to cooler nights, changing leaves, and the promise of snow. I've always loved winter. Something about the quietness of a nice snowfall. Nothing calms me more than sitting in my hot tub with snow falling around me.

After we've eaten, Liam is chomping at the bit to get home to his woman. Evidently, Liv found her dress early in the day, so they've been having drinks at Liv and Liam's house. I expect they are drunk by now. I find myself eager to see Harper, which is a highly uncomfortable sensation. I've never felt excited to see anyone more than once.

Upon entering Liam's house, I see Harper dancing on a

table. As she turns, she stumbles, and I move forward to catch her.

"Fucking hell, woman, what are you doing?" I spit out.

Her eyes are wide as she stares at me.

"Put me down," she whispers.

"No."

"Yes."

"God dammit, Harp, no! You're in no shape to be walking, let alone dancing on a table," I retort.

"You don't get to talk to me like that, Owen. You've made your feelings clear. So put me down," she snarls.

I look at her in shock. What? What feelings did I clearly put out there? I'm a little surprised at her outburst, but I'm even more surprised when she slaps me hard across the face as soon as I put her down.

"What the fuck was that for?" I exclaim, rubbing my cheek.

"You know exactly what it was for, asshole," she growls before flouncing into the kitchen. I try to follow her and apologize, but Liv tells me to leave. Liam backs her up.

I walk out to my car, completely confused. I've never had to explain myself before. By leaving her apartment, did I subconsciously tell her that I didn't want her? Or that it wasn't good for me? Shit. I absolutely do want her. But I don't want to want her. This is so messed up. I'm thirty-nine years old, and I don't know how to talk to Harper, a woman I've known for decades.

"Hey, O," I hear Nathan call out from behind me as he maneuvers a giggling Emily into his truck. His mom Kathryn sways as she attempts to boost herself into the cab of the truck, so I go and help her.

"Thank you, other unofficial son of mine," she says gleefully. I chuckle as I close the door.

"What's up?" I ask Nathan once he gets Emily situated. "Hey, wait. Where are the twins?"

"I left them at home with lighters and liquor," Nathan deadpans. I cock my eyebrows at him, and he chuckles. "Next-door neighbor has the girls and Jack. Seriously, man, we were just at my house. Did it not occur to you that they weren't there? Or that we were there all evening, and there wasn't any crying?"

"Uhh, I guess not," I say sheepishly.

"What the fuck, dude? What is going on with you? And what is going on with you and Harper?" Nathan asks. I shrug.

"I don't really know, man. I tried to ask what Harper was talking about, but she wouldn't answer me. Then Liv made me leave."

"That's bullshit. Something happened before now. Something made Harp hit you. What did you do?" he asks accusingly.

"Why do you automatically assume I did anything?" I ask defensively. He just raises his eyebrows and doesn't say a word. Yeah. I know. It's me. "Shit, man. I don't want to go into details. But I may have hurt her unintentionally. I don't know. It all got fucked up. I'm trying to help her, but she doesn't want to let me. And I left in the middle of the night, so I think she's pissed about that. Pretty sure she's still mad about the other time I did that, too."

"Owen."

"Yeah?"

"Did you just say you left her in the middle of the night? Twice?"

Fuck.

"Umm..." I stammer.

"Jesus. You slept with her?" Nathan asks, his eyes darkening. I take a step backward. Nathan is one of the most loyal people I've ever met. He had no problems taking a swing at

Liam when Liam broke up with Liv this spring. I know he'll pop me without qualms.

"Accidentally," I blurt out.

"Totally makes sense. She just fell on your dick."

"That's not what I meant."

"You know what? Don't even bother giving me the details. But fix this shit. You know better," he says, staring coldly at me. He gets into his truck and swiftly pulls out of Liam's driveway. I'm left staring at the retreating truck lights as I struggle to find an easy solution to this Harper debacle.

CHAPTER NINE

Harper

I can't believe it's come to this.

I certainly didn't expect an eviction from my landlord. He's never gone this far. He's just continued to raise the rent when I've refused his advances or ignored his comments of 'servicing' him.

I've already rented a storage space and moved a ton of things there. So I'll be able to continue leasing my salon, but I will have to live in the storage space.

With less than twenty-four hours until the landlord changes the locks, I've muzzled my pride and called Owen. His large SUV will help me move the rest of my things into the storage space. On cold nights, I'll just bring a sleeping bag and sleep at the salon.

I'm starting on my third bottle of wine when Owen arrives. I hate that I had to call him. But I can't call Liv or

Emily. Liv and Liam are getting married in a few weeks. Em is a new mom. So who else do I have? Owen is it.

I left the doors unlocked, so Owen strolls in when he arrives and gapes at me.

"Jesus, Harp. What the fuck happened?" he asks.

"I've been evicted," I tell him, then let out a very unladylike belch. His mouth drops open.

"What?" he breathes.

"Yep. I've been evicted. I convinced my landlord to let me keep the salon space. But I have to be out of here by tomorrow. So I need your help to move my stuff to my storage space," I tell him, my voice trembling.

"What are you gonna, I mean, where are you going to stay?" he asks. I shrug.

"I'll figure it out. I always do."

Owen stares at me.

"Seriously, Harper. Where are you going to stay?" he asks again.

"I'll figure it out. I just need your help moving some more of my stuff, okay? We can do it faster in your SUV."

He studies me and doesn't speak for a few minutes, then sighs and takes off his jacket.

"Okay. What do you need me to do?" Owen asks.

We pack my things in silence for an hour as I polish off the third bottle of wine.

"I ran into our favorite cougar this evening," Owen comments. I turn to him with a surprised look.

"Amelia McCallister?" I ask.

"Yep. Think she might have followed me out of town. I was an hour away at a hole-in-the-wall bar. No way she just chose that spot."

"Damn. She's a psycho."

"Yep. She got pissed when I turned her down, so she screamed out that I was hurting her," Owen tells me, and my mouth drops open in astonishment. "Couple of guys took me out back, ready to show me a lesson. Bartender had to intervene and explain that Amelia set the whole thing up."

"Holy shit, Owen! Are you gonna press charges?" I ask incredulously.

"No. Don't want to deal with her any more than I have to. She'd probably think I did it to get closer to her or some other bullshit."

"Wow. Guess I called at a good time then, huh," I say.

"You did manage to time it pretty perfectly as I was walking out of there and making sure Amelia didn't follow me," he muses.

We continue packing for a few more minutes before Owen speaks up again.

"Did your landlord contact you again and discuss raising the rent?" Owen asks quietly.

"Nope. Just left me a note evicting me. I tried to plead my case, but he wouldn't even look at me. Told me I could keep the salon if I paid extra for that. I had to say yes. I can't lose that space," I say sullenly.

"When did he evict you?" Owen asks, his eyes narrowing.

"Monday."

"Shit."

"What?" I ask him.

"Nothing. I'm really sorry this happened, Harp," Owen says quietly, refusing to make eye contact. He whips out his phone and starts typing furiously. "Gonna see if there's anything I can do."

"No, Owen, stop," I say, lunging over and grabbing his phone. "There's no point. One less thing he can hold over me, anyway."

Owen looks at me for a moment and then nods, putting his phone back in his pocket.

"Okay, Red. Let's get a load moved over. You okay to walk down your stairs?" he asks.

"Not my first time drinking this much wine, Owen. I'll be fine," I say with a flourish as I toss my hair over my shoulder. I give him a saucy wink, and he smiles.

We load up his SUV and take it to my storage shed. I splurged and got a climate-controlled locker. It goes below freezing in Colorado in the winter, and I don't know how long it'll be before I find an apartment within my budget. So I want to make sure my things will be okay.

Owen looks around the space and then cocks his brow at me.

"No."

"What?" I ask, confused.

"I know what you're thinking, Red. You're not living here," he says as he glares at me. I feel my cheeks blush as I look down at the ground.

"That's not what I was thinking ..." I whisper, trailing off as the lie fails to come off my tongue with ease.

Owen steps into my space and touches my chin with his knuckle.

"Don't lie to me, Red," he says quietly, his eyes studying mine.

"I'm not," I respond, and he chuckles.

"Yes, you are. I know you. You're not living here. End of discussion," he says.

"Excuse me! This is not the end of the discussion! What the fuck, Owen? You don't get to just waltz in here and tell me what to do!" I yell at him.

"In this case, I absolutely do. You are not going to live in a storage facility."

"Well, Mr. Hot Shot Attorney, tell me what I'm supposed to do with no fucking money. This is my only choice!" I yell furiously. Tears threaten to spill down my cheeks.

"I've got you, baby," he whispers as his arms come around me. I cry, sobs wracking my body as I finally let go. I've held onto this for so long that it's cathartic to finally let someone in to share this burden. Even if it's Owen. "Oh, sweetheart. I hate that you're going through this."

I struggle to remove myself from his embrace, suddenly embarrassed at my outburst. Wiping furiously at my face, I keep my head down as I focus on moving a few bins into the corner. I have just enough space for my couch, which will serve as my bed. Squeezing my eyes shut, I try to reel in my emotions.

"It's fine. Everyone has a rough period in life. Mine is just longer than most. I'll be fine," I say quietly, refusing to look at him. He comes behind me and puts his head on my shoulder.

"You're not staying here, Harp."

I whip around and stare at him.

"I don't have a fucking choice, Owen."

"Yes, you do!" he yells.

"What is my choice, then?" I yell back.

"You're staying with me, dammit!" he shouts.

"What?"

"You're staying with me, Harper. I have four bedrooms. You can have your own space. I'm not letting you do this. You're not alone anymore, okay? I'm not letting you stay in a fucking storage facility because you refuse to accept help from me. So you're staying with me," he says fiercely, his dark brown eyes alive with anger and heat.

"Owen," I whisper hoarsely.

His arms slide around my midsection, one hand skirting down to grab my ass and the other sliding into my hair. He yanks on my hair, and wetness pools in my panties. Damn this man.

"You're staying with me, dammit. That is the end of this discussion. Don't fight me on this. I'll win," Owen says as he leans down and bites the skin where my shoulder and neck meet. I whimper. "You're staying with me, baby. Say it."

I struggle to answer him. He slides his tongue along my collarbone as I reflexively grind against him.

"If I stay with you, it doesn't change anything between us," I whisper.

"It changes everything."

"No."

"Yes."

"Owen! I can't …" I say quietly as my fingers latch onto his hair.

"What are the ground rules, then? Tell me what you expect," he mumbles against my neck before sucking my earlobe into his mouth. Fuck. I moan incoherently. No one has ever turned me on like this.

"No sex," I blurt out.

"Hard no for that one, babe," he chuckles against my skin.

"I can't watch you with other women. I can't watch you bring others to your house, Owen. I can't," I whisper. He stops and leans his head up to look at me.

"Wait, you're talking about not having sex with anyone else?" he asks, and I nod. He stares at me for a moment, then gives me a sexy smile. "Can I have sex with you?"

My mouth drops open, and I'm unable to respond.

"I mean, if you're gonna be living there, we might as well enjoy ourselves," he says with a grin.

I shake my head vehemently.

"No. We can't muddy the waters. It will be too hard for me when you're done with me. It will be hard to see you around. We're together too often, Owen. I can't do that," I tell him honestly. He cocks his head to the side.

"What makes you think I'd be 'done' with you?" he asks with air quotes.

I bark out a laugh.

"Oh, come on. Out of the two of us, you're definitely the one who would move on. I'm the monogamist, not you," I tell him, laughing. He looks slightly hurt but schools his features quickly.

"I guess you're right," he says slowly. "Let's get back to your apartment and get the rest of your things."

I'm a little taken aback at how quickly he changed the topic, but I follow him out to his SUV. The ride back to the apartment is silent. We load up again and head back to the storage facility.

After the last of my boxes is inside, Owen turns to me.

"What furniture are you taking?" he asks.

"Just my bedroom furniture and the couch. Everything else was already in the apartment," I tell Owen.

"Okay. I can rent a U-Haul in the morning to help with the furniture. Grab whatever you need tomorrow, and we'll head to my house. Get you situated," he says, refusing to look in my eyes.

I grab my suitcase with my essentials and put it in his SUV. The quick ride to his house is tense and silent. When we get to his house, I'm barely in the door before he pushes me against it and slams his lips against mine.

I moan immediately as his tongue slides in to duel with mine.

"One last time, baby," he whispers against my mouth, and I nod enthusiastically. He lifts me up and carries me up the stairs. It still boggles my mind that he can lift me. I'm a bigger girl. But Owen carries me around effortlessly. He lays me on the bed tenderly, then stands over me.

"Gonna take my time with you tonight, Red. If this is it, I want to memorize every single part of your body. Need to know every part of you. Make you sing for me. Watch you come apart so many fucking times that I'll never be able to erase the memory. That okay with you?" he says quietly, his hand slowly stroking his cock through his trousers.

"Fuck, yes," I whimper.

He climbs on top of me and takes my lips in a kiss so deep, so searing, I think I'll never be able to kiss anyone again without feeling disappointed. Owen kisses like he was created specifically for the task. His lips are plush pillows, and his velvet tongue slides against mine with precision and skill. His man-whorish ways have definitely taught him how to kiss.

I figured he'd end up inside me quickly, but he did exactly what he said he would do. He worshipped me. I lost track of how many times I came. The entire time he whispered sweet nothings and dirty thoughts into my ear. When we finally came together, chest to chest, as he sat on the edge of his bed with our eyes locked, it was the most powerful orgasm of my life.

After cleaning both of us up, Owen wrapped his arms around me and told me he was holding me one last time before our new roommate arrangement began. He fell asleep immediately, but I was solidly awake. As his warm breath hit my neck, I knew I was so screwed.

There's no way I can live with the man I've crushed on for so long, especially when he's rocked my world multiple times.

I make a resolute decision to steer clear of Owen as often as possible until I can find another apartment. The lines have already been muddled, and my heart won't take much more. I can't take much more.

CHAPTER TEN

Owen

Last night was unexpected.

I knew her landlord was a greasy spineless asshat, but I didn't think he'd evict her. And yeah, I know it was probably because I confronted him. I can't let Harper find out about that.

I told Harper it would be our last time together, but I was straight-up lying. No way am I giving up. Sex with her is mind-blowing. I mean, Jesus. I haven't had sex with anyone but her for the last sixteen months. She doesn't know that, but it's true. There's no comparison. I know Harper wants a relationship and expects a future with someone. Still, I'm hoping I can convince her to try a 'friends with benefits' situation. Well, maybe that's not precisely correct. I've done it before, but I've always slept with other people at the same time. And I'll be damned if Harper is allowed to fuck anyone except me.

So it would be exclusive sex, but not dating. How do I express that tactfully? Gotta figure this out before I put my foot in my mouth *again*, and piss her off, *again*.

I roll over in bed and reach for her, only to find cold sheets. Fuck. I glance at the clock, and it's four in the morning. What the fuck? I throw off the sheets and go into my bathroom. She's not in there. Opening my bedroom door, I listen for any sounds. Nothing. The guest bedroom door is closed. I swear it was open earlier. I go and try the knob, only to find it's locked.

Holy fuck. Harper left *me* in the middle of the night and locked herself in the other bedroom. I'm completely gobsmacked. And I'm actually really hurt.

Jesus. Is this how women feel when I leave them? Is this what I've done with Harper? Wow. This is one hell of a reality check. Almost all of the women I fuck know the score ahead of time. I'm forcefully blunt when propositioning a woman. She needs to know I'm in it for a one-night situation, and I'll be out of there before morning.

But I never really expressed that with Harper. Maybe, all along, I knew it would be more with her.

As I slide back into my bed, I chuckle at the circumstances. Of course, the first woman to put me in my place would be Harper. I guess all of our arguing and disagreements over the past ten to fifteen years have been a weird kind of foreplay.

I fall back asleep, thinking of all the ways I can convince her to give me a chance.

HARPER DOES a ridiculous job of avoiding me for over a week. We awkwardly rented a U-Haul and moved the rest of her furniture to her storage facility the day after she snuck out during the night. Then it was like she had disappeared. I never saw her coming or going. I wouldn't think she still lived here if it weren't for the occasional dirty dish in the sink.

Then, the following week, I see her twice as she darts out the door in the morning. I've been getting up earlier, trying to catch her, and she always beats me. I know her salon doesn't open up before sunrise, so I have absolutely no idea what she's doing. And I'm not going to follow her. At least not again. She caught me trying to follow her once, went all Grand Theft Auto on me, and left me in the dust. I was so surprised I didn't even attempt to engage in a pursuit.

My divorce and custody case is ramping up, so I don't have the time to devote to aggravating Harper. At first, I just wanted to talk to her. Now, my feelings are hurt, so I'm regressing into previous behaviors that I know will piss her off. Simple stuff that doesn't require a lot of brain activity on my part but has always infuriated Harper in the past.

Leaving just a sliver of coffee in the coffee pot? Done.

Clothes in both the washer *and* dryer? Yep.

Pile of dirty dishes in the sink? You know it.

Putting Alexa on as loud as possible when I think she's sleeping? Yeah, I've done that, too. She's a light sleeper. I know this. I know everything about this woman, so it's pretty damn easy to incite a riot.

But she isn't fucking budging. I honestly think my juvenile behaviors are frustrating me much more than her. I'm generally a fairly clean and organized guy. Actually choosing to make a mess is incredibly difficult for me. But Harper isn't budging, the damn stubborn ass. She does a cordial wave if we pass each other in our cars. She remains so quiet in my house it's almost as if I don't have this incredibly sexy pseudo-roommate that has taken up residence in my dreams.

The week before Liam and Olivia's wedding, I worked eighteen-hour days. Unfortunately, the soon-to-be ex-husband of my client has really increased his behavior over the past two weeks, and his attorney is becoming much more aggressive. My client is understandably frightened, and I'm doing everything I can to ensure we are ready for the trial. With the very minimal extra time I have each day, I'm laying the groundwork to sue the hell out of Harper's landlord.

"I just don't understand why this is all so difficult," my client, Victoria, tells me as she wipes tears from her eyes. "I never thought he'd end up this way. He's the one that cheated. He's the one that left us. So now he gets to try and sue for custody? This is bullshit."

I look up from the papers I'm reviewing and nod.

"Unfortunately, Colorado is a no-fault state, Victoria. We've been over this. It means his actions don't impact the divorce proceedings or the judge's decision." But in my head, I agree entirely. It's bullshit. Her ex, Thomas, gaslit her for years, had multiple high-profile affairs, and left some incredibly vicious voice messages concerning their children. That last one is my smoking gun. He's suing for full parental responsibility, and it's very evident he's doing it just for clout and to stick it to Victoria.

"I can't lose my kids, Owen," she whispers brokenly. I reach over and squeeze her hand.

"That's not going to happen. Thomas is going down, Victoria. I promise," I tell her confidently.

If it weren't for having those voice messages, plus signed affidavits from multiple sources who are willing to go on the stand and testify how Thomas is a bad parent, I'd be more worried. I also happen to know the judge who has been assigned our case, and it's a woman with three kids. History shows female judges are typically more likely to rule in favor of the mother.

"Enjoy the weekend with the kids, okay? Just forget all about this trial. You all set?" I ask her, and she nods. I treated her and the kids to a weekend at Great Wolf Lodge. It's a fantastic hotel with an indoor waterpark. The location in Colorado Springs even has a ropes course, bowling, mini golf, and tons of other cool activities. If this doesn't go well and somehow Thomas manages to finagle custody, I want to be sure Victoria has amazing memories with the kids this weekend.

"Yeah, we're all set. Thanks again for everything, Owen. I couldn't have done this without your support," Victoria says, emotion clogging her voice.

"It's my honor to help you, Victoria." I smile warmly at her as she gives me a hug. As we are separating from this friendly hug, my door slams open, and a surprised Harper barges in. Her eyes almost bug out when she sees me with my arms around Victoria, and then her face contorts into pure malice.

"Harper, this is an unexpected surprise," I say. Victoria's face lights up.

"Oh, you're Harper! Owen has told me all about you," she says warmly.

"Really? Owen hasn't told me a thing about you," she snarls. Victoria noticeably steps backward toward me, shocked at the venom Harper spews.

"Jesus, Harp. Victoria is my client. I'm helping her with her custody and divorce proceedings next week."

Harper blanches.

"Oh, shit. Oh, God. I'm so sorry. I had no idea ... and, honestly, no right to say anything. Owen's just my roommate," she laughs awkwardly as she steps forward and extends her hand to Victoria's in greeting. Victoria is hesitant to accept, understandably.

"Oh. I'm sorry. From the way Owen described you, I thought you were his girlfriend. My apologies. It was nice to meet you, in any case. I have to get going. Thanks again for the reservation this weekend, Owen. I really appreciate it," Victoria says as she grabs her belongings and leaves.

"What reservation?" Harper asks.

"I got her a weekend at Great Wolf Lodge for her and her kids. Just wanted to give them one last weekend in case things go to hell next week," I tell her.

"Wow. That's incredibly decent of you, Owen," Harper says quietly. I chuckle.

"I can be nice, you know. You'd realize that if you ever let me see you for more than five seconds," I point out. A pink hue rises up Harper's neck as she refuses to make eye contact.

"Liv sent me to get Liam's ring," Harper says, effectively changing the subject.

"Oh, yeah. Hold on. I have it right here," I say as I rummage around in my desk. Then, handing it to her, our fingers graze each other, and I feel an immediate spark. Harper gasps, letting me know she felt it as well.

"Okay, thanks. See you tomorrow," Harper says as she turns and swiftly walks away.

"Harp, wait," I call after her. As she turns, I see her take a big inhale, but her expression has been shuttered. "Are you not going to be home tonight?"

"No, I'm staying with Liv. Her last night as a single lady, we wanted to celebrate with a good ole slumber party," she says, smiling shyly. I smile in return. It's the first smile she's given me in weeks.

"That sounds like fun, Red. I'm sure you two will have a great time," I say sincerely.

"Thanks," she responds.

"Are we okay?" I blurt out. Our eyes lock, and I can see uncertainty in her gaze. "I need us to be okay, Harp. I don't know exactly what I did to make you pull away from me, but I need us to be okay."

She gives me a hesitant smile as she schools her expression, and my heart drops. I can tell what she's doing. I've done it a thousand times.

"We're cool, Owen. Everything is fine. See ya tomorrow, roomie," she says as she turns and walks out.

Fuck.

Never thought I'd feel hurt by being called a roommate. But somehow, Harper thinking that's the only relationship we have is hurting me more than I ever thought it could.

CHAPTER ELEVEN

Harper

"Liv, you look so beautiful!" I cry.

God dammit.

I don't know why I bothered putting on makeup. It's about the fiftieth time I've cried today. Even waterproof mascara can't handle this chaos.

"I'm just so happy for you," I blubber.

"I'm a little concerned about you right now, Harp," Liv says under her breath, her eyes darting toward her mom. "What the hell is going on?"

"I'm just so happy for you. Finally, you're getting your happily ever after. It can happen! I'm just so happy …" I trail off as a sob overtakes me. "Jesus, what the hell is wrong with me! I don't know why I'm crying like this, Liv. It's your day. I'll get it together, I swear."

We stayed up most of the night talking and gabbing like

teenagers again. Even did each other's hair and painted our toenails. It was a perfect slumber party to end our time as Liv and Harp so that she could begin her life as Liv and Liam.

Honestly, I've been a complete wreck for a few weeks. The constant avoidance of Owen has been draining. The rent on my salon space is so high now I'm barely making any money. I've tried to find an apartment, but there's nothing even remotely in my budget. If it is in my budget, it's thirty to forty minutes away in Colorado Springs, and it would definitely qualify as what some may call 'the ghetto.'

Seeing Owen with his arms around his client yesterday threw me for a major loop. The sheer jealousy I felt instantaneously was absurd. There was no reason to act as I did, but I couldn't control it. I'm lucky I didn't lunge at her and tear her hair out. Beautiful hair, too. I'd love to get my hands in there and style it.

And when he asked if we were okay, I was tempted to tell him no. Tempted to say to him that it was *killing* me to live in his house. To be in his space. His cologne permeates all of the furniture there. Even when he's not there, it's like he is! He doesn't even know I've stolen a couple of his shirts, and I sleep in them. It's the only thing keeping me even remotely sane right now. Because that dry slump I talked about a few months ago? It's even worse now because I can't bring myself to orgasm. Yeah, you heard me correctly. My slew of different toys aren't working. It's like my girly bits *know* Owen is right there, and why bother getting off with a half-assed orgasm when Owen could send me to the stars over and over again?

So here I am, at my best friend's wedding, about to watch her marry the man of her dreams. The love of her life. And I'm fucking miserable because I need to come so badly. I just need to take the edge off. At least, that's what I hope is the issue. I really hope I just need to get some action.

AFTER THE WEDDING, of which I sobbed the majority of, Liv and Liam so dramatically raced up the stairs in their mountain house and got busy super fast. From the sound of it, it had to have been against the damn door. I've never been so jealous of someone in my entire life.

"You okay?" Em asks me quietly as we walk out to our cars.

"No," I answer her bluntly, my sullen expression evident.

"What's going on?" she asks.

"I need to get laid, Em. That's the issue. I'm in a dry spell, and I'm so turned on, and my toys aren't working, and I. Just. Need. To. Get. *Fucked*," I yell. The sound of my voice reverberates over the trees and against the stucco wall of the house.

"What the fuck?" I hear behind me, and I turn to see Owen glaring at me. "Seriously, Harp? Did you need to shout that out for everyone to hear? Jesus, woman. Get it together."

Oh, *he did not just do that*.

"You son of a bitch!" I scream, stomping up to him and slamming my hands into his chest. He steps back with the force of my shove, and I continue moving toward him. "How dare you judge me? How dare you! How many women have you slept with this *week*, Owen? I wouldn't be surprised if it was double digits. You certainly aren't home at all. So you have a lunch date and then grab another skank for dinner?"

"Did she just say he hasn't been home?" I hear Nathan whisper to Em, and she tries to shush him. "Oh, shit, he did mention something ..."

"Jesus Christ, Harper. I've been working. You *know* that. I've slept at my office. I'm barely functioning here. Not like you'd even acknowledge me if I was home. You ignore me all the time. So what the fuck am I supposed to do?" he snarls.

"I have questions, baby girl," I hear Nathan say again. I turn to them and see Emily has her hand over Nathan's mouth, and they're both staring at us.

"You don't have to tell us anything, Harper. We're leaving. Have a great night," Emily declares as she pulls Nathan over to their car. I'm suddenly aware of it being just Owen and I standing in the driveway. Once Nathan drives away, Owen grabs my arm and turns me toward him.

"You said we were okay," he says, his eyes boring into mine.

I stiffly laugh.

"Can't believe you thought I was being honest. No, Owen. We're not okay," I growl as I yank my arm away from his and walk to my car.

"How the fuck am I supposed to fix whatever is broken if you aren't honest with me, woman? Jesus!" he says, throwing his hands up in the air.

"That's the thing, Owen. There's nothing to fix. We were just a fuck, right? And I'm just a roommate. Once I find an apartment, we can go back to blissfully coexisting and antagonizing each other like normal."

His eyes don't leave mine as I get into my car and pull out of the driveway. One last look in my rearview mirror shows him still standing there.

AN HOUR LATER, I'm showered and relaxing in Owen's guest room. I don't hear him come home. In fact, I assumed he would stay out after my little outburst. So when my bedroom door suddenly shatters off the hinges, I scream in terror.

Owen stands there, his eyes wild.

"What the fuck was that for? Are you crazy?" I scream. He scared the shit out of me. I'm shaking.

"Yes, I am crazy! I'm crazy for putting up with you, woman!" he shouts back. I launch out of bed.

"What the fuck? I've done *nothing*." I claim.

"You know what? You're correct. You've done nothing. You've done nothing except avoid me like the plague. You've done nothing but take over my mind. You are in my head, in my dreams, in every fucking waking thought I have, and you didn't do that. I did. And I can't fucking stop, Harp. So you think we're nothing? The fuck we aren't," he roars.

"You can't be serious, Owen. We've had sex a couple of times. What's the big deal?" I say uncertainly.

"Three. That's technically a 'few' times, not a couple," he corrects me, and I roll my eyes.

"You're seriously gonna correct me on that technicality?" I say.

"You bet your sweet ass I am, Harper. Because that's the same number of times I've had sex in the last sixteen months, and I'll be damned if you keep making remarks about me hooking up all the time."

My mouth falls open in complete shock.

There's no way.

Owen is a man-whore. He has regulars. His black book is probably the size of an old-school phone book.

"You're lying," I whisper. Owen shakes his head.

"I may be some things, Harper, but I'm not a liar. And I've definitely *never* lied to you."

I stand completely still as I let his words marinate. His eyes take a slow perusal down my body, and I see heat overtake him as his nostrils flare, and his jaw clenches. I'm in a thong and a tank top. Obviously, I didn't expect a visitor tonight or my door to be shattered. That was kinda hot, though.

"Four."

"Four?" I ask, confused.

"Now it's four," Owen says as he lunges for me and crashes his lips to mine.

CHAPTER TWELVE

Owen

I'm done avoiding her.

I'm done trying to deny whatever this is.

Maybe I'll look back and regret some things I've said or how I've treated Harper, but I will not regret this. This moment, right here, I'll remember forever.

As my lips take hers, Harper immediately wraps her arms around my back and digs her nails into my skin. I'm almost disappointed I'm still wearing my suit from the wedding because I want to feel the pain. I need to feel everything she gives me.

I've got one hand in her hair and the other on her ass as I push her against the wall. Yanking on her hair, I pull her head back slightly so I can angle this kiss exactly how I want. Her tongue tentatively runs along the seam of my lips, and I growl. For as much of a ball-buster as Harper is, I love that she's more hesitant and submissive in the bedroom. Such a fucking turn-on.

"Tell me you want this, Red," I whisper as I bury my head in her neck and suck on her pulse point. "Tell me you're done avoiding me. Avoiding this. I need the words, baby."

I lean up, so I have her forehead against mine, our breath intermixing as we both pant. Her eyes struggle to open as she looks at me.

"Owen, please," she whispers as she leans up and places her lips on mine.

"Thank fuck," I respond as I grab her ass and lift her. Harper automatically wraps her legs around my waist, and I grunt as her hot center pushes down on my cock. "Gonna make you feel good, Red. Gonna make you feel so fucking good."

"Promise?" she giggles breathily as her hands glide into my hair. I groan as she drags her nails against my scalp.

"Have I ever let you down?" I say, and her hands stop. I open my eyes to see her with her eyebrow cocked. "Sexually, Harp. I mean sexually."

She giggles again, the sound going straight to my groin. It's different from her usual laugh. This is deeper, husky, and full of promise.

"I hate to admit this and give you an even bigger ... umm ... *ego*, but no. You haven't ever let me down sexually," Harper says quietly.

"Damn straight," I say harshly as I pull her legs from around my waist and set her down. "On your fucking knees."

I know I sound borderline violent, but I'm so turned on and I need to be in her mouth. And as soon as I say those words, Harper's eyes morph. She drops to her knees so fucking fast I almost think she fell. I can't help but caress her cheek as I watch her.

"Look at you. My spicy redhead doing what I ask. You

gonna suck my cock like a good girl?" I ask, and her eyes heat. Fuck. Does she have a praise kink? Just when I thought she couldn't get any better.

"Yes, sir," she responds, and I throw my head back and groan. Jesus. Didn't expect that. My dick is about to break through my clothes. I'm so turned on.

"Take it out, then," I tell her quietly, and she furiously undoes my belt and pants. As soon as her hand hits my cock, I hiss. Her tongue snakes out to touch the tip, and I almost come.

"Fuck my mouth, Owen," Harper whispers as she slides my entire length into her mouth, and I hit the back of her throat.

"Holy fuck, woman," I groan. My hand finds the back of her head, and I wrap her hair around my fist. I tentatively thrust forward, and she moans. I quicken my pace slightly and watch as her left-hand skirts in between her legs. As soon as she touches herself, she moans around my dick, and that's it. I'm no longer in control of my movements or my ability to hold in my orgasm. I watch as tears trail down her cheeks while I pummel into her mouth, and I come on a roar down her throat. She swallows every last bit.

My eyes close in bliss for a moment, and when I open them back up, she's softly lapping at my cock like it's the tastiest popsicle she's ever had.

"Did you like that?" I ask her quietly, and she nods enthusiastically. "Damn, baby. You're such a good fucking girl, sucking my cock like that."

Harper beams at my praise. I grab her underneath her armpits and drag her up into a standing position.

"That was the best blow job I've ever gotten, Harp. Not even a comparison," I blurt out. She gives me a brilliant smile.

"I aim to please," she says with a saucy wink.

"Well, you can do that any time you want," I tell her honestly. "Now, be a good girl and go to my bedroom. Sit on the edge of the bed and wait for me."

Her eyes darken, and she nods, but as she walks away, I yank her back to me and kiss her deeply. I could get used to this.

I head to the kitchen and grab a couple of candles and some water. If Harper's giving me carte blanche to be with her tonight, I'm gonna enjoy it. Gotta stay hydrated.

Heading to my room, I find her sitting perfectly still on the edge of my bed, her hands on her knees. She looks up at me expectantly. I lean against the doorframe and take it in. The vision of her waiting for me, waiting for my instructions ... Jesus. It's fucking perfect.

"You're so fucking beautiful," I whisper reverently. Harper doesn't respond, but I can tell she enjoyed the sentiment. I light the candles before moving to stand with her knees between my legs. I grab her chin and make her look up at me.

"We've had sex a few times, but I want to make something perfectly clear moving forward," I tell her. Her brow furrows in confusion as I continue. "From now on, I'm in control. This is my ballgame. You make so many decisions in your life, baby. You're in control of so many things. So let me be in control in here, okay? I'm gonna make you feel so fucking good, Red. But you gotta let me lead the way I was born to."

There's a moment where I can see an internal battle within her eyes. Harper is incredibly sexy as an independent and confident woman, but she needs to let go. She needs to let people in and let people help her. She doesn't have to handle everything. And right now? She needs to let me in. Let me worship her and bring her pleasure like she's never experienced.

I see the moment I've won. Harper's green eyes deepen to

the most exquisite aquamarine color I've ever seen, and the tension releases from her shoulders.

"Yes, sir," she whispers, and my cock jumps. I'm still mostly clothed, but I left my cock out after she sucked me off. Her eyes dart toward it as she quickly leans forward and licks the tip. I jump back.

"Uh uh," I tell her. "It's your turn."

She gives me a wicked grin as she whimpers and rubs her thighs together. I drop to my knees and pull her knees apart.

"What do you want, baby? Want me to kiss every part of your skin until you're writhing beneath me in frustration? Suck on those beautiful tits that haunt my dreams? Make you come on my tongue? What do you need, Red?" I say as I lean forward and inhale harshly, taking in her sweet and musky smell.

"Oh, fuck, Owen. I need your tongue, please," she moans.

"Good girl," I respond, and she moans again. Praise is definitely her kink, and I'm here for it.

Sliding the tiny thong she's wearing to the side, I flatten my tongue, lick from bottom to top, and then circle her clit at a leisurely pace, never touching the bundle of nerves. Her hands have found the back of my head, and she tries to forcibly move my head to where she wants it.

"Tsk tsk tsk," I say as I sit back, and she growls in frustration. "Good girls get rewarded, Harper. Are you a good girl?"

I see the battle in her eyes and how she's biting her tongue.

"Owen," she whines.

"Answer the question. Are you a good girl?" I ask as I slide one finger to her opening but don't insert it. Harper struggles to maintain her composure as her body reflexively pushes toward me. "Sit still, baby. I promise it'll be worth it."

Harper visibly struggles to follow my directions, but I patiently wait. It only takes a moment for her to settle down and breathe, and the moment she does, I slam three fingers into her and suck her clit into my mouth. Harper screams as I viciously finger fuck her.

"Eyes on me, Red. You look at me when you come," I demand as my tongue flicks across her clit rapidly. Her eyes pop open as I feel her orgasm beginning. Then, her walls begin to flutter, and her legs tremble around my head.

"Owen," she whimpers.

"Scream my name when you come, baby," I demand as I latch back onto her clit and send her soaring. She screams incoherently, but I hear 'Owen' a couple of times. I turn my fingers inside her and find her G-spot, tapping it repeatedly until she comes again. This time she lets out a stream of gibberish profanity that makes me chuckle.

"Holy shit, Owen," she pants breathlessly as she falls back onto the bed. I climb onto the bed until I'm covering her. I haven't wiped the evidence of her orgasm off my face, and she suddenly leans forward, licks my chin, and moans.

Jesus.

"Dammit, Harper, that was so fucking hot," I groan as I kiss her passionately. A woman who wants to taste herself? Yeah. That's ridiculously hot. I roll us, so she's on top, and she sits up. Her glorious hair settles around her head and shoulders like a firestorm.

"Need you to fuck me now, Owen," she whispers as she grabs my cock and impales herself on a guttural moan. "Oh, Jesus, you feel so good ..."

"Harper," I groan as my hands find her hips, and I begin to move her. Never seen anything as sexy as this. We're still wearing clothes. Her thong is pushed to the side, and my dick is barely out of my boxer briefs and suit pants. But this? This is the single most erotic thing I've ever seen in my life.

"Harder, baby, I need it harder," she whimpers. Other women have called me baby before. But Harper doing it hits a different chord. Like I've been waiting my whole life to hear that term of endearment come out of her mouth.

I shake my head to clear it. I don't know what I'm doing, thinking about Harper as an endgame. I need to fucking focus. She's riding me, and I'm thinking about word usage.

I grab her and slam her down hard, and she screams.

"Yes! Do that again!" she shouts, and I oblige.

"Damn baby, this fucking pussy was made for me," I mutter as I hammer into her from below. I feel her walls begin to clamp down, and I grab her hand and put it on her clit. "Are you close? I need you to come, Harper. Come for me."

Her head falls back as her pussy clenches me so hard I can barely move. The visual of her touching herself while I'm deep inside her has me coming the hardest I've ever come. My vision falters as I spurt stream after stream deep into her womb. A momentary vision of her carrying my baby comes across my thoughts, and I'm taken aback by a feeling of peace. Nope. No. Focus. No relationships. No babies. Jesus, man. Get it together.

Harper falls forward onto me as we both tremble through the aftershocks of our orgasms.

"You okay, baby?" I whisper into her ear as I slowly stroke her hair. God, I love her hair.

"Hmmm," she responds with a pleased sigh. "Yeah, I'd say I'm okay."

I chuckle as she slowly slides herself off of me and to the side of the bed. Once I get the feeling back in my legs, I jump up and grab a wet washcloth for her. When I walk back into the bedroom, the bed is empty.

"God dammit, Harper! Get your ass back in here!" I roar. She slowly rounds the corner from the hallway, her eyes wide. "Where the fuck do you think you're going?"

"Umm, back to my room?" she answers, confusion evident in her tone.

"Get in this bed, woman."

"What?"

"You heard me," I tell her, dramatically throwing out my arm to point to my bed.

"But," she stammers, "You don't do sleepovers. Everyone knows that. I know that."

I stare at her, surprised at her admission. Wow. I really don't do sleepovers, but here I am, almost begging this woman to stay with me.

"Well, tonight, I do. Get in bed," I tell Harper. As she walks to the bed and climbs under the covers, I feel a wave of relief. "Good girl."

I see her shudder, and I chuckle. "Fucking love that you're into that, Red."

"What?" she asks.

"Praise."

"Oh," she says with a light giggle. "Does that bother you?"

"Absolutely not. In fact, it's a major turn-on. I'd fuck you again right now if I didn't know how tired you are," I say as she yawns. "Now I just want to cuddle. You okay with cuddling?"

"Yeah, Owen. I'm okay with cuddling," Harper responds with a small smile.

I pull her toward me and let out a relieved breath. But, God, I've missed this. Her. I've missed her.

"Don't you dare think about sneaking out of here and going back to your room, woman. You don't have a door anymore, and I will come in there and make your ass red," I threaten, and her breath hitches. "Jesus Christ, Harper! How many kinks do you have?"

"I'm not sure," she giggles. "That may be a new one."

"You gonna let me find out?" I ask, and I feel her hesitation.

"I don't know, Owen. This is gonna get messy. We need to

think about things," she whispers. I squeeze my eyes shut as I contemplate her words.

"Yeah, baby. We need to think about some things," I say quietly. I fall asleep quickly as her breathing and scent lull me into a dreamless sleep. I shouldn't be surprised when I wake up, and she's not there.

CHAPTER THIRTEEN

Harper

I ran.

It was too much.

Owen was different last night, and it scared the crap out of me. I don't know how to handle my emotions with him. But if we keep doing what we're doing, I will fall for him. More so than I already have. And he's going to break my heart.

I wish I could call Liv and talk to her, but she's on a short honeymoon with Liam before heading back to work this week. Life of a principal, I guess. She really can't take much time off.

So, I do the next best thing.

I show up on Nate and Em's doorstep with donuts and Coke. I know Coke is Emily's vice. She won't turn down caffeine and carbonation.

The door swings open, and Nathan smiles widely at me.

"We've been expecting you," he says as he motions for me to come in.

"What do you mean?" I ask, looking past him to see into the house that their table is set for brunch.

"Well, you can't call Liv, so we figured you'd end up here. Brunch will be ready in about twenty minutes," he explains. "So talk quick. Because I'll bet my savings account Owen shows up before we sit down."

"You invited Owen?" I screech, and Nathan puts his hands up, motioning for me to quiet down.

"Jesus, Harp, chill. No, I didn't invite him. I bet he just shows up. And the twins are sleeping, so keep it down," he whispers. I cringe.

"Damn, I'm sorry," I say quietly. Me and my big mouth.

Walking into the kitchen, I see Emily whipping up a fruit salad while humming along to something on the Alexa.

"Hey, Harp. You ready to answer questions rapid fire?" Em asks with a glint in her eye. I sigh.

"Fine."

"Yes!" Emily hisses with glee, then high-fives her husband. They both turn to me and cross their arms over their chests.

"You first, baby girl," Nathan says as he looks down at his wife tenderly. Ugh. Sometimes I hate hanging out with them. They're just too cute with each other.

"Have you and Owen slept together?" she asks.

"Yes."

"How many times?" Nathan asks.

"How is that relevant?"

"It's not. I'm just nosey."

"That's fair."

"Answer the question," he demands.

"No."

"Fine," he huffs. "Are you living with him?

"Yes."

"Why?" Emily cries out, a look of horror crossing her face.

"Because my landlord has slowly been increasing my rent, trying to force me to sleep with him, and then he doubled it, and when I couldn't pay it, he evicted me," I say simply. Wow. That was easier to say out loud than I thought.

"Is that how Owen got involved?" Nathan asks.

"What do you mean?"

"Why did Owen learn about this before anyone else? Why didn't you call Liv or me?" Em asks.

"Because you were about to have babies when it started. And Liv was working things out with Liam. So I didn't want to burden either one of you with my problems," I admit quietly.

"Why not when you got evicted, then?"

"Because then you *had* the babies, and Liv was engaged. I'm a big girl. I can deal with my own shit," I tell her.

"But, why Owen? You guys kinda hate each other ... oh, now I get it," Em says with a weird smile.

"What?" I ask as I open a bottle of water and take a big gulp.

"Hate sex."

I immediately choke and spew water all over their kitchen.

"Jesus, Emily!" I choke out, coughing dramatically.

"What? The tension coming off you guys is ridiculous. I bet the sex is mind-blowing," she muses. Nathan swallows a chuckle as he bites his lip to hide a smile.

"Well, it's just complicated things."

"How did you end up living with him?" Nathan asks.

"I called him to ask if he'd help me move some stuff to my rented storage locker. I think he figured out pretty quickly I was going to live in it," I admit. Emily's mouth drops open.

"You have *got* to be kidding me!" she growls.

"What?"

"You could have lived here. Or Liv's. Even Kathryn would

have put you up! Why on earth would you *choose* to live in a storage locker, Harper? What the hell is wrong with you?" She yells. Nathan attempts to calm her down, but Em is not having it. "I can't believe this. I can't believe that you think so little of Liv and me that you truly believe neither of us would have helped you in your time of need. What the fuck? I'm so furious with you, Harp."

"I couldn't take away time that you should be spending with your daughters. I couldn't do that! Why is that so hard to understand? I'm an adult, and I can handle my own life. I don't need people to come in and clean up my messes," I tell her angrily.

"Depending on your friends is *not* the same as cleaning up your messes. It's not your fault your landlord is nasty. It's not your fault that you have a shitty lease. Everyone goes through dark times, Harp. We're your family. Why wouldn't we help you? None of us are perfect. We all need help at one point or another. I know you'd help me instantly if I needed it, right?" Emily asks, and I nod.

"It's just ..." I trail off, trying to figure out how to explain my reasoning. "I've been on my own for so long. I've dealt with everything myself. I've never needed anyone, so I don't know how to do it."

"You've never gotten help from Liv?" Nathan asks.

"No."

"Let me rephrase this. Have you ever *asked* for help from Liv? Because I know she's offered it to you countless times," he points out. Dammit. I forgot he's known me as long as Liv has. Fucking siblings.

"Well, I mean, maybe when we were teens ..."

"You know she stopped offering to help because she knew you wouldn't take it, right?" Nathan says matter-of-factly. My mouth falls open as I gape at him.

"What?" I breathe.

"She just stopped offering. She figured if you ever really needed help, if things got so bad that you couldn't find a solution, you'd come to one of us. I can guarantee she won't like knowing you went to Owen instead of her, though," Nathan says.

Before I can respond, the doorbell rings. Nathan looks down at his watch and chuckles.

"Right on time!" he says with glee as he turns to trot to the door. Em turns to me.

"Are you going to be okay with Owen here?" she asks quietly.

"Are you telling me the truth that neither of you invited him?" I respond, ignoring her question. She nods.

"Nathan said he just knew you both would show up," she says. "I swear, these Riggs boys have some kind of psychic power." I giggle at that. First Jack with the clairvoyant thing, and now Nathan?

Nathan comes back in with a sheepish Owen trailing behind him.

"Hey, Em. Harp. I swear I didn't know you were here," he says, his eyes pleading with mine.

"It's fine," I respond. I try to keep my eyes as blank as possible. My emotions are in turmoil, and I don't know how to respond to anything right now.

"Well, Harper explained why she's living with you, so there's that," Nathan says as we sit down at the table. Em had gone to the stairs and quietly called up to Jack, who quickly flew down the stairs and sat in his spot at the table.

"How long have you been living there, Harper?" Emily asks as she takes her seat.

"A few weeks, I guess," I answer. In some ways, it feels like months. In others, it feels like I just moved in yesterday.

"When did you get evicted?" Nathan asks. Before I can

respond, he looks over at Owen. "Oh! That's why you went to the greasy landlord!"

My eyes whip to his.

"You went to my landlord? When?" I ask, my voice trembling. He looks up at me, and I know. I can see it in his eyes. "You went before I got evicted, didn't you? That's why he turned on me so quickly and threw me out! I can't believe you, Owen! I never asked you to do anything! Why can't you stay out of my life?"

I stand up and throw my napkin on the table. I'm so furious my entire body is shaking with adrenaline. Owen stands up, too.

"I swear I didn't intend to get you evicted. I had no idea it would end up like that. I'm not sorry I got you out of his clutches, though," Owen says.

"Oh, really? That's great, Owen. I'm so glad you're happy with my lot in life and that I'm currently paying $5,000 a *month* to rent my salon space, and I can barely make ends meet enough to save for anything," I yell.

"I'm working on that," he mutters.

"What are you working on?" I ask.

He looks up at me. His expression is fiery and steely with resolve.

"Getting you out of that lease," he says.

My mouth falls open.

"I did not ask you to do anything!" I seethe.

I hear the twins begin to cry, and I know I'm to blame for waking them up, but I can't stop.

"I never asked you for your help. I didn't ask you to force me to move into your house. I didn't ask you to talk to my landlord. I didn't ask you for a damn thing! What the fuck is wrong with you? Why can't you respect my boundaries?" I scream.

"Harper, calm down," Owen says, and I see Nathan cringe in my periphery.

"Did you really just tell me to calm down? Are you fucking kidding me?" I roar. I slam the chair back under the table and stalk out of the kitchen. Owen grabs my arm as I pass him.

"Red, wait. We need to talk," he says.

I wrench my arm from his grasp.

"No. We do not need to talk. Do me a favor, Owen. When you see me? Walk the other way. Don't even look at me. You and I? We're done. I'll be out by the end of the week," I say.

I walk swiftly to the door as Em walks down the stairs with the girls.

"I'm sorry, Em. Sorry for waking them. I just can't be around Owen right now," I tell her as the tears begin to fall.

"It's okay. I know you're hurting. I'm sorry," Emily murmurs as she reaches out to give me a reassuring squeeze on my forearm. "I'll call you later, okay? Liv still has the townhouse. Maybe she will let you stay there. You'll have to tell her everything about Owen, though."

Fuck.

"I'll figure something out."

"No, Harper. You won't. It's time you realize that we are your family, and you need to accept our help," Em says with conviction. I nod miserably.

Thankfully, Owen's car is beside mine instead of behind it, so I can swiftly escape. I text Emily and ask her to keep Owen occupied for an hour so I can grab a bag of belongings. I can't be near him right now. Can't be in his space.

I head back to his house and pack as quickly as possible, shoving everything into grocery sacks and one suitcase. I'll sneak back during the day this week and grab everything else. Then, heading back to my car, I see a text from Liv.

> Liv: I don't know why you need this, but you can stay at my townhouse.

> Me: Thanks. I owe you.

> Liv: Are you okay?

> Me: No. But I will not ruin your honeymoon by telling you about it. Can we make plans for next weekend?

> Liv: Absolutely.

> Me: I hope you're having lots of sex and not thinking about anything else.

> Liv: We had to take a break. My pussy has a pulse and needs some TLC.

> Me: Tongues, Liv. Your pussy needs a tongue.

> Liv: What do you think he's doing right now?

> Me: And with that, I'm done texting. Go enjoy your HUSBAND. (Smile emoji)

I throw my phone down on the passenger seat and back out of Owen's driveway. I awkwardly detour through his neighborhood to ensure he doesn't pass me. I'm sure he'll figure out pretty quickly that I'm at Liv's, but I just want to avoid him. I'm thankful I have a spare key to Liv's to get inside without an issue. And since she has a garage, I'll be able to park there and hide from humanity.

Once I unload everything at Liv's, I call my favorite pizza

place and arrange delivery. Tonight calls for comfort food and wine. Fortunately, Liv hasn't cleared anything out besides her clothes and personal items. She still has wine bottles in a small fridge.

I pull up Netflix on her television and cue up the next episode of Gilmore Girls. It's my guilty pleasure. I've seen the show a hundred times and memorized most of it. But when I'm feeling down in the dumps, Luke and Lorelei can make me feel better.

Typically.

Tonight, however, I'm a mess. I begin sobbing ten minutes into the episode and embarrass the crap out of myself when the pizza is delivered. I'm hiccuping and trying to catch my breath. I scarf down the entire pizza in record time, then throw it back up. I end the night sobbing pitifully in Liv's tub and fall asleep on top of her bed in just a robe. I'm the definition of a 'hot mess.'

Just another reason I never should have gotten involved with Owen Taylor.

CHAPTER FOURTEEN

Owen

Emily wouldn't let me leave. I know this was strategic. She's giving Harper time to get stuff out of my house. You want to know how she managed to keep me there? She literally handed me both girls and then grabbed Nathan and walked out. I sat on the couch with twin five-month-olds. I don't know who was more confused at that moment: the twins or me.

Rushing back to my house, I barrel into her room and find almost all of the drawers empty. My heart falls into my stomach. Harper didn't even allow me to explain. First, we needed to talk about what happened last night, but then it got so much more complicated when Nathan had to drop that bomb. Never should have fucking told him anything.

I spend the day miserably sulking around the house. I queued up Harper's number so many times, ready to call her and plead my case, but never ended up pushing the button. I draft dozens of texts and delete them all.

Maybe this is for the best. Almost all relationships end badly, right? I mean, I have high hopes for Nathan and Liam, but everyone else just crashes and burns. Whatever I'm feeling about Harper has to be just about the sex. There's no way I'm actually falling for her. Right?

Dinner is pizza from my favorite place and a bottle of wine. I drink the whole thing while watching Netflix. Harper must have been on here last because it started that show Gilmore Girls that she loves. I end up watching it. Not bad. That kid Logan is a dick, though.

I finish the night with a long shower. As soon as my head hits the pillow, I regret it. I can still smell Harper. Her scent is all over the sheets. Should have changed out the bedding as soon as I got back, but I forgot. I sleep fitfully as memories of Harper flit through my dreams.

THE WEEK after Liv and Liam's wedding is a disaster. The trial for Victoria and Thomas goes much longer than we anticipated due to the amount of evidence Thomas and his attorney have included. It's all completely ridiculous things like receipts for personal care items for Victoria and text messages where they've redacted so much it's hard to discern what the texts were actually about. Thomas has the audacity to call a housekeeper as a witness, stating the housekeeper believed Victoria was an unfit parent.

Because of how Colorado decides on parental responsibilities, we have to look at so many different factors when one or both parents dispute the relationship. The relationship the child has with the parents, the mental capacity of the parents, their living situation and income ... the list goes on and on.

Thomas' attorney has been a shark. He's fought almost everything I've procured and has attacked Victoria's personality. He claimed she was mentally unstable. The judge ordered a psychological evaluation, which came back perfect. Then the attorney claimed Victoria leaves her children alone and goes out in a 'philandering manner.' His words, not mine. Victoria was horrified. She's been a model parent and, as far as I know, has only left her children when she's been working. She even took a job at their school so she could have the same schedule as them.

On the final day, after over a week of testimony and back and forth, I called her children to the stand. I had hoped it wouldn't get that far, but I need them to clearly state their preferences. I hate that I have to put a five and seven-year-old on the stand because their dad is a jackass.

"Hi, Blaire," I say quietly to the five-year-old, who is legitimately quivering in the chair next to the judge.

"Hi," she whispers.

"We can't *hear* her," Thomas' attorney snarls out, and I don't even need to say anything because the judge does.

"You better pipe down, counselor," she retorts.

I turn back to Blaire and give her a big smile.

"Did you have fun this weekend?" I ask her. She sits up straighter and gives me a big grin.

"Yeah! It was so cool! I even got to go on the big slides with my mommy!" she says gleefully.

"I bet that was amazing!" I respond.

"Yeah, and we even had room service and ate in bed. It was so awesome," Blaire says.

"That sounds great, Blaire. I'm so glad you had fun. Did you wish your daddy was there to enjoy it as well?" I ask.

"No," she says.

"Oh? Why?"

"Because he's mean. All he does is yell. He doesn't even

like us. I heard him tell that man right there," she points to the attorney, "that he just wants to stick it to my mommy. What does stick it to mommy mean?"

"Objection!" the attorney calls out.

"What grounds?" the judge asks.

"Umm ..."

"Overruled."

I turn back to Blaire.

"What else has your daddy said?"

"He doesn't talk to me much. He just gets mad. I don't want to be with him. Why do I have to sleep over at his house? I don't want to," she says with a pout.

"What do you do when you're at your dad's house?" I ask.

"Nothing. He locks us in our rooms," Blaire responds. Woah. What? This is the first I'm hearing about it.

"He locks you in your rooms? Are you sure?" I ask.

"Yeah. Molly and I can't get out. We tried. You can ask the housekeeper. She knows. She tried to unlock the door once, and daddy yelled at her," Blaire tells me.

Jesus. This is getting better and better. The housekeeper lied on the stand.

"Okay, Blaire, you did great. You can go sit back down, okay?" I turn to the judge. "I'd like to call the housekeeper back up for questioning if that's okay."

"Wait, I need to cross-examine Blaire!" Thomas' attorney calls out.

"No." The judge doesn't even look at him. She just demands we call the housekeeper back up. As soon as the housekeeper is on the stand, she begins to sob.

"Mister Thomas told me if I didn't lie, he would get me deported and take my family away," she blubbers.

"He threatened to deport you?" I ask incredulously. "Do you have any evidence of that other than verbal communication?"

"Yes, I have a text message," she tells me.

Holy shit. Not only is Thomas a complete jackass, but now he's breaking even more laws. This just keeps getting better.

The judge stops the trial.

"I don't need to hear anymore. There will be no cross-examination. I find in favor of Mrs. Wallace for both parenting time and decision-making. Mr. Wallace may have supervised visits should he want. I award Mrs. Wallace five thousand dollars per month in child support," the judge claims as she grabs her gavel.

"What!" Thomas roars out.

"Mr. Wallace. Your outburst is unacceptable. Should I raise the amount?" the judge asks.

"Five thousand dollars?" he says more quietly.

"The state of Colorado awards child support as twenty percent of the combined gross income for both parents for the first child and ten percent for the second child. Your gross income is two hundred thousand dollars. That is equivalent to five thousand per month," she states.

Thomas pales.

"And, considering Mrs. Wallace and your children have been living in a one-bedroom apartment for over a year while you've been living in your familial home with five bedrooms, I think it's clear she needs more money than you," the judge says. "Adjourned."

I turn to Victoria and see her silently crying. I let out a massive exhale. It's finally over.

"It's over. You got your girls," I say quietly.

"Owen," she whispers, "Thank you so much. I can never repay you for what you've given me."

"You bringing your girls up without that monster around is all I want, Victoria. Now go get them and celebrate," I tell her.

I don't want to rain on her parade. I'm half expecting Thomas to sue again over the child support amount. I wouldn't be surprised if Victoria is served new papers next week.

But for now, I'm victorious and thrilled that two little girls won't be forced to spend any time with their horrid father.

DRIVING HOME THAT EVENING, I swing by Liv's condo. I just have a feeling Harper is there. And what do you know, she is. She's standing out front talking to someone who appears to be dropping off food.

I don't even think before I slam into the driveway and pop out of my car.

"Harper."

Her eyes whip to mine, and her face falls.

"Go home, Owen."

"No. We need to talk."

The guy delivering the food graciously steps out of the way as I jog up to her.

"Owen, come on. I just want to eat dinner and relax. Can't we do this another time?" Harper whines.

"Oh, sure. Because you'll really take my calls right now," I say pointedly. I haven't tried to call because I know Harper won't answer. There isn't a more stubborn woman in the entire state of Colorado than Ms. Harper Williams.

"Well, you haven't tried to call, so how would you know?" she says accusingly.

"Honestly, I knew you wouldn't answer. I also expected you'd block me," I answer. "Please, let me explain what happened with your landlord. I need you to hear me out. Please."

She sighs loudly.

"Fine. But I'm eating while you do it. And I'm not sharing."

I follow Harper into Liv's townhouse. The new renovations look phenomenal. After that douche Xander trashed the place, Liv had to get a ton of work done. It looks great. It actually really suits Harper.

She sits on the couch and strategically places her take-out bag next to her, effectively forcing me to sit across the room. Alright, Harp. I'll play the game.

I explain how I went down the rabbit hole looking into her lease. How everything was by-the-book because of how the lease was written. I leave out that I'm royally pissed she didn't come to me to review the lease. I might be a tad dumb regarding this woman, but I'm not a complete idiot. She'd immediately have my balls in a vice grip, and not in a good way.

I then tell her how I ended up at the landlord's house. I explain how I had this whole plan of what I was going to say, but as soon as I saw the landlord and visualized him trying to force Harper to sleep with him, I lost my cool. I explain that I told him to stop raising the rent, and he slammed the door in my face. I maybe gloss over the fact that I threatened to press charges, but I'm hoping she understands that I implied it.

The entire time, Harper remains quiet. Finally, when I'm finished, I find myself nervously wringing my hands together, waiting for her to say something. Anything.

"Okay."

Wait, what? That's all she's saying?

"Okay?"

"Yeah."

"What the hell does that mean?"

"You explained. I said, 'okay.' You can leave now."

"The fuck I am!" I shout. "God dammit, woman, can't you give anyone a fucking break?"

Her mouth drops open.

"Why do you deserve a break, Owen? Why do you think I need to give you anything?" she asks as she shovels food into her mouth.

"Red, have I ever tried to hurt you with my actions?" I ask her, and she shrugs. "Seriously. I know we get our barbs in here and there, and we both love a good argument. But do you think I've ever gone out of my way to try and hurt you?"

I study her as she waits to respond.

"Please don't say yes," I murmur. "I know I fuck up tons of times. I know I say the wrong thing a lot. But baby, I've never tried to hurt you. It breaks my heart thinking that you're hurt."

I wince when I realize I called her baby. I know I shouldn't call her anything. But, for some reason, I can't hold in my thoughts right now. Harper unnerves me more than any other person I've ever met.

"No, Owen. I don't think you've ever tried to hurt me. But that doesn't mean you get off scot-free," she says softly. "You have hurt me. That hurts when you go behind my back and try to solve my problems without talking to me. It makes me feel worthless and unvalidated. Maybe we could have devised a plan together if you had talked to me first. But, instead, you bolted in the middle of the night. Am I correct? You saw him the day after we had sex at my apartment?"

I nod, a feeling of shame washing over me.

"I know whatever is going on with us has an end date. Or maybe the end date has already passed. Whatever. I get that you're not going to do a relationship. But we're going to be in each other's lives forever. You get that, right? We'll always be seeing each other. At kid birthdays, Christmas, concerts, and whatnot. So we need to be respectful of each other. And when you treat me like I'm a meaningless woman who can't solve her own problems, I don't want to be around you," she tells me.

Holy shit.

I had no idea I did that.

And how she felt.

"Fuck, Harper. I feel awful. I never meant for you to feel like that. Ever," I tell her as I rest my elbows on my knees and put my face in my hands. "Damn, woman. I'm so fucking sorry."

I hear rustling as she gets up from the couch and comes to kneel in front of me.

"Don't do it again, okay?" she says quietly. I raise my head to look into her eyes.

"Okay," I say quietly as I lean my forehead against hers. The floral scent that is so inherently Harper washes over me, and I feel a wave of peace. Of contentment. I wish I knew how she smelled this way so I could bottle it up. I went way too long before washing my sheets because I didn't want to lose her scent. "Will you come home now, please?"

Harper sighs and then rises, taking a step back from me.

"No. I don't think that's a good idea. I'm going to stay here until Liv sells the place," she tells me.

Fuck.

"I understand," I tell her as I walk to the door. "Thank you for taking the time to hear me out."

"You're welcome, Owen."

I take a deep breath as I wrap my hand around the doorknob.

"I miss you, Red," I whisper. I hear her breath catch behind me. "I miss you so much, and I don't know what to do about that."

It's a long moment before she responds.

"I miss you too, Owen."

CHAPTER FIFTEEN

Harper

By mid-November, I realize my life is about to implode in catastrophic proportions.

Liv put her townhouse up for sale, and it sold in twenty-four hours. The housing market in Colorado is absurd. And her townhouse is in a great location with a low price. She had a bidding war, which was fantastic for her.

Liv and Liam asked if I wanted to stay for a while, and I said no. I just couldn't do that to them. I know they don't need the money, but I felt like I was taking advantage of them by continuing to live there rent-free.

So, in four short weeks, I'm homeless again. I have my eye on a cheap studio apartment on the far western side of Colorado Springs. I can swing it financially if my shitty landlord doesn't raise the rent on my salon space again. I'll definitely be surviving on ramen, rice, and crackers for a while.

Thankfully, there are a couple different free food distributions in the county I can use to get fresh ingredients. Doubt I'll be seeing the medium-well inside of a steak for months, though.

I'm also late.

Yeah, that kind of late.

The kind of late where you relive all of your sexual experiences, trying to think of what might have gone wrong. Did I forget to take a pill, was it the wrong time of the month, yada yada yada.

But, in true Harper fashion, I'm also in complete denial and have avoided taking a test. Just willing for my period to show up. Begging it, actually. Praying to the period gods to smite me with a heavy flow, so I am not carrying Owen's child.

I don't even know if I want kids. But, listen, I have loved Jack since he was born. And watching Emily raise those two beautiful girls? So inspiring and incredible. But having that all on me? Eh. I don't know.

What I *do* know, however, is that Owen doesn't want kids. So if I am pregnant, I have to decide how to tell him. Do I give him an out? Tell him he can sign away his rights? I'd really have to move away. I can't tell the dad he doesn't need to be involved and then show up at every damn activity he's at with his kid in tow.

But for now, I'm going to continue to be in denial. I have too much else on my plate. No reason to stress about a possible baby that is months away if it happens.

***

EVERYTHING COMES to a head at Thanksgiving. We've always had Thanksgiving at Kathryn's house. I've been feeling nauseous all day, but I've chalked it up to anxiety about being in the same space as Owen for an undetermined amount of time. We haven't been together since he apologized at Liv's townhouse.

When I enter Kathryn's house, Owen is at the door.

"Hey, Red," he says quietly, leaning in to hug me. But he lingers. And I feel him smell my hair. I shudder reflexively and lean into him. "Missed you."

"Hey, Owen," I stammer.

"Hey, guys! Get in here," I hear Emily call from down the hallway.

"How long have you been here?" I ask Owen, who shrugs.

"A while."

"Why were you at the door?"

"Isn't it obvious?" he says with a half-smile. "I was waiting for you."

My heart jumps in my chest as I coyly smile in return. Owen slides his hand down my arm and intertwines our fingers together for a moment before squeezing and letting go.

Walking into Kathryn's kitchen, it's a flurry of activity and chaos. Em unceremoniously dumps Poppy in my arms and mutters something about sweet potatoes. Nathan does a similar action with Rose in Owen's arms, chasing after Emily. We both stand with babies in our arms, confused. The babies look equally confused.

As Poppy looks up at me, she reaches up and lightly touches my cheek. I feel a wave of maternal instinct come over me. I've never felt it before. I'm suddenly acutely focused on Poppy and her wants, her needs. I'd do anything for this little creature right at this moment. She lays her head against my shoulder, and I almost sob. This is the most poignant moment of my life.

As soon as Emily returns, I hand Poppy to her and let everyone know I'll be back. I have to go to the store, telling them I forgot something. I barrel down the road and shout out my frustration when I see the local King Soopers is closed already. Damn holiday hours. I head a couple more miles and find a Safeway still open.

Running in, I grab three pregnancy tests. Because everyone will think I'm nuts if I come back empty-handed, I grab a bouquet of flowers for Kathryn as a thank you for hosting.

I don't even make it back to Kathryn's. I hightail it to Liv's condo and rip open all three tests. After peeing in the cup, I set a timer and place all three tests into the cup. Once they are adequately soaked, I put them face down on the counter and hit the timer.

It's the longest three minutes of my life.

I don't need to read the directions when I turn them all over.

Pregnant.

Pregnant.

Pregnant.

I HEAD BACK to Kathryn's in a daze. I probably shouldn't have done the tests now because I have to face everyone, and I'm not ready to share this news yet. I'm not ready to face my future. I'm not ready...I'm not ready for Owen. His response. His reaction.

I'm quiet the entire dinner. Owen is quiet too. It's like he subconsciously knows something has happened and studies me the whole night. No one asked about my sudden grocery trip, and Kathryn was thrilled with the flowers.

After dessert, Owen excuses himself to the bathroom, and I make a very mad dash out of there. I don't want him to catch me. I want to get home and live in denial for another day. Or week. Maybe even a month.

I shouldn't be surprised when he shows up five minutes after me and lets himself in.

"How the fuck did you get a key?" I screech at him.

"Liv gave it to me," he says nonchalantly.

"I'm gonna kill her," I seethe.

"No, you're gonna tell me whatever is going on. Never seen you so quiet, Harp. What the hell has you so rattled?" he asks.

"It's nothing. Seriously."

"Did something happen with your landlord?" he asks.

"No. Really. I swear. Nothing happened with him," I tell Owen. He doesn't look convinced.

"Yeah, I'm not leaving until you talk to me, Red. So you might as well just get on with it ..." he trails off as his face pales.

Holy shit.

I left the pregnancy tests on the table after I saw the positive results.

"Oh my God," I whisper.

"Is that ..."

"Owen, I didn't want you to find out like this. Oh shit," I mumble. He looks up at me with pained eyes.

"Are you pregnant?" he asks, and I nod as tears fill my eyes. He looks back down at the tests and studies them before looking back at me. "Is it ... is it mine?"

I nod as my throat lets out a small sob.

"It's yours. I haven't been with anyone else, I swear." I'm blabbering now.

"I believe you, Harp. I trust you," Owen says quietly as he looks back at the tests. His hand reaches up and cups the back of his neck. "I just ... wow. This isn't how I thought today would go."

"Yeah, me neither."

We stand in silence for a few moments. I don't know how to continue. How to tell Owen that he doesn't have to do anything. I won't force him. But holding Poppy tonight? It made me want this baby so much.

"Owen, I just want you to know I didn't plan this. I didn't even think I wanted kids at all," I say.

"But you're keeping him?" he asks, his eyes suddenly very intense.

"Yeah," I say with a smile. "I'm gonna keep him. Or her."

"We can ask Jack, see what he says," Owen says with a small smile. My smile falls.

"You don't have to. I mean, I don't expect ..." I trail off. His eyes whip to mine.

"This is my baby. I'm gonna be in his life. You got that?" he says deeply. I'm stunned by the intensity of his words.

"I didn't think you wanted kids," I blurt.

"Didn't think I did either. Until right now," Owen murmurs. His eyes again meet mine. "What do you need, Harp? Have you made any appointments yet? When do you need to move out of here?"

"I literally just took the tests, Owen. It's Thanksgiving. I doubt any doctors are taking calls right now," I say dryly, and he chuckles. "The new owners are closing on the townhouse in two weeks. I found a studio in Colorado Springs I can afford, and I'll be able to put the deposit down next week."

"The hell you will," Owen snarls. Those intense eyes narrowed and turned angry. "The mother of my child will *not* be living in a studio apartment in a shitty area of town."

"Yeah, I don't think that's your decision to make, Owen," I retort. "It's what I can afford, and it's available now."

"Woman, I swear to God! Why won't you let me help you?" he says exasperatingly. "Come back to my house, please! I can help you with the pregnancy. Going to appointments. Getting you food that doesn't make you sick. Holding your hair back when you barf. I want to be involved! Please, Red, let me be involved."

The wounded look in his eyes does me in, and I let out a massive sob. Owen's arms immediately surround me as I cry into his chest. I'm so overwhelmed.

"Please let me take care of you. Please," Owen whispers against my hair. "Don't shut me out, Red. Please."

"Okay," I whisper. He stiffens momentarily.

"Okay?" he asks, and I nod against his shoulder. He exhales and squeezes me tighter. My arms find their way around his waist, and I hug him back just as tightly. "God, I've missed you, Harp."

I don't respond. I don't have the words. Looking back, I now realize that many of my outbursts and crying fits over the last few weeks were hormonal. I wish I knew how far along I was. How long have I been pregnant and not known? Today is the first day I've had real nausea. So many unknowns.

"Can I ask you a favor?" Owen whispers against my neck. I shiver as his lips ghost over my skin.

"Yeah?"

"Can I stay tonight? I really want to hold you, Red. I need to hold you," he says as his voice trembles.

"Okay."

"Thought you'd make it more difficult for me," he says, chuckling.

"I think I really need to be held tonight, Owen," I admit. He takes my hand and leads me up to the bedroom. We undress silently. I try not to look at Owen but feel his heated stare. As I take off my shirt, he stands in front of me. His hand covers my stomach in a tender caress before he drops to his knees and places the lightest of kisses all along my stomach.

"I don't know what our life will be like, little one," he croons to my womb, "but I'm so glad I'm your daddy. I can't wait to meet you." He kisses my stomach once more and then walks into the bathroom.

My emotions are whirling. That was the most exquisite thing that has ever happened to me. I don't know how I'll ever survive a lifetime of being connected to Owen this way.

CHAPTER SIXTEEN

Owen

I'm pleasantly surprised when I wake up the following morning with my arms still wrapped around Harper, my hands cupping her stomach reverently.

I'm going to be a dad.

This is how life is supposed to be, a voice whispers in my head.

I know the moment Harper wakes up, as she stiffens against me momentarily and then melts back into my embrace. Her hand covers mine on her stomach. I slide my hand out from under hers and squeeze our fingers together.

"Hi," she whispers.

"Hey," I say quietly as my head dips to kiss the side of her neck. "You sleep okay?"

"Yeah, actually. I slept really well," Harper says with a yawn. "Could probably go back to sleep."

"Is the salon open today?" I ask her.

"No, thankfully. I decided to close. Just needed a break. And Tori wanted to do Black Friday shopping, so she was thrilled I didn't want to work either," Harper tells me.

"How about I make us some breakfast, and we can talk?" I ask, and she nods.

Sliding out of bed, I immediately miss having Harper in my arms. I run to the bathroom to pee and brush my teeth, thankful that Liv always has extra things stored in the townhouse for unexpected guests, like toothbrushes.

Harper heads into the bathroom after me, and I run downstairs to see what I can make. I really enjoy cooking. It's relaxing for me, and creating new recipes and concoctions is rewarding. Plus, most recipes are for two people or more. While I like leftovers, I can't stand eating the same thing over and over again. I'd rather cook a small meal for myself each day instead of being forced to reheat the same meal repeatedly.

Harper stocked the fridge, so I easily found ingredients for omelets. I'll need to research what Harper isn't allowed to eat now. She doesn't realize it, but I will take care of her. I'll make sure she's eating enough. Getting her vitamins. I'm going to be at her beck and call for the next nine-ish months. Shit, how far along is she? I wonder. Maybe the baby is coming sooner rather than later.

As Harper descends the staircase, I stop what I'm doing and stare. Her beautiful hair is settling on her back in glorious waves of red, and I now see she has that gorgeous pregnancy glow everyone talks about. I didn't realize it before. Pregnancy looks good on her.

"What?" she asks. I can't even withhold my thoughts if I try.

"You're so fucking beautiful, Harp," I say quietly, and she blushes immediately. "Sorry. I hope that doesn't make you uncomfortable. But you look ... damn, woman. You look amazing. Pregnancy is a good look for you."

"You say that now, but wait until I'm the size of a whale," she jokes, and I walk over to her, taking her chin in my hand.

"You'll still be beautiful then, baby. You're making a human. That's the most amazing thing I've ever seen. I'll still think you're beautiful," I tell her. Her eyes hold mine for a moment before she steps back and looks toward the kitchen.

"What are we making?" she asks.

"I'm making omelets. You can sit there and let me cater to you," I tell her with a wink. "Wait. Are omelets okay? Have you had any nausea or anything?"

"Yesterday was the first day I felt yucky. But, honestly, I chalked it up to being nervous to see you," she admits. She takes a seat at the bar while watching me cook.

"In all honesty, I felt pretty nauseous, too, thinking about seeing you." I pull the eggs out of the fridge, set them next to the stove, and then grab butter and veggies.

"Liar," she says with a smile.

"Never lied to you, Red. I've told you that," I say as I turn back to the stove and crack the eggs.

"I didn't mean that ... damn, Owen. I'm sorry," she says remorsefully. "I was just teasing. I'm sorry."

"It's okay, sweetheart. Just believe me when I say I don't lie to you, yeah?" I ask, and she nods.

We're silent for a few moments as I begin making the first omelet, both of us obviously lost in our own thoughts. I want to ask Harper so many things. Want to tell her to give it a shot with me. A real shot. A real family.

"I think we need to address the elephant in the room," Harper blurts out. I turn to her, and before I can speak, she continues. "I think it's best to lay down some ground rules for moving forward. So we can co-parent successfully."

I turn to flip the omelet, so she doesn't see my face fall.

Co-parenting means no relationship. It's not what I want at all.

"What kind of ground rules are you thinking, Red?" I ask softly. I want to know where her head is at before I put my heart out there.

"Well, I don't want this kid to be confused. We're friends. Friends with a kid. We can be in the same room together and participate in all the kid-related shenanigans without getting into arguments. We'll come up with a parenting arrangement, so we each get equal time. We can do this, Owen," she says confidently.

I'm silent. Marinating on Harper's words, I try to come up with a valid argument where I'm not disregarding her thoughts while also letting her know that I want more. And I just can't come up with anything without sounding like a narcissistic asshole.

"If that's what you want, Harper," I finally say as I plate the omelet and place it in front of her. Her brow furrows as she studies me.

"What do you want, Owen?" she asks, and I sigh.

"I just want you to be happy. That's all I want," I say honestly. As long as Harper is happy, I can make anything work. She doesn't need to know that I want more with her. Not now, at least. Maybe we can revisit it down the road.

"Should we get it in writing?" she asks. I'm acutely aware she's now asking me the legalities as an attorney and not as the baby daddy. I fill up two glasses of orange juice and set them at the bar.

"I don't think there's any rush, Harp. We don't even know how far along you are. We'll get it all figured out before the baby comes, okay?" I tell her as I continue making my own omelet. I hear a subtle moan and whip around to see her eyes closed as she blissfully chews a piece of egg.

"Oh my God, Owen, this is so good. When did you learn how to cook?" she moans, and I chuckle.

"Learned how years ago. Right after law school, I guess. Had to figure out how to feed myself because I refused to survive on takeout and freezer meals," I say.

"Your mom didn't teach you?" she asks.

"Nah. She was too busy complaining about my dad and how miserable her life was without him to teach me anything," I tell her.

"Oh, shit, Owen. I'm sorry. I didn't know that," she says quietly.

"It's okay. I don't have a good relationship with my parents. But it's fine. I've come to terms with it," I say.

I plate my omelet and sit beside Harper, eating quietly for a few minutes until Harper finally speaks up.

"Do you think it was after Liv and Liam's wedding?"

The last time we were together.

As I take a trip down memory lane, my eyes close reflexively, reminiscing about that amazing night. God, the sex had been spectacular.

"I don't know, maybe," I say nonchalantly, trying to keep my voice level, so she doesn't know what I'm thinking about. "If it was, that would put you at around five weeks pregnant?"

"I think technically it goes from the date of your last period, so more like seven weeks," she answers.

"What if it was the time before that?" I ask, thinking out loud.

"Oh, well then, I guess around eleven weeks?"

"What about the time before that?" I ask, my voice dropping as my dick twitches in my joggers. I'm aching to touch her. Aching.

"Fifteen weeks, I think," she says breathlessly.

"Which time was it that I made you come so many times you blacked out?" I ask huskily.

"Eleven weeks," she mumbles. I can see her chest quickening as her breathing elevates. She's as turned on by this discussion as I am.

"You know, since we're moving forward as co-parents and all, can I just say I have a few regrets?" I say as I stand to take my plate to the sink.

"You do?" she respond, and I see how her eyes shine with a glimmer of hurt momentarily before she shutters her expression to one of placid nothingness. Harper is the queen of schooling her face, so she doesn't show anything. Well, most of the time. I'm the fortunate soul who can bring out her fiery side.

"Yeah, I do," I say as I come to stand behind her. Leaning down, I place my mouth next to her ear. "I regret not spending more time with my face between your legs. I regret not spending more time with you in the shower, watching your face as you come on my cock. I regret not taking you from behind in front of a mirror so I could watch. I regret never having you outside. In public. Where we could get caught. I regret not covering you in my cum, marking you, so everyone knew you were mine. I regret never waking you up by sliding into you and fucking you awake. I regret never telling you how you're the last person I think about at night and the only woman I see in my dreams. I regret so much, baby. So much."

Harper whimpers as she leans back into my chest.

"What are you doing to me, Owen," she whispers.

"Only the same things you do to me, Red. Making me wild. And hungry. And fucking feral. For you," I say as my tongue slips out to touch her neck.

"This isn't a good idea," she stammers as her hands slide up and reach around my neck, holding my mouth to her skin. I suck gently on her pulse point and reach around to cup her tits. Jesus, they're so much bigger. They were fantastic before, but now they're damn near perfect.

"I disagree. I think this is the best damn idea I've ever had," I tell Harper as I pepper kisses along her shoulder blade.

"It muddies everything up, Owen. We need clear black and white, not gray ... oh, fuck ..." She trails off as I pinch both nipples and twist. "Oh shit, don't stop."

"Not gonna stop, baby. Gonna make you feel so fucking good, alright?" I say, turning her slightly so I can see her face. "Need the words, Harper. Need to hear you say you want this."

"Yes, I want this," she breathes.

"Good girl," I praise, and she fucking beams at me. I groan. This woman is gonna be the death of me with how fucking perfect she is for me. "God damn, woman. You're so fucking amazing."

I pull off her shirt and find she's completely naked underneath. Jesus. She gives me a coy grin.

"What the fuck, woman?" I say. "Were you hoping this happened too?"

"Maybe a little," she says quietly as her hands find the hem of my shirt, and she drags it up my torso. Harper surprises me again by leaning forward and dragging her tongue along my abs as she lifts the shirt, then finding my nipple and catching it between her teeth. Holy ... well, fuck. I liked that. Huh.

"Liked that, didn't ya?" she says cheekily as she nibbles on my other nipple. I growl at her, my hands threading through her hair as I drag her mouth to mine. My lips slant over hers in a searing kiss, our tongues dancing together. She tastes like orange juice and cherries. I assume it's some kind of flavored lip balm, and it's fucking intoxicating. She moans into my mouth as my hands slide down and grab her ass. I break off the kiss, panting.

"Typically, I'd be all for taking this slow and memorizing every curve of your body, but I fucking need you," I tell her, and she whimpers.

"Me too, Owen. Me too. Make it hard. I need you to fuck me hard," she whispers as her hand slides into my joggers and fists my cock. Now it's my turn to groan.

"Fuck, Red. Stop or I'm coming in my pants, and I'd much rather come in you," I grunt. Harper giggles like the little vixen she is. She loves undoing me as much as I do her. I lift her, and she wraps her legs around my waist.

Too many steps to make it up the stairs. Couch is too far away. Bar is too high. Fuck it. There's this little decorative desk off to the side of the kitchen, and that's as far as I'm able to make it before I deposit Harper on top. I have my dick out in a few seconds, and I'm thrusting into her wet heat a moment later.

We simultaneously groan. In wanton need. In relief. In a feeling of coming home. I have a voice in my head screaming at me that I need to live in her, embedded in her, until our souls are one.

"Move, Owen," she whispers, and I'm forced out of my trance.

"Hard and fast, baby," I tell her as I hammer into her. Her pleasured cries fill the room as I piston in and out. The desk she's sitting on slams against the wall as the sounds of our skin slapping together and the wetness between Harper's legs noisily joins the party. I almost come just from hearing it all together in a fucked up harmony. Harper's hands find my hair, pulling until our heads are against one another. I open my eyes to see her staring at me. "Harper ..."

"I know."

Never been like this. Never felt such exquisite lust and passion. Never felt like I found my match. I don't know what to do about that.

My hand wraps around her neck, holding our foreheads together as our eyes don't look away. I grab one leg and pull it onto my shoulder, hitting inside Harper so deeply that she screams. I feel her walls begin to clamp down on me as my vision starts to waver. I can feel the most amazing orgasm of my life starting in my legs, flowing through my spine, and finally into my balls as my dick swells inside her. I slam into her at a frenzied pace, coming so forcefully I forget to breathe. One last thrust, and it breaks the camel's back, literally. Well, it breaks the desk. I hear the wood splintering, but it takes me a moment to fully comprehend what's happening.

Harper cries out as gravity begins to take her down. Her legs automatically cinch around me, and I'm pulled down with her. I manage to swivel, so I land on my back, and she lands on my front, and I brace her so her stomach doesn't hit me at all.

"Shit, Harp, you okay, baby?" I say breathlessly. I can hear the concern in my voice. But, Jesus, I just found out she's pregnant. I can't lose the baby now. Because I know that I'll lose Harper, too.

Her head is against my chest, and she doesn't speak.

"Harper, baby, talk to me," I say nervously.

I hear a sound come out of her, and I finally grab a handful of hair and pull her head up to see she's silently laughing. The sound I heard was a very unladylike snort.

"What the hell was that?" she cackles. "Holy shit, we broke the desk! How the fuck am I supposed to explain that to Liv?"

"Just blame me. Liv expects it from me," I deadpan, sending Harper into more hysterics.

"That's one way to celebrate having a baby, huh," she muses, setting her chin down on my chest and looking at me with giddiness in her eyes. I place my right arm behind my head and thread the fingers of my left hand through her hair.

"Yeah, that was something," I comment.

"Great way to start our new chapter as friends and co-parents," she says, and my entire body stiffens.

"What do you mean?" I ask, trying to keep my voice steady.

"Sex complicates things, Owen. The baby needs to be the priority. Plus, if we continue, I'm likely to fall for you, and we both know you don't want that," she says, her eyes downcast as she moves to stand up. I wince as I slide out of her.

"I never said that," I mutter.

"What was that?" she calls as she walks into the bathroom.

"Nothing."

Shit.

I have to figure out a way to tell her I'm not feeling that way. That I think I'm falling for her. And I want her to fall for me. How do I tell her that? When everything anyone knows about me subtracts from my current feelings?

CHAPTER SEVENTEEN

Harper

Moving back in with Owen has been weirdly déjà vu. Well, except we didn't have sex like the first night I moved in here in September. Owen has remained cordial and respectful but has kept his distance. So it's been ... odd.

In all honesty, moving back to Owen's took a lot of stress off my plate. I was barely making ends meet. The salon lease wrung me dry every month. Some weeks I had to choose between filling up my car or grabbing more groceries. I walked a lot in November.

I'm rarely nauseated, which has been a blessing. In fact, I've been ravenous for food. Anything and everything makes me salivate and hyper-focus so much that I can't complete simple tasks until I get that craving covered. I now realize I should have never made fun of Emily and her odd pregnancy cravings because I'm either equaling her in weirdness or beating her.

Today's craving was mac and cheese on top of a Panera cinnamon bagel. Tori, my only stylist on staff, gagged as I scarfed it down. She's the only person, other than Owen, who knows I'm pregnant. I didn't intend to tell anyone until I was seen by the OB, but she overheard me making the appointment.

I couldn't get into the OB until mid-December. I wanted to use the same OB Emily used because she had great things to say about him. Owen picked me up and took me to the appointment. He graciously looked away when I had to undress from the waist down, which made me giggle. It's not like he hasn't seen it all before, but whatever.

I sat on the examination table and swung my legs back and forth.

"You nervous, Harp?" Owen asks quietly, and I nod.

"Yeah. Yeah, I'm nervous," I respond.

He reaches over and grabs my hand, squeezing it tightly in his.

"Gonna be okay, Red," he whispered.

"I'm just already so attached to the bean," I say softly.

"The bean?" he repeats, a grin spreading across his face.

"Yeah, the bean. It's what I've been calling him," I say.

"I love that you think it's a 'him.' I think so, too," Owen says, as there's a knock on the door before the door opens.

"Hello, Harper, I'm Dr. Thomason," an older man says warmly as he extends his hand to shake mine. "And you're dad?"

"Yes, sir, I'm Owen. Baby daddy," Owen says with a chuckle. My heart skips a beat. I kinda love hearing him call himself the baby daddy.

"Good to meet both of you. I understand you're a friend

of Emily and Nathan Riggs?" he asks as he washes his hands and sits down at the ultrasound machine.

"Yes, we're all good friends," I answer. He smiles softly.

"Do they know yet?" he asks.

"No, no one knows," Owen responds. The doctor gives me a weird look.

"You should tell them at Christmas," he says.

How odd.

"Yeah, maybe," I answer uncertainly. I really want to see the bean and ensure everything is okay first.

"Well, your vitals look great. Let's get started with the ultrasound," Dr. Thomason says as he begins to position the exam table precisely as he needs. "Put your feet in the stirrups, please."

"Why the stirrups?" Owen says, and I can see the horror on his face as it dawns on him what that means. "Hold up, you're going *up* there? You do an ultrasound *that way*?"

I stifle a giggle with a cough.

"Uh, yes, the first ultrasound is done vaginally. It's the best way to see an embryo early in pregnancy. By around twelve weeks, we'll be able to do the ultrasound on the abdomen," Dr. Thomason says as he inserts the wand. I wince slightly when it hits my cervix. I'm about to make an inappropriate joke when the doctor pulls the wand out. "Well, never mind. You're definitely at least twelve weeks. Let me switch out the wand."

My eyes whip to Owen's as we both process that tidbit. Holy shit. I'm already in my second trimester? I had no idea I was even pregnant!

Suddenly, a swift thump-thump-thump-thump sound takes over the room.

"There's your little one," Dr. Thomason says. "Let's get some measurements, but I'd say you're probably around fifteen or sixteen weeks." He flips the screen around so Owen and I can see, and my eyes immediately fill with tears. There's the baby's profile. Nose, arms, the whole thing. I'm overcome with emotion. I don't even realize that Owen has pulled his chair right up to me and buried his head in my hair.

"Oh my God," I whisper.

I'm a mom. That's my baby.

"Actually, I'm calculating you're about seventeen weeks along, Harper. Your due date is May twenty-second. Would you like to know the gender?" the doctor asks.

"Holy shit, you can tell that already?" I yell out, and he chuckles.

"Yes, I can tell. Would you like to know?" Dr. Thomason asks again.

Owen raises his head up, and I see his eyes are red.

"Can we ... can we find out? Please, baby, I really want to know," He whispers.

"I really want to know, too," I tell him with a smile. I turn to Dr. Thomason and nod.

"Congratulations, mom and dad. You're having a boy."

I let out a strangled sob as I realize Owen and I were both right in calling it a 'him' from the beginning. Owen pulls my head toward his and gives me a tender kiss. I can feel the emotion and happiness in that kiss. It pulls at my heartstrings. He rests his forehead against mine for a moment.

"Thank you," he whispers.

"For what?"

"For giving me this gift. For making me a dad. For everything, Red."

"I'm pretty sure you were an equal participant in making this gift, Owen," I tease him, and he gives me a boyish smile.

"You know what I mean. I never thought I'd want kids, but ... this is everything. You get that, yeah?" he asks, and I nod. I know exactly what he means and how he feels. It is everything.

Dr. Thomason prints off some ultrasound pictures for both of us, then excuses himself, so I can get dressed. Owen is staring at the images while I get dressed. The look of adoration on his face is priceless.

"You okay?" I ask him, and he looks up at me with a breathtaking smile.

"So much better than okay," he says with a grin and a wink, causing me to inhale sharply. I wish he wasn't so handsome. This would be easier if I didn't feel my body pulling toward him.

After leaving the OB office, we grab lunch before returning to my salon. When Owen pulls up, we sit silently in his car for a few moments, lost in thought.

"When do you want to tell everyone?" he asks.

"I don't know. Should we tell them at Christmas?" I ask.

"As long as we're together when we tell everyone, that's all I want," Owen says.

"Together? But I thought ..." Owen cuts me off.

"I mean in person. I don't want you to tell them without me there. Relax, Harp," Owen says with a chuckle. "Good to know where your head is at, though. Noted."

I don't miss the slightly pained look in his eyes when he looks back at me.

"Owen ..."

"It's fine, Harp. Really. I need to get going. I have a deposition. I might be running late tonight, so don't count on me for dinner," he says as he puts both hands on the wheel and looks out on the road, effectively dismissing me.

"Oh, okay," I murmur. "Thanks for going with me today, Owen."

He looks over at me, and his expression is masked.

"Anytime, Red." He gives me a saucy wink, and I awkwardly smile in return.

I get out of the car and barely have the door closed before

he pulls away. I watch his tail lights disappear in the distance before heading back into my salon.

"Hey, girlie! How did it go?" Tori calls out from the back.

"It went great. Don't you have a client soon?" I ask as I walk toward her.

"No, the heifer canceled on me. Had the audacity to expect *me* to fit her in on Saturday because she *needs* her highlights done before her husband's work party, and then got mad when I said I was fully booked. Fucking entitled rich bitches," she mutters.

"Put it in her computer file so we can track how often she cancels. If it becomes a pattern, we will tell her she isn't welcome here anymore," I say.

"Will do. So! Tell me about the appointment! Did your man go? How far along are you? Only one crotch goblin in there, right?" Tori asks in rapid succession.

"Owen went, and he's not my man. Only one baby. And I'm seventeen weeks," I tell her. Her eyes widen comically as she gapes at me.

"Holy shit! Seventeen weeks? How did you not know?" she asks. "I barfed so much I basically lived next to the porcelain god for months!"

"I really don't know. I've only been nauseated a couple of times so far. My belly just started popping out this week," I say as my hands subconsciously cup my still-small baby bump.

"Wait, if you're that far along, did you get to find out the gender?" she asks, and I nod. "Well, what is it? Come on, Harp! Give me the deets!"

"Okay, but you have to promise not to tell anyone. We aren't telling our families until Christmas. So you just have to keep your trap shut for two more weeks," I say.

Tori makes a motion like she's zipping her lips, then throws away the pretend key. I giggle.

"Okay, crazy lady. It's a boy," I tell her, and she shrieks, jumping up and down with glee.

"I knew it! I knew it would be a boy. Oh, Harp, you're gonna love being a boy mom. It's the best!" she says.

"You just referred to your kids as crotch goblins," I point out, and she shrugs.

"I still love the little hellions. They've just made it so that I color my hair a hell of a lot more often," she says with a wink.

I chuckle as I get my station ready for my next appointment. I catch my reflection in the mirror and see the glow that Owen mentioned. I look fresh. Happy. At peace. I've never looked or felt this way. Never would have thought I'd be ending this year pregnant, let alone be pregnant with Owen's child. What a way to end the year.

CHAPTER EIGHTEEN

Owen

I'm chomping at the bit to announce Harper's pregnancy at Christmas dinner. I've never been this excited about anything before. I know there will be many questions, but I hope everyone is happy for me. For us. Regardless of what relationship I wish Harper wanted with me, I'm thrilled we're having a child together. A boy. My son.

"Everyone ready for the white elephant gift exchange?" Emily calls out. We all shuffle into their family room and gather around the tree. Liv and Em decided a white elephant gift exchange was the most logical for our group, as well as the most economical. Gifts had to be under forty dollars and would work for both sexes. We all went around and picked a present.

Liv and Em decided to make their own rules. Instead of each person opening the present immediately, thus allowing someone else to 'steal' the item, they felt we should all open the gifts simultaneously. Then we had one chance to barter a steal if we wanted.

I open mine to find a coffee mug and a Dutch Bros gift certificate. The mug says, "Nice Butt." But, even worse, at the bottom of the mug, it says, "Can I wear it as a hat?" My eyes narrowing, I look around the room and see Liam leering at me. Fucking jackass. Should have known it would be one of the guys who put that in the pile.

Nathan ended up with a motorized tube guy, like the things you see at car dealerships. Emily got a family game night package with kid-friendly games, popcorn, and ice cream toppings. Perfect for their growing family. Monica, who is finally settled in Colorado after an extremely tumultuous year in Oklahoma, snagged an outdoor wine tote bag and immediately threatened all of us that we weren't allowed to steal it. She's one hell of a feisty Italian.

Her boyfriend Marcus, who none of us like, ended up with a fantastic gag gift that I submitted. I'm so fucking thrilled he ended up with a toilet timer, Poop-Pourri, and a dozen rolls of toilet paper featuring Joe Biden and Donald Trump. He glared at all of us. He's a douche. We're all just hoping Monica drops him quickly.

Harper squealed when she opened up a miniature fridge. When I asked what the hell it would be for, she explained it's great for keeping skincare products cool. Whatever. Girls are weird. Liv was thrilled to unwrap a charcuterie board set, and Liam scored a survival kit.

As we're cleaning up the wrapping paper, Liam clears his throat.

"Actually, I have one last gift I'd like to give my wife," he says, his eyes shining at that last word. He loves calling Liv his wife.

"Baby, we said nothing else!" Liv hisses.

"You'll like this, I swear," he says as he gingerly bends down to snag something from inside the Christmas tree branches. Liam is recovering nicely from being shot a few weeks ago after Liv's ex tried to kidnap her from her school. Dickwad got a bullet in his skull for attempting that.

Liam hands Liv a small box. She opens it with trembling hands and gasps. "Oh, Liam!"

Liam takes out a necklace and stands behind Liv to put it on her.

"It's beautiful, baby," she whispers, leaning up to give him a kiss. Harper's eyes narrow as she looks at the necklace. I look closer and see it appears to be a gold outline of a mother holding a baby.

"Liv?" she says quietly and waits until Liv's eyes are on her. "Are you pregnant?"

Liv beams, nodding. Harper shrieks and hugs Liv, jumping up and down. Em joins the fray but doesn't appear as shocked as Harper. Nathan looks pleased as well, so I assume they already knew. This necklace presentation was just for Harper and me.

"Congrats, mama," I tell Liv as I give her a quick hug. "When are you due?"

"The beginning of July," she responds.

Holy shit. Our babies will be only a few months apart.

I look at Harper, and she shakes her head ever so slightly, silently telling me not to speak up. She doesn't want to ruin Olivia's moment. While I understand that, I'm incredibly disappointed. I've been looking forward to telling them all week.

On the way home from Nathan's, I'm quiet.

"I didn't want to ruin their moment, Owen," Harper says quietly.

"I know. I understand. I can be sad, though, right? I want to tell them and have everyone be excited, too," I tell her.

"Do you think they will be excited?" she blurts out.

I turn to look at her.

"Why wouldn't they be?" I ask her incredulously.

"Well, it's you and me. We aren't together. He wasn't made the same way Liv and Liam's baby was made," Harper says.

"Um, I can guarantee you it was made *exactly* the same way, Harp. Married people have the same kind of sex," I say dryly, and she giggles.

"I mean that they wanted a baby. She went off birth control. They were actively trying for a kid. You and me? This was a complete accident."

"Poppy and Rose were an 'accident,' as you say. But I bet Em and Nathan would never call them that. They'd say the girls are a blessing," I tell Harper.

She shrugs, chewing on her bottom lip.

"I just don't want to be judged by any of them," she whispers as I pull into my driveway. I park my SUV in the garage, shut off the engine, and then turn to her.

"None of them will judge us, Red. They're going to be thrilled," I tell her as confidently as I can. I'm not sure I truly believe my own words. They won't judge Harper. But they sure as hell will judge me. I'm the loose cannon of this group, the man-whore who can't keep it in his pants. If a side has to be picked, I know the entire group will choose hers. And I don't blame them at all for it.

I help Harper grab our presents and leftovers from the car, then head inside. Harper begins to head up the stairs, but I call for her.

"Hey, Harp? Can you come back down here for a sec?"

"I'm exhausted, Owen, and I want to take a bath. Can we talk tomorrow?" she says with a yawn.

"Oh, I just wanted to give you something really quick," I

tell her as I pull a small box out from inside the tree, just like Liam did.

"I thought we weren't getting each other gifts," she says warily.

"I know. I couldn't help myself with this one, though," I tell her warmly. Harper opens the small box to find a necklace similar to what Liam gave Liv.

She gasps as she pulls the double heart pendant out of the box. A larger white gold heart holds a smaller rose gold heart within it. Knowing Harper would freak out if she knew where I got it, I removed it from the Tiffany box and put it in a standard jewelry box. She doesn't need to know how much it cost.

"When I saw this, I knew you had to have it," I tell her softly as I take it from her trembling hands. "I like to think it's your heart and little man's heart, beating together as one."

A tear slips down Harper's cheek as she sweeps her beautiful red locks up and away from her neck, and I clasp the necklace.

"It's breathtaking, Owen. Thank you. This means so much to me," she says quietly. I can't help but lean down until my nose is against her neck as my arms circle her from behind.

Harper lays her hands on my arms, allowing me to hold her. I think she knows I need this. Right now, at this moment, I need this connection with her and with our baby. I wish I could tell her everything I want to say. How much I want her. Need her. Cherish her. But the only thing I can give Harper right now is what she's made perfectly clear: space and a friendship with me.

"You know I'd do anything for you, right?" I say softly against her neck as I breathe her in. Her perfect floral scent soothes my anxiety. I can feel my heart rate lowering in just the few moments I've held her.

"I know," she whispers.

"Merry Christmas, sweetheart," I whisper against her skin,

pressing the lightest of kisses against the pulse point that drives me wild. I hear her quick intake of breath as I force myself to pull my arms from her.

Harper turns, her fingers reverently touching the pendant.

"Merry Christmas, Owen."

She walks past me and makes her way upstairs. I hear the bath in the guest room running a few moments later, and I walk to the fridge and grab a beer. I rest my hands on the cool granite countertops and drop my head.

I don't know how I will survive the next five months as Harper's roommate and friend when I want to bury myself inside her every fucking moment. I better sign up for a wine of the month club because I foresee a lot of drinking to take the edge off.

CHAPTER NINETEEN

Harper

A week goes by in a blink of an eye. We still haven't told anyone about the baby. I'm growing less and less thrilled with the idea of dropping a bomb on the entire group, so I tell Owen I think we should divide and conquer. I'll tell Liv and Em while he tells Nate and Liam. We each make plans for lunch on New Year's Eve to deliver the news.

Liv, Em, and I head into Colorado Springs to hit one of our favorite Mexican restaurants. Liv and I have been queso snobs for as long as I can remember. So if a new Mexican joint opens up, we will judge it based solely on this one appetizer. If they refer to it as a 'cheese sauce', we're out. Nope. We need it to be spicy, cheesy, and bonus if the place adds a chunk of spicy meat.

"Liv, is this going to be okay?" Em frets about the choice. Oh, I hadn't even thought about that. She's still in her first trimester. I really lucked out with hardly ever having nausea.

"Yeah, I think it'll be fine. You know me, I never turn down queso," Liv says with a giggle.

"Well, I'm grabbing a massive margarita while we're here. Harp, tell me you're drinking too. I don't want to be the only one getting blitzed," Emily laughs. I awkwardly chuckle.

"Um, no. Not today," I say.

"Oh, are you saving it for tonight?" Liv asks as the server brings the chips and queso and puts it in front of her. The wicked gleam in her eye as she takes a massive scoop and shoves it into her mouth makes both Em and I laugh.

"Dang, woman, slow down," I tease.

"What the baby wants, the baby gets," she mutters. "So why aren't you drinking today? You're not doing some stupid fad diet, are you? I swear, Harp, you have a banging body. No stupid diet where you avoid alcohol, or only eat carbs, or only eat yellow things is going to change that fact."

"Okay, *one time* I did a fad diet, Liv. You gotta quit bringing that shit up," I say.

"Yeah, and you puked for like three days afterward."

"Well, technically, it worked then, didn't it?"

Liv snorts around another mouthful.

"Fair point. So why aren't you drinking?" Liv says as she takes a swig of her ice water.

"Because I'm pregnant," I blurt out.

Liv spews water across the table, directly onto Emily.

"Oh, shit," I murmur as my two best friends stare at me with shock clearly evident on their faces.

"I'm sorry, I must have misheard you. Can you repeat that?" Liv says sweetly as her eyes narrow to slivers.

"I'm pretty sure you heard me correctly," I say quietly. "I'm pregnant, Liv."

"And who exactly is the father?" she bellows.

"Jesus, Liv, calm down," Emily hisses. "People are looking. You're causing a fucking scene."

"What does it matter who the father is?" I ask.

"Because if it's who I think it is, I'm going to cut off his balls and feed them to him," she snarls.

"Um, okay, you really need to chill," I say, staring at her. Liv's face is red, and her chest expands rapidly as she breathes. I have no idea why she's so worked up over this.

Suddenly, Liv's eyes fill up with tears.

"Are you really pregnant?" she cries. Emily's eyes widen at the insane change in Liv's mood. Hormones. Fucking hormones.

"Yeah, Liv. I'm really pregnant."

"Oh my God, we get to be pregnant together!" Liv gushes, jumping to her feet and hauling me up to hug her. She squeals as she dances side to side. I look at Emily with big eyes, and she shrugs. "When are you due? Maybe we'll be in labor together! Well, I hope not. I don't want to be baking this munchkin any longer than I have to. How are you feeling? Any nausea? I'm puking every morning. It's awful, but then I feel fine. So random."

"Um, that's a lot of questions right in a row, bestie," I murmur.

"Dang. I'm sorry. I'm just so excited now! I can't believe ... wait. Who is the father? Dammit, Harp, please tell me it's not Owen," Liv says, her voice lowering dramatically.

"Then I guess I won't tell you that it's Owen's," I say nonchalantly.

"God dammit!" Liv bellows, and again, most of the restaurant stares at us.

"Olivia! Calm down!" I whisper.

"When did this happen? It was Thanksgiving, wasn't it? I knew I shouldn't have given him the key to my townhouse, but I figured he'd at least apologize. Didn't think the fucker would knock you up ..." she pouts. I chuckle lightly. Liv only cusses with me when she's really pissed.

"Uh, no. We actually found out on Thanksgiving. That's why I was so off at dinner. Owen didn't know yet. He caught me with the tests when he came over after dinner," I confess. Liv's eyes dart to mine.

"How far along are you, exactly?" she asks.

"Nineteen weeks. I'm due in May."

"Holy shit," Liv whispers.

"Yeah."

"How did Owen take it?" Emily asks.

"Much better than I thought he would, actually. I figured he'd either go postal and yell at me or haul ass out of there like his pants were on fire. He did neither. He got down on his knees and kissed my stomach," I admit. Both ladies are quiet as they process that information.

"Wow. That is ..." Liv trails off.

"Not how I thought Owen would act, that's for sure. That was incredibly sweet of him," Emily comments.

"Yeah. He's made some comments over the last month. I don't know, like maybe he wants to try things with me? It's very confusing, and I'm hormonal and emotional, so I don't know what to trust," I tell them.

"Hold *up*," Liv says bluntly, throwing up her hand to stop me from talking. "Nineteen weeks? *Nineteen*. Harper Elizabeth Williams! That means you had sex with him this *summer*!"

"Okay, I swear to God, Liv, if you don't settle the fuck down, I'm going to find some duct tape and muzzle you. Everyone just heard that," I hiss.

"Crap. I'm sorry. But I have questions! How long has this been going on? Why am I just hearing about this now?" Liv says. "Over the summer, you insinuated something had happened with the two of you and that he was involved with the issue with your landlord. I guess I just never thought you'd have fully slept with him."

"Yeah, well, I did. The first time was the summer before last, though," I admit. Her mouth drops open. Emily stares at me wide-eyed. "I think it was the first night you were with Nathan, Em. Owen followed me home, and we got into a big fight ..."

"And then you had some great hate sex," Em says with admiration in her eyes. I nod and smile. She gets it. "Oh, shit. I forgot you told me months ago about sleeping with Owen. I can't believe how long this has been going on! But you two always seemed like it would be combustible, so I'm not surprised. Why have you held this all in and not talked to us more about it?"

"Everyone had chaos in their lives. I didn't want to become a burden. Jesus, Em, your sister shot you, and then you found out you were pregnant with twins and married Nathan immediately. Liv, your relationship with Liam was a fucking roller coaster from the beginning. I didn't want to add stress to your already crazy lives," I say quietly.

"That's not how families work, Harper," Liv asserts. "We're here for one another. We help one another regardless of what's going on in our own lives. I'd never tell you to take your drama elsewhere, Harp. You're my best friend. Don't do this again. You come to me when you need to talk, vent, get advice, or whatever. I don't care what I'm doing. Well, I'll definitely call you back if I'm doing my husband." She gives me a saucy wink as she shovels another massive chunk of queso into her mouth.

"I'm here, too, Harp. We love you. We want to support you with everything. I get that you've been independent for most of your life, but it's okay to have support from friends. It doesn't make you any less of a woman if you let us shoulder your burden sometimes," Em says. I nod.

"I know. I won't do it again. Thanks, ladies. I'm so thankful for both of you," I say as my voice trembles. "God dammit. These hormones are killing me."

Liv laughs, and Emily gives a knowing smile.

"So, how are things really going with you and Owen? Are you friends? Friends with benefits? What?" Liv asks.

"Friends, roommates, acquaintances, I guess. I made it clear on Thanksgiving that I felt we needed to draw clear lines and focus on co-parenting. He's really excited about the baby, and I think it's best to focus on him," I say.

"Wait ... him?" Em says quietly.

"Oh. Oh yeah, it's a boy," I whisper with a beaming grin.

"Oh my God! Oh, Harp. Oh, you're gonna be the best boy mom ever!" Liv says reverently, which makes my eyes fill with tears.

"I didn't think I wanted kids, guys. Not even when you had the twins, Em. I just figured that wasn't going to be part of my life. But the moment I found out I was pregnant, my axis shifted. It was like I had been waiting for this moment. Like my life finally had a purpose. I can't wait to meet this little man," I tell them.

"And ..." Emily says hesitantly, "Are you sure you don't want any kind of relationship with Owen?"

"It's not about whether I want one or not. I'm trying to be logical and realistic here. Owen isn't made for relationships. He's the guy you fuck to get over your relationship. The one you never see again. And if we even tried a relationship, it would end horribly. Crash and burn with no survivors. I'd get invested, and he wouldn't. We all know that! I don't want to chance that because we're raising this kid together. Besides, Owen just wants sex. There's no way he wants a relationship, especially with me," I say.

"Not one fucking part of that was true, Red. And the fact that you think so little of me? Wow. Noted. I'll be sure to stay out of your space from now on," a deep voice pipes up from behind me, and I swivel to see all three guys with varying looks of emotion on their faces. Liam shows regret. Nathan shows sadness. And Owen shows straight anger, annoyance, and a heavy dose of hurt.

"Shit, Owen, I'm sorry ..." I start, but he holds up a hand to stop me.

"No. You've said your piece. Obviously, your opinion of me is still complete shit, even though I've been faithful to you over the past year and a half. Guess I didn't need to, huh," Owen says harshly with a wry smile, but I can see the pain in his eyes.

"No, you misunderstood. I just don't think it's a good idea to get involved when we need to focus on the baby," I tell him.

"Hold up: what baby?" Liam calls out.

God dammit.

"You didn't tell them yet?" I ask Owen.

"Obviously not."

I'm completely crestfallen. Not only did I just say some incredibly hurtful things about someone who will be in my life forever, but I also accidentally just told his best friends about my pregnancy.

"Thanks, Harp. Thanks a lot. Always an experience with you," he says with disdain as he walks away.

Nathan looks over at me and shakes his head before following Owen back to the door. Liam looks at me with borderline disgust in his eyes.

"You better fix this, Harper. You're slowly breaking him, and you don't even fucking realize it. He'd do anything for you. Figure this out," he says before leaning down and giving Liv a quick kiss on the forehead. After he leaves, I turn to Liv and Emily.

"Why were they here?" I ask quietly. Emily looks down guiltily but then raises her eyes to mine, forcing her chin up.

"I thought it would be fun if they showed up. I invited them. I didn't know you'd be dropping a pregnancy bomb on us or that you'd blurt out all that nastiness about Owen right when they walked up," she says defensively.

"Harp, I know you're scared," Liv says softly, placing her hand over mine and giving it a squeeze, "But Owen is trying here. Obviously, he cares about you. He wants to be in your life just as much as your son's life. So why won't you give him a chance?"

"Because!" I whisper hotly. "He's going to break my heart. I just know it! He'll decide he wants out. Or I'm too much for him. Or he wants someone different. Sex with one person for the rest of your life isn't all it's cracked up to be. Having to answer to someone else, have someone in your space, all of it. He will end up choosing himself over me, and I can't have that happen!"

Tears fall down my cheeks, and I furiously swipe at my face.

"Oh, Harp. I had no idea you felt this way," Em says gently. "How long have you had feelings for Owen? Are you in love with him?"

My head whips around to stare at her, and the words are on my tongue to disagree with her. Tell her she's crazy. That there's no way I could be in love with him.

But my heart overrides my mind and speaks the truth no one knows.

"I think I've had feelings for him for as long as I can remember. Love ... I don't know. Love is a lot. I'm scared to love him. He's going to break me," I confess.

"But, you're so mean to him!" Liv sputters. "I knew you were attracted to him, and I've teased you about loving him, but I didn't think you actually did!"

"Defense mechanism," I mumbled, shoveling chips into my mouth. "Easier to be mean. I was trying to convince myself that I didn't actually want him. A big ole dose of self-preservation. I'm not even sure if I'm actually in love with him. These damn pregnancy hormones are *killing* me. I can't trust myself with anything."

"Jesus, Harp. You have to explain this to him. He needs to know. He deserves the truth," Emily says.

"What the hell am I supposed to say? 'Hey, Owen, sorry I was so mean to you, but I've had a thing for you for years, and I think you're going to break my heart, so I can't be with you?'" I jokingly say. Emily and Liv don't smile. They look at each other and then look back at me.

"Yeah, you need to say something like that. Owen deserves to know why you're holding back from him. Even if you aren't willing to move forward with any kind of romantic relationship with Owen, he deserves to know why," Liv says.

Fuck.

I know she's right.

But the thought of putting myself out there with Owen makes me feel like puking.

"Let's get our food to go and head home. You need to find Owen," Emily tells me, and I nod.

Boy, I sure do wish I could drink alcohol right now. This conversation would be so much easier one bottle of wine deep.

CHAPTER TWENTY

Owen

I burst out of the restaurant furiously.

I can't believe I just overheard Harper telling the girls what she thought of me. How she truly perceives me.

I've made zero headway with her over the last eighteen months. I thought we were moving forward. I was trying to give her space. Show her what a respectable guy I could be. How I'd put her and our son first. Fuck, I haven't had sex with anyone else since the first time I touched Harper. Haven't even thought about anyone. Lord knows I tried. But once I had her, no one else could compare.

But to know she still thinks I'm just looking for some ass? After all this time, and every single fucking time I've told her that it's only been her this entire time, she still believes my past.

"Owen! Buddy, wait up," Nathan calls, jogging up to me when I reach Liam's SUV.

"What?" I snarl.

"Yo. I'm not the enemy here, bring down a notch," he says. "Seriously, dude, did you knock her up?"

"Yeah."

"I should deck you for fucking with her, man. Thought you knew not to go after Harper," Nathan says angrily.

"Yeah, well, that didn't work out, now did it," I snap back. In frustration, I run my fingers through my hair and rub the back of my neck. I feel a migraine coming on. Haven't had one in a couple years, so this could be a doozy.

"How far along is she?" he asks.

"Like nineteen weeks," I answer. Nathan's eyes widen comically.

"Jesus! How long have you known?" he yells as Liam walks up.

"She's nineteen weeks? Holy fuck, man, why didn't you tell us? Damn. Congratulations," Liam says warmly. "Wow. Never would have thought Harper would give you the time of day, to be honest."

"Why's that?" I ask, my eyes narrowing.

"Well, you're ... you. You two fight like cats and dogs. And she's ... a handful."

"I'm me? What the fuck does that even mean?"

"You have a flavor of the night, not even a flavor of the weekend. Your black book is probably the size of a phone book," Liam jokes.

"I haven't been with anyone but Harper in a year and a half," I tell him.

"Seriously?" Liam gawks at me.

"Yeah. Seriously. No one but Harper."

"Damn. How come none of us knew?" Liam asks.

I shrug in response. "I don't know. Maybe in my head, I

knew she was different, and I didn't want anyone to spoil our little bubble. Honestly, we've only been together like that a handful of times. But I also know she and I have both been fighting it."

"So, when did you find out about the baby?" Nathan asks.

"We found out after Thanksgiving dinner. Didn't want to tell anyone until she got in to see an obstetrician. Then we were going to tell everyone on Christmas, but …" I trail off.

"We announced Liv's pregnancy instead," Liam finishes. I nod.

"Was your plan to tell us at lunch?" Nathan asks, and I again nod. "Then I changed our plans and said we would surprise the girls."

"Yeah. I figured maybe Harper hadn't told them yet, so we could tell everyone together," I explain.

"Dang, man. I'm sorry about how this all worked out. How do you feel about the baby?" Liam asks. I can't help but smile, whipping out my wallet where I keep the ultrasound pictures.

"I'm fucking over the moon, man. So ecstatic. It's a boy. I'm gonna have a son," I tell them, and both guys whoop and give me man-hugs.

"Why did you storm out of there, then? Do you want more with Harper?" Nathan asks as we pile into Liam's SUV.

"I don't know. Yes. No. Yes. I want more with her, but I don't know what the fuck I'm doing. I feel … more. More than I've ever felt before. I want to be with Harper, but she's fighting it, and I don't know how to come to terms with that," I admit.

We're silent as Liam pulls out of the parking lot and heads west toward Mountain Springs. My mind is going a million miles per minute thinking of everything Harper said. A blind spot has developed in my eye, a definite precursor to a migraine. Fuck. I don't have any meds on me.

"For what it's worth, O," Liam says quietly, "I think you're going to be an amazing dad."

"Agreed," Nathan says with a nod.

"This deal with Harper, though …" Liam trails off.

"What?"

"I don't know. Could be really messy. I can see that you care about her, though."

"Doesn't matter if she thinks otherwise," I murmur, leaning back and resting my elbow on the door handle so I can cover my eyes with my hand. I can already tell this migraine is going to be a bad one. My eyes are having trouble adjusting to the bright Colorado sun.

"What are you going to do?" Liam asks.

"I don't know. But listen, guys, I'm getting a migraine. Can you drop me off at home? I need to get my medicine," I say quietly.

"Sure thing, man. Absolutely," Liam answers.

My two best friends know about my migraines. Blind spots in my eyes, sensitivity to light and sound, overwhelming pain, and the inevitable nausea and vomiting. It's a really fun course of events. They remain silent as we get closer to home. Liam even turns off the radio so it can be as quiet as possible.

I'm cursing myself as Liam pulls into my driveway for not having a spare tablet in my wallet. Most guys carry condoms, which I also do, but I almost always have an emergency Imitrex in my wallet. Can't believe I forgot to replace it after my last migraine.

As I open the door, I'm overcome with a wave of vertigo, and my knees buckle. Fuck, this migraine came on so fast. Nathan jumps out of the passenger seat and grabs my elbow.

"I got you, man," he whispers as he walks me to the front door.

"My neighbors are gonna think I got completely blitzed at brunch," I joke quietly.

"Fuck 'em. You're not friends with any of them anyway," he says nonchalantly. He's right. My neighbors are all families. They look down on me and my whorish ways. Bet they'll all love knowing I finally knocked someone up.

Nathan gets me onto the couch and then asks where my medication is. After I answer him, he roots around in the kitchen until he finds it. Then, he brings me a glass of water and my medication and waits until I take it.

"You okay here, or do you want to go to your room?" he asks.

"My room. Can you help me? I don't think I can make it on my own," I whisper. I'm having one hell of an aura with this migraine. The room is spinning horribly.

"Yeah, buddy. I got ya," he says, helping me to stand. He slowly leads me up the stairs and into my room. I immediately collapse on my bed. "You need anything else? Want me to stay in case you need help?"

"Nah, man. I'll be okay. Not my first migraine rodeo," I painfully whisper. My entire body is throbbing. It hurts to breathe at this point.

"Alright. I'll check on you later today," Nathan says quietly as he closes the door.

I focus on my breathing. In and out. Slow and steady. Just willing the medication to take the edge off this pain. I feel like a steel trap is slowly and methodically pushing against my skull. The pain reverberates through every molecule of my body, and the force makes my organs revolt. I feel like I'm going to puke, but I'm also hungry. Do I need to pee, or is my bladder just freaking out? I don't fucking know. Jesus. This is the worst one I've had in years. Time is slowing. Not sure how much time has passed. Ten minutes, an hour...who knows. Time is now relative.

Nausea begins to overwhelm me, and I know I'm going to throw up. But with the room spinning, I'm unsure if I can make it to my bathroom in time. I know I can't walk, so I slide off the bed until I'm entirely on the floor. I attempt to get up onto all fours, but I can't seem to keep myself upright. So, my only option is to army crawl toward the bathroom and hope I make it in time.

I hear a weird noise, and it takes me a moment to realize it's my own painful moaning. Fucking hell. I'm glad Harper isn't here to witness my misery.

And as if my one thought seemed to conjure her up, my bedroom door swings open, and there my angel stands.

"Owen! Oh my God," she cries out. "Nathan texted me and told me to check on you."

"Gonna puke, baby, help me," I mutter as I try to get to my knees again. Harper's arms come around my midsection as she assists in getting me to stand. I lurch to the bathroom and fall to my knees as soon as I reach the toilet, violently retching into the basin.

"Oh, sweetie," Harper croons, rubbing my back. I empty out what feels like a week's worth of dinners before resting my head against the rim of the toilet.

"Well, this isn't emasculating at all," I whisper, and Harper quietly chuckles.

"Nothing wrong with being sick, Owen. It happens to everyone," she responds quietly. "Do you think you're done? I'll help you get back to bed."

"Need to brush my teeth first. Mouth feels like cotton and tastes like ass," I mutter. Harper helps me stand, and I brace against the wall while she puts toothpaste on my brush and hands it to me. I brush my teeth with my head against the wall, my eyes squeezed shut. Vomiting, for some reason, almost always makes me feel marginally better in the throes of a migraine. But this one isn't letting up. I feel awful.

"Okay, sweetie, let's get you back to bed," Harper says as she helps me clean the toothbrush.

"Like that," I mutter.

"What?"

"You calling me sweetie."

"Oh."

"How come you're allowed to take care of me, but I'm not allowed to take care of you?" I ask bluntly.

"It's not that simple, Owen."

"Yes, it is. Why won't you let me love you?"

"You love me?" she breathes.

"Of course I do. How could you not know that?" I whisper as I slide under the covers.

"You mean as a friend, right?" she says after a moment.

"No."

"Owen ..."

"Fuck, Harper. I'm in love with you. How come you don't see that?" I murmur. Maybe I said that in my head? I really don't know. Feels like I'm partially asleep. Maybe this entire conversation is in a dream. "Stay with me, please. Let me hold you."

I'm almost asleep when I feel the bed shift as Harper climbs in. I immediately yank her toward me and bury my head in her hair. I vaguely hear myself whisper how much she means to me and how I don't think I can live without her. But again, I feel like it's all a dream. Maybe it's my subconscious, and I'm thinking about what a perfect world would be. Me and Harper. And our son. A family. Thinking of our family, I finally fall into a deep sleep as the migraine medication takes effect.

CHAPTER TWENTY-ONE

Harper

I'm sitting ramrod straight in Owen's bed.

I have no idea how he's fallen asleep wrapped around me like this because I'm so stiff my calf muscles are spasming.

He just told me he's in love with me.

And that he wants us to be a family.

And how no one compares to me.

Was it the medication talking? Is he having a stroke? What the hell is going on? All Nathan told me was that Owen was sick and I needed to help him. So the girls and I flew back into town so I could get there quickly to check on Owen. My heart flew into my throat when I opened his door and found him moaning incoherently on the floor. I'm still not entirely sure what has transpired.

When Owen's breathing deepens ever so slightly, I shift to pull my phone out of my maternity jeans. Yep, I had to switch to maternity clothing this week. Thank goodness Tori had a bunch of things she gave me. Maternity clothing is ridiculously expensive. I'll continue to wear leggings as much as possible since those fuckers stretch amazingly.

I shoot off a text to Nathan asking for more information.

> Nathan: He gets migraines.

> Me: That's all this is?

> Nathan: It's obviously something, Harp. Jesus.

> Me: I mean, I thought maybe I needed to call for an ambulance. I found Owen on the floor. He just threw up a ton.

> Nathan: Yeah, when he gets a really bad one, they can be like this. He's had them for as long as I've known him.

> Me: I never knew he suffered like this.

> Nathan: It's not like he broadcasts it.

> Me: I get that. But I figured it would at least come up in conversation.

> Nathan: He's not gonna tell a woman he's interested in that he ends up in the fetal position on the floor and can barely walk, Harp.

> Me: He's not interested in me like that.

> Nathan: Woman, get your head out of your ass. He's interested in you. You're the one holding this up.

I hesitate before responding. Owen sighs next to me and tightens his arms around me. God, this feels so right. So perfect. Why am I fighting this?

> Me: I'm scared, Nate.

> Nathan: I know. I was, too, when things got serious with Em. But I think you're gonna regret not taking this chance with him, Harp. He's not the guy you've pegged him to be.

I don't respond after that. Owen finally shifts and turns over, letting me out of his warm cocoon. I slip out of bed and tiptoe out of his room. I'm tempted to take a long, hot shower, but right now, my clothing smells like Owen's cologne, making me feel like he's still holding me tightly.

I head downstairs, turn on Owen's television, and queue up another Gilmore Girls episode. I notice it's not at the spot I saved on Netflix, which means Owen has been watching it. I giggle, thinking about him getting invested in this very obvious chick show. Maybe Nathan is right. Maybe Owen isn't the guy I've conjured up in my mind.

THREE HOURS LATER, I hear Owen rustling around upstairs. I was about to check on him when I heard him. I made chicken noodle soup for him because I wasn't sure what he liked to eat after a migraine. As I listen to him trudging down the stairs, I busy myself by wiping imaginary stains off the counters.

"Hey, Harp," he says quietly.

"Hey, how are you feeling?" I ask.

"Like I've been run over by a truck," he says, grimacing slightly. He looks over at the stove, and his eyes widen in surprise. "Did you cook?"

"Yeah, I made you some chicken noodle soup. I wasn't sure if you'd be hungry, but it can be reheated. Soup always makes me feel better when I'm sick, so I figured …" I trail off. He gives me a small smile.

"Thanks. I love chicken noodle soup. That sounds great." Owen gets a bowl from the cabinet before looking at me. "Are you going to eat some, too?"

"Uh, sure. Yeah, I can eat some," I say hesitantly. Owen is literally acting like nothing happened today. Does he not remember?

Owen hands me a bowl, and we both silently add the soup before heading into the living room.

"I don't normally eat on the couch, but my whole body hurts, so I want to be comfortable," he says softly.

"That's fine, Owen. Whatever makes you feel the best," I whisper in return. We eat quietly for a few minutes.

"Damn, woman. This is really good," he mumbles, and I lightly chuckle.

"I can't cook much, but I make really good soups," I say.

"Noted."

"How's your head now?" I ask.

"Still hurts, but it's manageable. I'll feel pretty crappy for a day or two, but nothing like it was when I came home today …" he trails off, and I can see he remembers what happened today.

"Owen …"

"No. I'm not going to discuss it," Owen says sharply as he

heads into the kitchen and puts his bowl in the sink. He rests his elbows on the counter and puts his head into his hands.

"Owen, I'm sorry," I murmur.

"I really don't want to hear it right now, Harp. I'm gonna need some time. Knowing now what you really think of me ... yeah. I'm gonna need some time. Is this what the soup was? You felt guilty?" he asks, gesturing to the stove.

"No. No! Absolutely not. You're sick. I just wanted to help," I stutter as I stand and walk to the kitchen, putting my bowl next to his in the sink. His expression is so volatile and intense that I subconsciously take a step back into the living room.

"I don't need your help. You don't take mine, so why should I take yours?" Owen counters. I open my mouth, but no words come out. He's right.

"I don't know what I'm doing here, Owen. I don't know what to do with you," I whisper brokenly. He looks up at me, and I know the pain in his expression mirrors mine.

"You don't know what to do with me. Jesus, Red. You make it sound like I'm a problem you have to take care of. You don't need to handle me. I'm a big boy. I'm well aware that you don't want to be with me. I'd rather you be horrible to me all the time than this Jekyll and Hyde bullshit you're pulling now. Nice one minute, then pushing me away the next."

"I don't mean to do that, Owen, I just ..." he throws up a hand to stop me as he stalks toward me.

"Enough. Let me make this perfectly clear to you because, apparently, you aren't getting it," he says deeply.

Owen reaches up and cups my cheeks with both hands. His thumb caresses my lower lip, and I can feel him trembling.

"I've never said this before. I've never felt this way, Harp. I'm in love with you. Don't you see that? I'm in *love* with you. I love you. I want to be with you. I want us to be a family. I don't know what to do to get that through your thick skull and how to make you trust me," he says passionately, his eyes never leaving mine.

"Owen," I breathe, my heart beating so fast I'm sure he can feel it at his fingertips.

"I need you to trust me, baby. I need you. This is it for me, okay? You're it for me," he whispers as he leans forward and touches our lips together in a featherlight kiss. "I love you."

A sob overtakes me as I think about what I said at lunch. How I basically undermined him and said he was just in it for the sex.

"Owen, I'm so sorry about what I said earlier. About you. I'm sorry ..." I blubber. He rests his forehead against mine.

"I know," he murmurs.

We stand silently for a few moments, breathing each other in. Owen finally speaks as he removes his hands from my face. My arms come from around his waist as he steps backward. I didn't even realize I had embraced him.

"I can't play this game with you anymore, baby. I can't be halfway. Either we're all in, or we aren't. I want to be with you. I want to go on dates with you. Wake up next to you. Bring you lunch to the salon. Rub your feet after a long day. I want to be the person you come talk to when you've had a bad day, and I want you to be that person for me. I want everything with you, Harper," Owen says. He waits a moment to see if I respond before continuing. "But I can't sit here and wait for when you *might* want to be with me. I can't just sit on pins and needles whenever I see you and wonder what you're thinking."

"Owen. I'm just ..." I hesitate.

"Tell me straight up what you're thinking, Red. Please."

I take a deep breath, close my eyes, and speak from the heart.

"I'm scared shitless, Owen. I'm scared you're going to break me. You'll figure out I'm nothing special, and you'll leave, and then I'll end up like your mom and just be so nasty and hurtful toward our son. I'm scared to go all in because I'll get lost in you, and then when you leave me, I won't survive. And I'll still have to see you all the time, and it'll make me feel the heartbreak over and over again. You'll want something else eventually. Someone else. I won't be enough for you."

I exhale as I open my eyes and see Owen staring at me in shock, his eyes red with emotion.

"Baby," he whispers. "You really think that?"

I nod.

"Harper. There's no one better than you. Fuck, I wish you could see that," he murmurs.

"That's bullshit, and you know it. I'm fat, and I don't have a filter. We argue all the time. I say what's on my mind, which constantly gets me in trouble. I've seen the girls you take home. Blonde and perky, and they're all the size of twigs. I'm not your type," I huff. Owen laughs.

"Baby, you are exactly my type. For the record, I've only ever brought you home. You're the only woman who has been in my bed," he says, and I gasp. "Yeah. The blonde women you think I favor? Nah. I went after the opposite of what I really wanted, *you*, because it was easier. It didn't blur the lines. If I fucked a redhead, I knew I'd say your name."

"I don't understand," I mutter.

"Yeah, you don't understand. I've had a thing for you for years. I ignored it as best I could because I knew you wouldn't be on board. But now? I'm through ignoring it. Ignoring you. So this is what's gonna happen," he says as he takes a step toward me. "I'm gonna move out for a week or two."

"What?" I cry.

"Let me explain."

"No, Owen, you can't move out!"

"Baby, let me explain. I'm gonna stay at Liam's, I think. Or maybe a hotel. I don't know yet. But it's to give you some space. I want you to think about what you want from me. If anything. I've laid my cards on the table, and now you need to do the same. Fuck, create a pro and con list if you want to. Bounce ideas off Liv and Em. Just really hash this out. Because baby, I'm in this. You're it for me. And I want to be it for you. I want you all in with me. And you need time to figure out how you really feel," he tells me as he grabs my hand and pulls me into his arms.

"What if I can't figure it out?" I whisper. A flash of pain crosses his eyes as he leans his forehead onto mine.

"Cross that bridge if we come to it," he murmurs.

"Owen, I'm scared," I admit. He sighs against me.

"I know, baby. I know."

"Will you let me know where you're staying?" I ask, my voice trembling slightly.

"Yeah."

"What about my doctor's appointment next week?" I ask, suddenly remembering the ultrasound we have scheduled.

"I'd still like to be there if that's okay," he says, and I let out a relieved breath as my forehead drops to his shoulder. His arms squeeze me tighter.

"I don't want to lose you," I whisper brokenly.

"You'll never lose me, baby. You just need to decide which version of me you want in your life."

"What are my choices?" I ask teasingly.

"The acquaintance you see at special events who is cordial. The friend who irritates the crap out of you for no reason. Or the man who loves and worships you like the goddess you are and gives you everything you deserve," he whispers reverently as he places a tender kiss against my temple.

"Holy fuck," I mumble, and he chuckles. "This new Owen is a lot to take in."

"I know. I've felt this way for a while, Harp. But I think hearing what you thought of me today really put it all into perspective. It's time for us to shit or get off the pot. All in or nothing at all. I'm thirty-nine years old, baby. I don't have time to play games," Owen says. "I'm gonna go pack up some stuff, okay?"

I nod and watch him walk upstairs. He's back down with two bags packed in just a few minutes. He sets them by the door and then takes a deep breath. He turns to me and gives me a breathtaking smile before stalking over and yanking me to him, covering my lips with his in a searing kiss. His tongue skirts into my mouth as he sucks on my tongue, his hands grabbing my ass and kneading. I moan into his mouth. He breaks off this kiss, and we both pant. "Just wanted to give you something to think about this week."

"I'll definitely be thinking of that," I mumble. Owen chuckles and then drops to his knees to tenderly kiss my baby bump.

"Bye, little man. I'll see you next week," he whispers. My eyes fill with tears at the sheer poignancy of that action. I really have gotten Owen all wrong. He's so much more than I thought.

Owen turns to me and gives me one last look, emotion written all over his face. "I love you, Harper. And if you decide you don't want to be with me, it's okay. I'll be okay. I'll always be here for you and our son. But if you *do* want to be with me, just know I'll never make you regret it."

"Okay," I stammer as I watch him walk out the door.

As I hear his car pull out of the driveway, I can't help the tears falling. Did I just lose my happily ever after?

CHAPTER TWENTY-TWO

Owen

Hardest fucking thing I've ever done was walk away from Harper. Hands down, the hardest thing. But I can't play this game anymore. I want to be with her. I want everyone to know she's mine. I don't want to co-parent with her. I want to parent in the same fucking house and have both of them with my last name.

My eyes widen at my own thoughts. Holy fuck. I want to marry Harper. Jesus. I want everything with her.

As I drive aimlessly down the main drag through Mountain Springs, I call Liam.

"Hey, buddy," he answers.

"Hey. Any chance you can put up an old friend in a guest room? Or give me the keys to the mountain house for a week or two?" I ask casually.

"What the fuck did you do."

"Hey, now, that's not necessary."

"Obviously, you aren't at home, so explain how Harper kicked your ass out of your own house."

"I left willingly. I maybe gave her an ultimatum," I admit.

"Damn, that migraine medicine makes you all kinds of fucked up, huh," he muses. Yeah, he's probably right. I'll undoubtedly regret this in the morning, but nothing I can do about that now.

"I'll explain it all as soon as you tell me if I can stay with you. If not, I need to find a hotel," I say forcefully.

"Yeah, come over. You can stay here," Liam chuckles.

Ten minutes later, I'm in their living room and explaining it to Liam. Liv left a minute before I arrived, and I assume she's on her way to my house so she can hear it all from Harper. I let it all out. How Harper helped me with the migraine, then cooked me soup. How I completely lost it and told her I was in love with her and wanted to be with her, and how she basically freaked out.

"Damn, man," Liam says quietly.

"Yeah."

"So you told her she had a couple weeks to decide if she wants to be with you?"

"Yep."

"What are you gonna do if she says she doesn't want to?" Liam asks.

"Be fucking sick and unhappy for the rest of my life," I admit. "But I don't think she will do that, Liam. I really don't. I think she's in love with me, too, but she's so scared that she doesn't trust herself. I see the way she looks at me. But she's got blinders on when it comes to me. She doesn't see how I look at her. That my fucking world rises and sets with her."

"Yeah, we all see that. I've thought you would have gotten with Harper a few years before now," Liam says.

"Well, technically, I did ..." I mumble.

"Well, yeah. I know that. Didn't think it was a big deal, though."

"But I haven't been with anyone else, Liam. I couldn't. There's no fucking comparison. Harper is ... fuck, man. She's everything," I admit.

"Wow. That makes so much more sense. Also kinda explains why it's been incredibly awkward for the last two years. Whenever you guys are together, the tension is ridiculous," he chuckles. Yeah. I know.

"That ended up being a weird kind of foreplay, honestly," I tell him. He gives me a leery grin.

"Hate sex. Yeah, I can see that. But you two really do have some weird chemistry. I bet she's a fucking hellcat in the sack," he says with a grin.

"Hey, watch it. Don't talk about Harper like that," I warn. Liam barks back a laugh.

"Never thought I'd see the day when Owen Taylor would get territorial over a woman. This is so fucking amazing," he cackles.

"Yeah, well, don't get used to it. Harper might decide we're better off as friends and co-parents," I say.

"Jesus. How are you gonna handle that if it happens?"

"Don't know, man. I really don't know. I'm just gonna pray she decides to be with me."

"How will you handle dating her while she's living with you and pregnant with your baby?"

"Fuck if I know, man. I've never dated anyone, period. So this is all new to me. I'm just winging it. All I know is I want to be with Harper in whatever way she'll let me."

"I get it. I really didn't date anyone before Liv. Felt like I was holding out for her. Maybe it's the same with you and Harper."

"Could be. I don't know. I'm still apprehensive. All I

know is heartbreak. Watched it with my parents, and I see it nonstop in my office. So I'm hoping Harp will give me the benefit of the doubt when I invariably fuck up."

"That's all you can do, man. Just hope for the best. None of us can predict the future. You sure you're ready for all of this with Harper, though?"

"What the fuck does that even mean, man? Not like we can take back the whole 'getting pregnant' part," I retort. I can feel my hackles rising. Liam shrugs.

"No, I mean the part about you wanting a relationship with her. That's all new territory for you, O. I'm just thinking you're not prepared for all of that," Liam says sheepishly.

"I'm ready for it. I've basically been in a monogamous relationship with her for a year and a half. No one else compares, man. This is it. Today just made me realize I was done playing the game with Harper. Now she knows where I stand. It's up to her to decide if she wants to be with me or not," I say finally.

We hear the garage door open, and Liv comes in. She bypasses Liam and comes straight to me, giving me a huge hug.

"I am so proud of you," she whispers in my ear before letting go and walking to her husband.

"You're proud of me?" I ask incredulously.

"Yeah. You put yourself out there, for the first time in your life, for a woman. For Harper. She needed that. No man has done that for her. She needed to know that you'd be there for her, regardless of her choice. We all know what she *should* choose, but Harper is stubborn, so it might take her longer than you'd be comfortable with," Liv tells me.

"So you think she should choose me? To be with me?" I ask quietly.

"Yeah, O. I do. We've all seen the changes over the last year in your life. Hindsight and all. I can see when you and Harper first hooked up and how you've been different since then. Looking back further, I can tell you've always kept an eye on her and watched out for her. Maybe subconsciously, you were laying the groundwork for your relationship now," Liv explains.

"I've never felt like this, Liv, and I'm petrified she's going to choose the safety net of co-parenting," I confess. "I don't know how I'll do that. How I'll be close to her without being able to touch her. Tell her that I love her. I just don't know what I'll do if she doesn't choose me."

Liv and Liam look at one another, appearing to communicate silently. Maybe I should have gotten a hotel. They're too damn cute when I'm feeling this heartbroken. Fucking true love and all that bullshit.

"Listen, man, let's take it one step at a time. If it's meant to be, it'll be. You're more than welcome to stay here as long as you need. If, and I do mean *if*, she decides she doesn't want to be with you, we'll get it all figured out," Liam tells me. If it's meant to be? What kind of crap is that? Harper and I *have* to work out. We have to.

"Thanks, guys, I really appreciate it. Anytime you want me out of here, just say the word," I tell them.

"Well, I finished the basement guest room, so I suggest you stay down there," Liam says sheepishly.

"Oh? Why'd you move it down there?" I ask.

"We wanted to have the nursery next to our bedroom," Liv explains.

"Don't you have more bedrooms up there?" I ask.

"And we intend to have more kids. So when guests come, we want them in the basement, so ..." Liam trails off. Oh, shit. I get it.

"Ahh. Because then there's a whole floor between you and

your guests in case you get ... loud," I say pointedly, staring at Liv. She blushes beautifully and buries her head in Liam's shoulder. I can't help but chuckle. Liam looks at me with a wicked grin and nods. He's already told me Liv is a screamer. Probably wise that I stay in the basement and keep headphones on at all times, so I'm not scarred for life hearing my best friend and his wife go at it.

I grab my bags and head into the basement. He's got a great setup with a game room and reclining couches, perfect for watching movies or sports. A full bathroom means I'll only have to go upstairs to eat and when I leave for work. I left all of my suits at home, figuring I'd head over during the day when Harper is at work this weekend. Unfortunately, both of our offices are closed for New Year's Day tomorrow, so I'll just hide out in Liam's basement all day. I'd rather do that than risk the chance of running into Harper and begging her to pick me. My emotions are at an all-time high right now, and I don't trust myself not to do something stupid.

"Hey, Owen?" I hear Liam call from the top of the stairs.

"Yeah?"

"We're heading to Nate's to watch the ball drop. Do you want to come? Liv said Harper isn't going," he tells me.

"Nah, I'll stay here. I don't want to bring the mood down with my drama," I tell him.

"Alright. We've got tons of food and some beers up here. So help yourself, and Happy New Year," he says.

"Happy New Year, man, and thanks again," I call back. After hearing the basement door close, I slump onto the couch and wait until they enter their garage. Once I can tell they've left, I whip out my iPad and pull up social media. Nothing says 'I'm alone and sad on New Years' better than stalking your love interest across all platforms.

I spend the next four hours surfing through all of Harper's social media accounts. She has hundreds of Instagram pictures, a fairly active TikTok account, and tons of stuff on Facebook. I brought down a six-pack of beer from Liam's fridge, and once I finished that, I found a bottle of whiskey that I began siphoning through. I'm sufficiently drunk at two in the morning when I hear someone upstairs. Assuming it's Liam, I call out to him.

"Hey, man, come down here! Check out Harper's post from eleven years ago. Did you know she wanted a cat?" I screech and then cackle at myself. "Wait, does that say cat? Oh, shit. I meant *car*. Fuck, I think I'm drunk."

"I'd say you are," a female voice says from the stairs. I whip around to see Harper staring at me, a wild look in her eyes. She's wearing pink unicorn flannel pajamas and massive unicorn slippers, complete with a glittery horn sticking out of the toes.

"What are you doing here?" I gawk.

"I needed to see you."

"Why?"

"Because I just needed to see you, Owen."

She comes over to me and straddles me.

"Holy fuck, this is an amazing dream," I murmur as dream Harper takes the bottle of whiskey out of my hands and puts it on the table.

"Not a dream, hotshot. I need you, Owen. I can't think straight after that kiss, and I need you," she whispers.

"You can't make an objective decision about us if we fuck, Harper," I tell her, my eyes closing against my own volition.

"Maybe I need you to remind me of what it's like with you so I *can* make an objective decision. Sir," she whispers, and my eyes pop open. My dick is fucking steel immediately.

"Fuck, woman, I can't say no to that," I groan as I yank dream Harper's mouth down to mine. Jesus, this feels so real. But it can't be real. I'm just so drunk my dreams are incredibly vivid tonight. Harper begins to grind herself into me, and I'm already so close to coming I have to grab her hips and hold her still. "My show, baby. I make the rules."

"Yes, sir," she whispers breathily as she climbs off and drops to her knees on the ground next to the couch. "What would you like me to do?"

"Suck my cock, baby," I tell her, and she jubilantly yanks my sweats down until my dick pops out. I don't even have time to think before she's got me completely down the back of her throat, and her lips are pressed against the base of my cock. "Holy fuck, woman! Jesus, slow down a little ... oh, shit, do that again ... yes, woman, yes! Suck hard ... fuuuuuuck!"

I come so hard I see stars. The orgasm hit so fast that I think I blacked out momentarily. I'm half asleep before I feel a hand slowly stroking my thigh.

"Are you okay?" I hear Harper's sweet voice ask.

"Are you real?" I ask again. "Cuz I think this is a dream, and I don't want to wake up."

"I'm real, Owen," she says softly.

I slide until my head is on the couch and throw my legs over the armrest. "Then get up here and let me taste that sweet pussy."

Harper giggles as she stands, kicks off her slippers, removes her pajama pants, and throws a leg over onto the couch. She attempts to crouch, but I grab her ass and slam her down onto my face, my tongue spearing into her drenched channel as she screams. I'm a mess of lips, tongue, and teeth, and I edge her to orgasm until her entire body shudders.

I yank her body down until her core is above mine, and I open my eyes to look up at her. Dream Harper. The love of my life.

"I love you, baby," I tell her as I thrust up, impaling her completely. Harper throws her head back in bliss. I begin a punishing rhythm as she holds onto the back of the couch. I feel her orgasm start as her walls tremble, and Harper holds her breath. Finally, she comes on a silent scream, and I can see her mouth my name. I thrust once, twice, and a third time I come with a guttural roar. Harper drops to my chest in exhaustion.

I'm half asleep when I feel her push off me, my dick sliding out of her. I feel her pull my sweats up to cover my cock, but I can't find the energy to open my eyes.

"I love you, Red. Please choose me," I mutter.

I feel her step away from me, but not before dream Harper replies, "Please don't break my heart, Owen."

"Never, baby," I mumble as sleep overtakes me.

WAKING UP IN THE MORNING, I can't tell what really happened. My dick feels like it fucked someone, but my memories are garbled. I have a hell of a hangover. A six-pack of beer and an entire bottle of whiskey are not good on a thirty-nine-year-old body.

Heading upstairs, I see Liam with his head in his hands, looking just as miserable as I feel.

"You okay, man?" I ask as I meander to the cabinet where I know he keeps the painkillers.

"Hangover. And it was too loud," Liam moans.

"It was loud at Nate's? How many people were there?" I ask.

"No, man. It was loud here. What the fuck were you and Harper doing down there? We could hear it upstairs. I'm scarred, O. Scarred," he says with an exaggerated shudder.

I turn around to stare at him.

"What?" I breathe.

Liam looks at me, confused.

"Harper was here?" I ask quietly. "That wasn't a dream? She was here?"

"Holy shit, O. How drunk were you? Yeah, she was here.

She got here at the same time we got home. That's how I know she showed up. You guys were so fucking loud. Did she choose you, then?" he asks with a smile.

"Guess not, considering she's not fucking here," I snarl.

"What did she say?"

"I'm really not sure. Something about being unable to make a decision because she was too horny or something like that," I murmur as I rub my forehead. This fucking Tylenol is taking way too long to take effect. Oh, shit. No wonder I got so fucked up last night. "Shit, man, I drank after taking the migraine medicine yesterday. No wonder I thought she wasn't real."

"She said something about Instagram?" he comments, and my head pops up.

"What did she say about Instagram?"

Fuck. I know what Harper said.

"You were commenting on her pictures."

Yep. And I remember what I commented.

"Did you really comment tons of times about how much you love her?"

I groan, sliding my head into my hands on the table next to Liam.

"Fuck. Yes. Yes, I did."

"Well, I can tell you're embarrassed about it, but obviously, it worked. Harper showed up here, didn't she?"

Oh. She did.

"What should I do now?"

"I don't know, man. Maybe lay off Instagram, though. But I'm sure you can figure out less conspicuous ways to show her you love her."

You're damn straight.

"You're absolutely right, Liam. I'm gonna need your help," I tell him as a broad smile covers my face. He furrows his brow and shakes his head.

"Fuck. You're gonna ruin my day, aren't you."

"You're gonna help me win her back, buddy."

"Great. Just what I wanted to do on New Year's Day." Liam rolls his eyes, but I see a hint of a smile. My friend is a closet romantic, and I know he'll do anything for love.

CHAPTER TWENTY-THREE

Harper

I know I shouldn't have gone over there. But damn, I don't regret that at all. Owen was right, though. It did muddy my mind quite a bit. Of course, it's all his fault. After seeing the dozens of comments on Instagram, pictures even going back five or ten years, about how much he loves me, I couldn't stay away. I had to see him.

And the sex? Jesus. Sex with Owen is always amazing, but this was out-of-this-world amazing. Mind-numbing, spectacular, brutal, carnal, and delicious sex.

But now that I'm back at Owen's house without him, I'm second-guessing everything. I barely slept overnight once I left Owen. Now it's lunchtime, and I'm sitting at the table waiting for my water to boil for my cheap Ramen noodles. I can't find it in myself to eat Owen's food when he's not even living here, so I've resorted back to my cheap ways. So, here I sit, stewing on every little detail about the last twenty-four hours with Owen.

I'm so far into my mind with overthinking that I don't hear the doorbell. Suddenly someone is pounding on the door. I open it and find a disheveled Liam holding a massive bouquet of flowers.

"He should have just given me the fucking key. This is what I get for letting him stay with me. Here, woman. I better not fucking be his gopher-slash-delivery boy the entire time he's staying with me. This shit will get old," he mutters as he thrusts the bouquet into my arms.

"Oh, wow," I whisper. The bouquet is beautiful. It's completely white, with roses, gerbera daises, and mums. Baby's breath, eucalyptus, and faux-beaded flowers make up the remainder of the bouquet.

"Yeah, that was a bitch to get today. Not many florists open on New Year's Day," Liam mutters, staring at me expectantly.

"Are you expecting a tip or something?" I blurt out, and he finally gives me a smile.

"No, but you could send me back with a message for your man," he tells me pointedly.

"He's not my man," I stammer.

"Yes, he is."

"Liam."

"Harper," he parrots back in my whiny voice. "He's yours. He's been yours for a while. So don't fight this like I did. Don't miss out. You're having a kid together, and you're fucking perfect for each other. No one in the world will take his shit and dish it right back to him like you will."

"That is true," I say offhandedly, my mind already running.

"Don't make him wait forever, Harp. He'll wait for you. But it'll hurt him. And I know you don't actually want to hurt him," Liam says as he gives me a cordial smile and walks back to his car.

"Liam!" I call out, and he turns to look at me. "Tell him thanks, and I'll see him at my appointment. And ... tell him I miss him."

Liam gives me a big smile.

"You got it, Harp."

I take the gorgeous flowers into the kitchen and look for a vase. Shocking that a single man in his late thirties doesn't have a vase. I snort to myself as I find a water pitcher and put the flowers there. It'll have to do until I get back to my apartment to get a proper vase.

The doorbell rings again, and I assume Liam forgot something.

"Did you forget something ... " I trail off when I find Nathan standing there.

"Hey, Harp," he says warmly.

"Um, hi?" I answer hesitantly.

"This is for you," he says as he thrusts a box into my hands. "From Owen. I mean, duh. Of course, it's from Owen."

I open the box and find my favorite sour candies. I've had an insane sweet tooth for the last month. I didn't even realize Owen noticed or that he knew what my favorites were.

"You might as well stand here. There's more coming," Nathan says sheepishly.

"What?" I ask.

"There's more deliveries coming. Owen's got one hell of a game plan to win you, Harp."

"I guess he does," I murmur as I look behind him and see Emily ready to walk up the driveway.

"Hey, girlie," she says as she hands me a bag.

"Hi," I mumble as I look in and find the only flavored water I like. I've been trying to keep my caffeine intake down under what the doctor recommended, but I can't stand plain water. My favorite carbonated and flavored water is hard to find sometimes.

"He went to three different groceries to find it," Em tells me.

"Really?"

"Yeah."

"Wow. I'm ... this is surreal," I comment absentmindedly. I hear giggling as I see Liv and Liam chatting on the driveway, so I don't see Em slip into the house.

"Hey girl, this is your last present," Liv tells me as she hands me a small box. It's a jewelry box, and I open it to find emerald studded earrings.

"Holy shit," I whisper. "These are beautiful. Why the emeralds, though?"

"It's the May birthstone," Liv answers knowingly. I stare at her in disbelief. "Didn't you know that? It's your son's birthstone."

"It also happens to be my birthstone and my favorite color," I comment.

"I'd bet you my entire savings that Owen knew that, Harp. He loves you. He knows everything about you," she says kindly. "Let's go inside. Em and I want to talk to you."

I wave to the guys, and as I'm about to shut the door, I see movement in the back of Liam's SUV. I can't fully recognize his face, but I know it's him. Owen watched this whole exchange.

"Thank you," I mouth to him, and I blow him a kiss. Then, closing the door, I lean against it and close my eyes briefly. I'm completely overcome with emotion.

"Alright, it's time for a come-to-Jesus chat, my friend," Liv announces as she motions for me to move into the kitchen. Em is emptying a bag I didn't even see her carrying. I moan when I see she has more queso from the Mexican place we were at yesterday. Holy shit. Was that really only yesterday? Feels like a lifetime ago.

"Okay. Give it to me," I tell them.

"Are you talking to us or the queso?" Liv asks with a smirk.

"Both."

"Good call."

Once the bowl of queso is passed to me, I shovel a massive amount onto a tortilla chip and jam it in my mouth. Ahh, pure bliss. Once you find good queso, there's no going back. It's a food group in my pyramid.

"I'm just going to be blunt. You're in love with him, but you're scared, and you need to just suck it up and give in to him," Emily says, and I choke a little bit.

"Damn, Em, tell me how you really feel," I say dryly.

"I don't have a lot of time. The twins will be hungry soon, and I'm the one with the working boobs. Kathryn can only do so much," she says with a shrug. "I know I've only known you for a small amount of time. But I've seen the connection you two have from day one. I've seen the way he watches you when you aren't looking. How your eyes follow him whenever he's near. And now that I've had so many months to learn your personalities, I can say with one hundred percent certainty that you are perfect for each other. There's no one that is going to match your will better than Owen, Harp. He is going to challenge you, absolutely. But he'll love you at the same rate. And he'll be the person for you that you need."

My eyes fill with tears as the doorbell rings again.

"Who could that be?" I wonder as I walk to open the door.

"Yo, I heard there's a pity party?" Monica says with a wink. "Damn, I knew I was late, but I didn't think y'all would already have her crying."

"Oh, shut up. Get in here," Emily says.

I'm staring at Monica.

"Why are you looking at me like that?" she asks me warily.

"Everyone else brought gifts from Owen, so I just assumed …" I trail off. Don't I sound like a greedy nitwit.

"My lovely personality is your gift, my friend," she says cheekily. "He was trying to track something down that I was supposed to give you, but whatever it is, he couldn't get it in time. So I come baring no gifts but my sarcasm and sass."

"Well, I happen to love sarcasm and sass, so that's fine with me. I'm actually relieved. I don't think I could take much more today. I'm wound so tightly right now," I tell Monica, my voice trembling as tears again fill my eyes.

"Wound so tightly? Even after your two am sexcapades in my house?" Liv asks, and I whirl to face her.

"What? He told you?" I seethe, downright furious that Owen would blab about that. *This* is the Owen I expect.

"Jesus, Harp, *no*! You guys were so loud. Seriously the walls were shaking. Liam and I couldn't sleep. We ended up having sex just to cover up your noises," she tells me. A wave of shame crashes over me as I realize how quickly I threw judgment on Owen when I had no reason to.

"God, I feel horrible," I moan. "I automatically assumed he would brag and break my trust like that. This is why I can't be with him. I can't seem to fully trust him, but I assume he'll trust me in return. I expect it from him. So why can't I give it to him?"

"You have a lifetime of hurt and having people leave you over and over again, and you know too much about Owen's past. You have to find a way to move past that. Frankly, Owen hasn't been with anyone but you in almost two years. That has to count for something, right? He's been faithful to you in his own way," Em tells me gently.

"I'm scared. I'm falling for him, and I'm scared he's going to either break my heart or make me change myself so completely that I don't recognize the person I will become," I say miserably.

"Why would you think that? Owen has never expected you to change. He loves you just as you are, Harp," Liv comments.

"Hey, if you don't want him, can I have him?" Monica pipes up.

"What?" I growl.

"Well, if you don't think you want a relationship with him, can I at least take him for a test drive?" she asks.

"Don't you have a boyfriend?" I snarl.

"Eh. Marcus would understand. I mean, look at Owen. He's *hot*. Who can say no to him? I bet he'd ride me like a fucking stallion, and I'd enjoy every blissful second of it," she muses with an evil glint in her eye. "Can one of you give me his number? I want to text him real quick."

"Uh, sure," Liv says, showing Monica her phone. Monica immediately begins texting and bites her lip, giggling to herself. She waits a second before her phone vibrates and reads the text with a triumphant smile.

"What ... what did he say?" I ask quietly. I almost don't want to know.

"He's meeting me for dinner," she answers.

"Are you fucking serious?" I yell, standing up and walking toward her. "Get the fuck out of my house, you little tramp. How dare you come in here and try to steal him away from me!"

Monica stands, so we are chest-to-chest. Well, not chest-to-chest. She's fucking *tiny*. Like five foot nothing. Monica still seems larger than life as she defiantly tilts her chin up to me.

"I never said I was texting Owen, Harper," she says with a devilish grin.

"You didn't text Owen and ask him to dinner?" I ask.

"Nope. Well, I did text him. I told him I was rooting for

the two of you, and he said thanks. That's it. I'm meeting Marcus for dinner. That's who answered my text," she explains.

"Why did you do that?" I whisper, falling back onto the couch and covering my belly with my hands. Little man is kicking up a storm, obviously feeling my frustration and emotion right now.

"Because you needed to see how you really felt. You love Owen, and you'd fight for him. And that's what *he* needs, Harp. Yeah, he was a man-whore before. But no one has ever fought for him. All he sees is broken relationships and devastation. No wonder he doesn't want to go long-term with someone. But you were ready to take me on at the thought of me even having dinner with him. That's love," she comments.

"Holy shit," I breathe.

It is love. I'm completely in love with Owen.

CHAPTER TWENTY-FOUR

Harper

Five days later, I'm heading to my twenty-week checkup and ultrasound. Owen is meeting me here ... well, I think he is. We haven't talked since I left him that night at Liam's. And I've literally thought about nothing else but him from that moment. I've reminisced about the amazing things he's said to me over the past few months. The way he holds me and rests his forehead on mine, like I somehow give him strength through that small touch. He always smiles when we argue, even when he is wrong. The way he makes me feel when he's deep inside me, looking at me with such intensity and determination. I've never felt this way with any other man.

I'm nervous to see him again. My anxiety is through the roof right now. Liv and Em brought me dinner last night, and we mapped out what I would say to Owen. I needed an outline because sometimes my mouth gets the best of me, especially when I'm nervous or feeling awkward. And no one on the planet unnerves me more than Owen.

Waiting in the obstetrician waiting room, my eyes are peeled to the door. My knee bounced so hard that another pregnant woman in the room asked if I was okay. I think she assumed I was on something. I probably do look like I'm tweaking from something. Lovely.

When I'm called back to the exam room, I'm worried. I fire off a quick text to Owen, asking where he is. Maybe he forgot? Or got stuck in court? I change into the gown and prepare for the exam, hoping he is just running late.

"Hi, Harper. How are you feeling?" Dr. Thomason says warmly as he comes into the room. "Is the daddy coming today?"

"Um, hi, I'm feeling fine, and I honestly don't know where he is," I confess, and a weird sob bursts from my throat. "Oh, God. I'm sorry. This is so embarrassing. We had a fight, and I thought he was coming today, but maybe he's not? Maybe he changed his mind about me, and I was going to tell him I wanted to be with him today ..."

I'm blabbering on and don't realize that the doctor has placed the probe on my stomach. The sound of my baby's heartbeat takes over the room and settles my nerves instantaneously.

"Knew that would work," he says with a wide smile. "Hormones, I get it. Don't worry about where he is. I'm sure something came up. Let's take a look at your little guy and do the measurements we need today, okay? Focus on this little nugget. Everything else will sort itself out."

I stare in awe at the screen. My son is doing gymnastics in my womb, and it's remarkable to see the movements on the screen as I'm feeling them in real life. Dr. Thomason talks me through the different measurements he's taking. He explains that he's measuring specific organs to check for development, saying that they can see when there is a potential birth defect if an organ is not measuring correctly. He confirms that my little nugget is still a boy, and I let out a relieved breath. I figured he wasn't wrong at the first ultrasound because how can a penis appear and then disappear on the screen. But I'm sure stranger things have happened.

Dr. Thomason assures me that everything looks great and schedules my next checkup at twenty-eight weeks. He also tells me he'd like to do another ultrasound at that point. Because I'm of 'advanced maternal age' and am considered a 'geriatric pregnancy' at thirty-five, he's cautious and wants to ensure everything goes smoothly.

"Whoever decided to call it a geriatric pregnancy needs to be shot," I mumble under my breath as I get dressed. Once dressed, I grab my phone and see no response from Owen. Fuck! Did he change his mind?

I walk out to my car and get in. Sitting for a moment, I try to collect my thoughts and maintain my composure. I want to call him, but I'm incredibly afraid of what I might hear from him.

It's now or never. Clicking on Owen's name, I hit 'call' and wait.

It rings and rings and rings.

Voicemail.

"Hello, you've reached Owen Taylor. Please leave your name, number, and a brief message, and I'll return your call as soon as possible."

"Hey, O, it's me," I stammer. "Um, is everything okay? You missed the ultrasound. I thought you were coming, but maybe I misunderstood. Can you call me back, please? I'm worried."

I end the call and throw my phone in the passenger seat.

Pulling out of the parking lot, my phone rings through the

car speakers. It's Owen calling back. I hit 'answer' on my car screen.

"Hey, is everything okay?" I ask.

"Hello, are you a friend of Owen Taylor?" a female voice asks, and my heart plummets.

"Yeah," I murmur. "Who is this?"

"Oh, I'm sorry. My name is Sophia Hampton. I'm a nurse at Silver Crest Hospital in Colorado Springs. Mr. Taylor was involved in an automobile accident and was brought to our emergency room via ambulance. He's currently in surgery," she tells me.

"What?" I cry out.

"Are you in the area? Can you come to our hospital? We were able to unlock his phone and return your call. It didn't appear he had any family numbers saved," she tells me.

"I'll be there in thirty minutes," before ending the call and immediately bringing up Nathan's number.

"Hey, Harp," he says after one ring.

"Nathan, Owen's been in a car accident!" I scream.

"What?"

"A hospital just called me, he's been in an accident, and he's in surgery!"

"Okay, where are you?"

"I'm driving there now." I hear the panic in my voice as I begin to hyperventilate.

"Come pick me up. I'll drive you. You're in no position to drive, sweetheart. Come to my house," he orders.

I'm a half mile from his house, and Emily meets me in the driveway. I jump out of the car and run to her.

"Oh, Harp," she murmurs as I cry into her shoulder.

"I was gonna tell him after my appointment that I wanted to be with him. What if I don't get that chance?" I sob.

"We don't know anything yet, Harp. Get to the hospital and speak to someone, then call me, okay? Nathan called

Liam, and Liam is on his way there. He was working in the city today anyway. I'm calling Liv after you leave. We're all here for you," she says soothingly. Nathan jogs out of their house and gives his wife a quick kiss before ushering me back to my car. He climbs in the driver's seat, and I don't even question it. I know I can't focus enough to drive.

"Deep breaths, Harp. Focus on breathing right now. Don't stress. It's not good for the baby," he cautions.

"I can't lose him, Nate," I whisper. "He doesn't know how I feel. I have to be able to tell him."

"He knows how you feel, Harp. Trust me, he knows," he says quietly, patting my hand. I stifle a sob as I try to focus on taking deep breaths. My hands find my stomach, and the little nugget kicks hard. He kicks so hard my exterior actually jolts to the side, and Nathan chuckles. "Damn, kid. That's one hell of a kick."

"He must know I'm taking him to see his daddy," I say wistfully. God, I hope Owen is okay. I can't do this without him. The thought of losing him makes me realize he's my fucking anchor.

When we arrive at the hospital, Liam is waiting for us.

"I was able to get back and talk to an ER physician to get more details. Owen was t-boned at an intersection, and the other car was going about fifty miles per hour. The other guy ran a stoplight. Owen was just at the wrong place at the wrong time," Liam tells us as we walk into the ER waiting room.

"What are they operating on?" Nathan asks.

"Sounds like a ruptured spleen, but there was some internal bleeding they weren't sure about. Owen may have broken a couple ribs and evidently has some really nasty cuts on his face when the window shattered," Liam explains. "They're letting us go back into a more private waiting room. I guess one of the nurses here was his client and helped her win custody of her kids. She wanted to do something for us, especially after I told her you were pregnant, Harp."

I can barely process any of the information Liam just spewed at us, so I follow Liam mutely to a smaller waiting room further inside the hospital. I sit in the corner and wait. Wait for my future, wait for my world to end ... I don't know. I just wait.

"HARP, WAKE UP."

"Damn, she's really out. Maybe we should let her sleep?"

"No, man. She needs to hear this. She'll want to hear this."

I open one eye to look up at Nathan and Liam, who are arguing back and forth loudly about whether they should wake me up.

"Um, guys, you're kinda loud," I tell them. For a moment, I've forgotten where I am. Who I'm here for. "Oh my God, *Owen*! Do we know anything? Where is he? Is he out of surgery? Is he dead? Oh, fuck, he's dead, isn't he? I know it. Just when I found him, he'd go and die on me ..."

Liam covers my mouth with his hand, effectively stopping my emotional spiral.

"He's fine. He's out of surgery. They repaired his spleen and didn't find any other internal injuries. He's awake and asking for you," Liam says gently.

"He's alive?" I whisper, and they both nod. "Where is he?"

"Room 217."

I don't even ask where that is or ask if they'll help me find it. I take off running. We're already on the second floor, so I'm barreling into Owen's room in fifteen seconds.

"Owen," I whimper when I see him. His face is mangled. Jagged cuts stretch along his left cheek, and his nose looks bloodied and broken. Cuts dot along his left arm as well. But his eyes ... his eyes are full of love and adoration as he looks at me.

"Baby, come here," he whispers as his voice cracks. I walk over to the right side of the bed and hover.

"Owen, I love you," I whisper brokenly. "I love you so much, and I was gonna tell you today after the appointment, I swear. I was gonna tell you that I wanted to give us a shot, and then the hospital called, and I thought I was gonna lose you ..."

"It's okay, baby. I know. I know you love me. You just needed some time to realize it," he says tenderly, his right hand cupping my face reverently. "I love you, too. Love you so much, Red."

I bend down and place a very soft kiss on his lips, afraid to do anything that might hurt him. I try to back away, but he clamps his hand down on the back of my head and keeps our lips attached. "Not getting away from me that easily, baby," he whispers against my lips. His tongue lightly traces the seam of my lips, and they part as I gasp. His tongue gently caresses mine until we break apart due to someone clearing their throat behind me.

"So, I guess you guys are good then, huh," Liam teases with a big smile. "About fucking time."

When I turn to address him, Owen grabs my hip and pulls me down so I'm sitting on the bed next to him, and his hand possessively splays across my stomach. Little bean immediately kicks me hard.

"Holy shit, that was a big one," he murmurs.

"Yeah, he kicked so hard in the car on the way here. I saw it in my peripheral vision," Nathan comments as he walks into the room. "Glad you're on the mend, brother."

"Thanks, man," Owen says quietly. His voice is raspy from the breathing tube, and he keeps clearing his throat, but the smile never leaves his face.

"Liam is gonna give me a ride home, okay, Harp? You okay to drive? Figured you'd want to stay longer," Nathan says to me.

"Yeah, I'm not leaving," I blurt out. All three guys chuckle.

"I figured," Nathan says with a grin.

Once Nathan and Liam leave, Owen rubs my back before pulling me toward him. "Lay with me, baby."

"I don't want to hurt you," I say.

"You're not gonna hurt me. Don't lay *on* me. Next to me is fine. I just need to feel you here, Red. Need to know this isn't a dream and that you're really mine," he whispers. I take off my shoes and slide my legs onto the bed, laying on my side, so I'm facing him. "Figured you'd lay the other way so I could spoon you."

"You need to feel me, but I need to see you. I've never been so scared, Owen. I thought I lost you before I really even had you …" I trail off as emotion clogs my throat. Owen brings his hand up to tuck one unruly lock of hair behind my ear, then lightly drags his fingers from my temple down to my neck.

"I know, baby. You're the last thing I remember thinking about. I saw the car a split second before it hit me, and I figured that was it. When I finally had you, I'd be gone, and I'd never get to see little man grow up," he says as his eyes redden and his voice trembles.

"Oh, Owen," I whisper.

"This is it, okay? You and me. End game. I'm all in, baby, are you?" he asks.

"I'm all in, Owen. I love you."

"I love you too, Red."

CHAPTER TWENTY-FIVE

Owen

You'd think that I would be miserable, cooped up in the hospital, forced to recover under the watchful eye of doctors. But I don't think I've ever been this happy. It could be the meds talking. The docs have me on some pretty powerful stuff. But it's most likely because Harper has barely left my side. She's only left to grab showers and some needed items, like my laptop. I was able to take some time off, but I can continue preparing for upcoming cases while in a hospital bed just fine.

That is when I'm not wrapped up in Harper.

I've learned so much about her over the past few days that I didn't know. Things that have made me fall in love with her even more.

My favorite ginger has a soft spot for all kinds of critters and would willingly destroy a car if it saved the life of a squirrel or rabbit.

She thinks baseball is pointless but loves football, especially the Denver Broncos.

She can't sleep well without a stuffed animal that her grandfather gave her, and she hides it under her pillow. His name is Snuggles. I've been told to accept this and not try to talk her out of it.

Harper also eats colored things only with the same color. So all yellow skittles get eaten together. All strawberry Starburst are consumed in a row. In fact, she eats around her plate, never taking bites from a different item before finishing the original item. First, the carrots. Then the mashed potatoes. Then the chicken.

I'm actually a little surprised I didn't notice that last quirk since I've been secretly studying her for years.

We also had so many random conversations about odd subjects. Like discussing whether or not one should put on both socks and then shoes or one sock and shoe and then the other sock and shoe. Or the benefits of daylight saving time. Turns out, for as much as Harper and I fought throughout our history, we agreed on almost everything. Well, almost.

We may have had a hell of a disagreement about living arrangements. Now that we're together, I just naturally assumed Harper would stay with me, and we'd raise our son together. But she fully intends to rent an apartment, and we'd still make a co-parenting arrangement while dating.

The fuck we will.

I'll be damned if she's leaving my bed again. Gonna fight tooth and nail to keep her at my house. I want her to spread herself all over the place like fucking glitter. I want the Harper Stamp of Approval everywhere. I want pictures of us on the walls, throw pillows she picks out and special knickknacks that only mean something to us on shelves. I want ... no, I *need* my closet jammed with all of her clothes. I want her sexy as fuck thongs tumbling out of the dresser drawers. I want the bathroom counter covered in all the products she thinks she needs.

I'm shelving the issue for now since Harper hasn't found a place she can afford. And she's unwilling to take any money from me. I intend to enlist Nate and Liam to help me get a plan together. Maybe even their wives. They know Harper as well as me, maybe even better. So they'll know where to hit her and get the biggest impact.

I need Harper. Not willing to go even a day without her by my side.

A FEW DAYS after my accident, I was released from the hospital with strict instructions to avoid heavy lifting or strenuous activities. Fucking ER doctor even specifically told me to wait a week or two to have sex. Harper snorted at that. I'd mount her in the damn hospital parking garage if I could. Something about her right now, with that pregnancy glow, makes me fucking feral. Want to cover her in my seed like a damn psycho.

As I gingerly climb into Harper's sedan, I'm acutely aware of its size.

"Can this even fit a car seat?" I ask, checking out the back seat.

"I think it can in the middle," she answers.

"Is that safe?" I ask.

"I assume so? I really don't know."

I think for a moment, trying to decide how I can broach the subject of buying her a new car. But before I can say anything, she continues talking.

"If I could afford it, I'd love an SUV. Too far out of the budget right now with the rent for the salon," she says.

"I'm still working on that, baby. I'm gonna nail that asshole to the wall, one way or another," I tell her, my voice getting all growly and aggressive. She shoots me a side-eye and chuckles.

"Down, boy," she murmurs.

"Can't help it. He messed with my woman. My baby mama. I'll figure out a way to deal with him at some point," I say.

"Is your car totaled?"

"Yep."

"Dang. That sucks," she says softly.

"Yeah. I already called the dealer. They're finding me another one. It's obviously a good car, and I feel safe driving it. I'll definitely feel safe driving our kid around in it, too. Not so sure about you driving this around, though ..." I trail off, letting Harper stew on my words. I don't have to wait long for the blowup. I laugh to myself, knowing she'd come for me.

"You self-righteous snobby prick! How *dare* you judge my car? Oh, look at me. I'm Owen. I'm a stuck-up lawyer, and I'll *only* drive an Infiniti. You lowly heathen driving a Honda, you must not love your child as much as I do," she bellows.

"Hold up. I never said that," I say. "Harp, do you honestly think that? That I think I love our son more than you?"

"Well, no, but ..." she hesitates.

"Oh, baby. I know the circumstances are awful right now. But I know you'd do anything for our child. I hate that you're self-conscious about finances. I hate that you won't let me help you," I say quietly.

"I've always been self-sufficient, and that's not going to change," she says assertively.

"What happens when we get married, Harp?"

Her head whips to mine, and I refuse to break eye contact.

"What?" she breathes.

"When we get married. Are we still going to play this

game? Where you have all your financial problems, and I'm not allowed to help? Will we still have separate bank accounts? Or will you finally see us as a fucking team and understand that whatever is mine is also yours?" I stare at her as I finish. Her eyes comically widen as she sputters.

"Owen ..."

"I'm not proposing today, Harp, so you can get that terrified look off your face," I say, chuckling. "But it's coming. You're it for me, baby. This is it. I want the whole nine yards. Marriage, kids, white picket fence, dogs. All of it. But we can't do that until you realize we are equal. It doesn't matter how much money either one of us has. We're in this together."

A single tear slides down her cheek as she pulls into our driveway and directly into the garage. Turning off the engine, we sit quietly for a few moments.

"Let's go inside, Red. I'm drained. Will you take a nap with me? Been waiting all week to have you back in our house, in our bed," I tell her. I don't miss how she shudders when I emphasize 'our' house and 'our' bed.

I gingerly climb out of her car and shuffle toward the garage entrance. They stopped giving me the powerful pain medications yesterday, and I'm definitely feeling it. Gonna be a long recovery, especially with my ribs. I know I'm incredibly fortunate that nothing worse happened.

Harper brings in my bags and follows me upstairs. I first head to the bathroom. It's a relief, pun intended, to not have a nurse watching me pee. When I emerge from the bathroom, I stop dead in my tracks. Harper has removed her sweater and maternity jeans, wearing only a tank top and cheeky panties. She looks like a fucking wet dream come to life. She stretches her arms high above her head, extending her baby bump out, and I groan. She's so sexy.

"Jesus, woman, don't tease me," I croak as I adjust myself

in the sweats Harper brought me at the hospital. She whips around and gasps.

"I didn't know you were there, I swear!" she cries out. I laugh.

"I know you didn't, baby. You standing there fully clothed would make me want you. Can't stop thinking about New Year's and you surprising me ..." I trail off as I see her eyes darken. She's thinking about it, too.

"Owen, we can't. I want to, God, do I want to, but you're hurt. I won't put you in any more pain. I won't," Harper says vehemently, her eyes wide with depth and love.

"I know," I sigh. "Can't blame a guy for trying."

"Come on, stud. Let's take a nap. Then, if you're nice, maybe I'll give you a hand job. The doc didn't say anything about orgasms, just about intercourse. Right?" Harper says with a saucy wink.

"You are the perfect woman, you know that?" I reply with a grin.

"Yeah yeah," she mumbles as she climbs into the bed and holds the comforter out so I can slowly shuffle myself in. Once I'm flat, I yank her toward me, slide my arm around her, and bury my face in her hair. I may have dreamed about fucking her all week, but I honestly dreamed about this more. Holding her. Breathing her in. Smelling the scent that is so uniquely Harper. This feeling, right here, blows every other feeling I've ever experienced right out of the water.

"I love you, sweetheart," I mumble into her hair as I drift off to sleep.

"I love you, too," she whispers.

CHAPTER TWENTY-SIX

Harper

It's almost two weeks before Owen shows signs of recovering. The surgical incision site is healing nicely, and he isn't in much pain there. But his ribs have been problematic, as well as his overall pain from the accident. As a result, he's been working from home and hasn't been cleared to drive yet.

I still go to the salon every day. I'm in the second trimester of pregnancy, so I have to take advantage of my energy level and ability to get things done. Every client who has had a baby tells me that the third trimester is horrid. I'm not entirely sure who to believe, considering I didn't even know I was pregnant until the beginning of the second trimester. So, everyone who said the first trimester was awful wasn't correct for me. Who knows what the third trimester will bring?

Liv and I try to catch up over lunch the second week. It's been really lovely being pregnant with her. You'd think we planned it, which obviously, I most certainly did not. But there is something so peaceful about my best friend experiencing the same firsts as me, and our men are best friends as well. It just couldn't be any more poetic and perfect.

Liv, however, has had an awful first trimester. I'm two months ahead of her, and she's miserable. Evidently, she's nauseated all the time but never gets sick. She's lost weight, which, as our group's resident bean pole, she can't afford to do. Liam is her gopher, running all over the county trying to track down anything that possibly sounds good to see if she can stomach it. Once he returns home, the item Liv wanted typically doesn't sound good anymore. Liam is a trooper, though. He says he'll do anything that brings even a small smile to her face because she's growing a tiny human and deserves everything she wants. Swoon.

Two weeks after Owen was released from the hospital, Liv and Liam invited all of us over to their house for dinner. Liam intends to grill out since it's been in the forties. When it isn't snowing in Colorado, you take advantage and do anything you can outside. Never know when Mother Nature will lash out in anger.

Owen has slowly become more and more sullen as the days go by. I know he's frustrated with how slow his recovery has been, but there's something else bothering him, and I don't know what it is. He's begun lashing out at everyone for mundane things, easily angered and quick to pop off at even minor inconveniences. He argued with a mom in the Walmart parking lot because she parked on the line. Smarted off to Nathan about some random sports fact and yelled at Liam for making an inappropriate pregnancy joke about his own wife.

I'm the only one who can keep him calm. At night, climbing into his bed, he wraps his arms around me and exhales so strongly that I think he's finally relaxed. For some reason, the stress of everyday life is eating away at him right now, and the only comfort I can provide for him is to be held by him every night. Not that I'm complaining. At this point, if he were to even go out of town for one night, I wouldn't be able to sleep. I need to know he's there. Feel him.

Upon arriving at Liam's, Owen quickly gets out of the car and trots around to open the driver's side for me.

"Wow," I comment. "I'm impressed."

"Are you impressed that I opened the door for you?" he says, his eyes narrowing.

"No, how quickly you got over here. That's the fastest I've seen you move since the accident," I correct Owen, and he relaxes.

"Oh, I thought you were gonna poke fun at me for opening the driver's door ..." he trails off.

"No, sweetie. I love that you do that. No one has ever done that for me," I admit quietly. His eyes soften, and he lifts one hand to cup my cheek.

"I'll do anything for you, Red," he whispers as he trails his fingers down my neck, onto my shoulder, and then finally down the length of my arm before twining our fingers together. "You ready to head inside?"

I'm an absolute puddle of wanton need and hormones as I stare at Owen. His eyes darken as he realizes how turned on I am by that one simple touch.

"Owen ..." I whisper as he steps toward me, crowding me into the side of my car.

"Are we done with this doctor-mandated sex cease-and-desist? I need you, baby," he whispers against my lips, his tongue sliding out to trace the seam of my lips. I moan as my hands latch onto his suit jacket. The kiss turns erotic and lewd immediately. One of his hands clutches a chunk of my hair while the other cups my ass. I slide my hands underneath his jacket to feel closer to his skin and pull one leg up so my center can be closer to his rock-hard shaft. He groans as I rub myself against him. With my heels on, he's the perfect height. I could come right here, pinned to the side of my car, in Liam's driveway at sunset.

Someone clears their throat.

"Do I need to pay for this show? Or was it a freebie?" I hear Nathan tease. Owen and I break away, but his eyes don't leave mine. His dark brown orbs are almost black as they swirl with lust, love, and need. I should feel embarrassed, but I don't. Everything about this moment is perfect ... even the interruption by our best friends.

"Tonight, Red. Tonight, you're mine," Owen whispers before kissing me and pulling me off the car. "Head inside. I, uh, I need a minute. Gonna recite the attorney oath of admission a couple times."

I giggle as Emily walks up and grabs my arm, pulling me toward Liam's house. She's holding one car seat while Nathan has the other, and Jack trails begrudgingly behind his parents. "Dang, girl! That was hot! Thought you weren't supposed to be doing anything strenuous for a while?"

"That's the first time he's kissed me like that since his accident. I don't know what came over him. That was ... intense," I finish. I'm fanning myself. Holy hell. That was incredibly erotic.

Owen comes inside a couple minutes after me and gives me a flirty wink as he grabs a beer and chats with the guys. I sit in the living room with Em, Liv, Monica, and the twins. The girls are almost nine-months-old, and mobility is coming sooner rather than later. Poppy rolls everywhere. Rose likes to get up on all fours and bounce back and forth. I just know they're going to terrorize this house.

"Where's Marcus?" I ask Monica. She gives me a weird smile.

"I didn't invite him," she tells me.

"Oh? Why?"

"None of you like him. I know that. I'm basically just using him for sex anyway. Dumber than a box of rocks, that one. But he has an amazing cock," she whispers loudly.

"Can we not say the c-word in front of my babies?" Emily asks.

"Yes, because your nine-month-olds are definitely gonna repeat that," Monica says, rolling her eyes.

"We don't know what is imprinting on their brains. I'm just being proactive. I swear Monica, if their first word is 'cock' I'm beating the shit outta you," Em warns.

"Because that's *much* better than 'cock', Em. You threatening to beat the shit out of me. Just for that, I'm going to start whispering every bad word I can think of in their ears when you aren't watching," Monica threatens.

"Then I won't let you sneak over here and drink all of Nathan's special whiskey," Em threatens back. Monica's eyes widen.

"You wouldn't dare," she seethes.

"Yep. A mom's gotta do what a mom's gotta do," she says victoriously.

"Damn. Hit me where it hurts," Monica says, pantomiming getting punched in the stomach dramatically.

"I know where your loyalties lie. Liquor and Mexican food," Em says with a laugh, and Monica nods.

"Regardless, I don't think I'm going to keep seeing Marcus anyway. He's starting to show a temper that I don't like," Monica admits.

"Oh, shit, Mon. What's been going on?" I ask.

"Nothing, really. Marcus just gets pissed off at stupid stuff. He's too dumb to get this mad about things. I don't have the time or energy to deal with thirty-five-year-old temper tantrums," Monica explains.

Monica really has fit in perfectly with our crew. She had a tough go of it originally with Liv because Liv thought there was something going on with Mon and Liam. Their relationship is weirdly platonic, like a sibling relationship. But, once Liam explained his feelings to Liv, she was much more welcoming and made an effort to get to know Monica.

I suddenly hear voices escalating from the other room. Monica jumps up to go see what's happening.

"Holy shit," she exclaims. "Owen and Liam are fighting!"

Liv and I both jump up and run to the other room to find Owen has Liam in a headlock.

"Take it back!" Owen yells.

"No!" Liam shouts back, but his voice is muffled against Owen's side.

"Owen, stop!" I shout. I don't know why they're fighting, but it's only been three weeks since Owen's surgery. I don't want his incision to open up.

Owen looks at me and immediately lets go of Liam.

"Thanks, Harp," Liam murmurs.

"Don't fucking talk to my woman, you piece of shit," Owen snarls. Liv and I both gasp. This is so atypical for our guys.

"Owen, what is going on?" I ask as I approach him slowly. I'm treating him like a damn gazelle. Afraid he's going to spook, and I don't want him to bolt.

"He said you were easy pussy, and the only reason I'm excited for the baby is that I didn't want to be left out," he says bluntly. I whirl to face Liam.

"Is that true?" I whisper hotly. Oh, I'm fucking furious. I'm half tempted to let Owen take another stab at him. Liam has four inches on Owen, but Owen is a scrappy bugger. I have no doubt Owen would win, even three weeks post-op with bruised ribs.

"Well, I mean, it's not exactly as it sounds, Harp," Liam stammers.

"Did you or did you not say I'm 'easy pussy'?" I ask with

air quotes. "And how incredibly narcissistic of you, Liam, to assume Owen would only want a kid because you were having one. We found out about our baby before you did. Maybe you were the one jumping on the bandwagon. Did that ever occur to you?"

"Well, no ..."

"And did anyone ever question your goals when you began fucking around with Olivia? Because, man, you were hot and cold for *months* with her. Months, Liam. Yet none of us ever judged you or made disparaging comments. Well, to your face, at least," I tell him with disdain oozing from my voice.

"Harp ..."

"At New Year's, you waxed poetic about how you thought I was slowly killing him and how I needed to trust him. What the hell, Liam? You obviously don't trust either one of us."

"Fuck, Harper, I didn't mean ..."

"No. You don't get to whine and try those fucking puppy-dog eyes you pull on Liv. She's *your* easy pussy, so you deal with that. But me? And Owen? We're *fine*. We're *great*. Don't go trying to fuck up our life just because you think you can," I state. Liam opens his mouth to speak, and I throw up a hand to stop him. "No. I don't want to hear it. Owen, can we go home? I don't want to be here since we are obviously not welcome in this house."

"Harp, I'm so sorry," Liv whispers to me. I grab her hand and squeeze it.

"I know. Get your damn husband in line. He owes us both an apology, but definitely Owen. That was incredibly hurtful and uncalled for," I whisper in her ear. She nods.

Owen retrieves my coat from the guest closet and slides it across my shoulders. We walk outside and get in my car silently.

"Baby," Owen says, reaching over to grab my hand, "I'm sorry."

"You have nothing to apologize for. That was all Liam," I tell him.

"I could have handled it differently. I don't know why, but the moment Liam started talking about you, I was just filled with rage."

I sit for a moment as I try to find the words to explain how much that meant to me.

"No man has ever fought for me before. Stood up for me," I whisper. Owen tilts his head to study me.

"No?"

"No."

"I'll always fight for you, Red. I love you," he says tenderly as he leans across and gives me a soft kiss. "But can we go get some food? I'm starving. I was looking forward to grilling out."

I laugh as my stomach grumbles.

"Me too. Burgers or steaks?" I ask, turning on my car and pulling out of Liam's driveway.

"Burgers. Quick and easy. Just how I like it," Owen says with a gaudy wink.

"Oh, please. You love a challenge, and you love to drag it out. Keeping the suspense and all that crap," I murmur as Owen drags his hand up my arm and settles it in my hair at the base of my neck. The track his hand took is riddled with goosebumps.

"That is true. But I make you feel good, don't I?" he asks quietly as his hooded eyes take a slow perusal of my body. He grins when he sees how tightly I've clenched my thighs together.

"That you do," I answer breathlessly.

"How fast can you eat?" he asks as his hand begins to massage my neck.

"As fast as fucking possible," I mutter. "Stop massaging me, or I'll wreck the car."

"Let's keep our car accidents to one per month, baby," he jokes.

"One per year would be better. One per lifetime? I'd like that. No more hospital beds," I say, shuddering. The image of him in the bed, hooked up to all the machines right after surgery, is something I'll never get out of my head. It's burned into my long-term memory.

"I know. I'd feel the same way if that had happened to you," he says quietly.

I run through a drive-thru for meals and then head back to Owen's house. I guess I shouldn't call it Owen's anymore. It's mine, too. I know he will not let me move out of here without a fight. But I'm not telling him that. Like him, I enjoy dragging things out. Gotta see how far I can push Owen. See how far I can challenge him.

Owen inhales his food as I drive home and begins feeding me french fries as I approach the house.

"Eat up, Red. I've got plans for us tonight. You need your energy," he whispers before leaning over and kissing the side of my neck. I let out a wanton moan. Second-trimester sex drive is through the roof. I'm so incredibly turned on I could probably come just by him kissing my neck.

Once in the garage, I grab the takeout bag and shovel the burger into my mouth. Owen looks at me with his eyebrow cocked and a bemused smile.

"What?" I ask with a mouthful. "I have plans, too."

Owen throws his head back as his laughter bounces off the garage walls. Oh, what an amazing sound. I haven't heard him laugh like that in ages. My Owen is coming back.

I hustle inside and eat as quickly as I can.

"Do me a favor," Owen says as he hangs up his coat, "Wait ten minutes and then come upstairs. And if you don't want to be self-conscious about your breath, brush your teeth. I plan on kissing you as much as possible tonight, so I need you to focus."

"Holy hell," I whisper.

"Yeah. Game face on, baby. We're gonna have fun tonight," he says as he jogs up the stairs.

I stand still for a moment, just envisioning what he might be planning.

"Finish your damn burger, woman!" Owen calls from upstairs.

"Are you watching me?" I shout back.

"Nope. I just know you so well. Know you're in your head right now. Eat and then get that perfect ass up here."

I giddily finish the burger, wash my hands, brush my teeth, and then impatiently wait until it's been ten minutes.

"Get your ass up here, Red."

"Yes, sir."

Game time.

CHAPTER TWENTY-SEVEN

Owen

She had to hit me with a 'yes, sir.' Fuck. That's my damn kryptonite. I'm not necessarily a straight dominate, but for some reason, getting Harper to submit to me is one hell of a turn-on. I think it's because she's so independent and in control of everything. When she lets me take control, I know she fully trusts me. And that is quite the aphrodisiac.

I've lit candles and started light jazz music on my Bluetooth when Harper struts into the room. I don't even think she realizes it, but she automatically cradles her baby bump, and it's the cutest thing. Her eyes slowly slide down my body as she takes in my state of undress. I already removed my suit coat and unbuttoned my shirt, but I haven't removed it yet. Seeing the look of lust in Harper's eyes, I know I guessed correctly in leaving the shirt on but unbuttoned.

"You totally know what you do to me," she mumbles,

and I give her a devilish grin. I do. She knows exactly how to bring me to my knees as well. We are one hell of a pair.

"I had a hunch, Red. Is it the unbuttoned shirt that does it? The lack of tie? Seeing my abs?" I ask.

"Yes," she responds with a breathy laugh.

"All of the above, huh," I muse, and she nods. "Come here, baby."

Harper slowly approaches and stops to stand in front of me. A look of uncertainty crosses her face.

"Are you sure you're feeling up to this? I don't want to injure anything else," she worries.

I reach up, cupping her face with both hands, and bring her mouth to mine. She hums into my mouth when our tongues slide together, and I groan. The kiss turns ravenous as her arms slide around to clutch my back, and my hands are lost in her glorious locks.

"Can't wait another day. Another minute. Hell, can't wait another second, baby. I need you. Right fucking now," I mutter as I drop to my knees and place adoring kisses all over her abdomen. I grab ahold of the waistband of her maternity pants and yank them down, catching her underwear along the way.

Harper yelps and tries to step away. Her feet get caught in her pants, and she falls onto the bed.

"What did you do that for?" I ask, chuckling.

Harper furiously untangles her feet and crosses her legs, cutting off my view of her perfect pink pussy.

"It's just..." she stammers.

"What, baby?" I know what she's going to say. But I want her to say it. I need her to say it. To be honest with me. I may like submissive Harper in the bedroom, but I want honest Harper, too. She needs to always tell me what she's thinking and how she's feeling.

"I haven't gotten waxed since before Christmas, and it's been a long day, and I haven't showered…" she trails off.

"Thank you for being honest with me, baby," I tell her. "But I don't care what is going on down there. You have hair? Fine. You want it waxed bare? Great. You want that weird ass triangle some women put there? Whatever. I really don't care. I just want my mouth on you. I want my tongue to spear inside of you. I want to suck your clit so fucking hard you see stars, and I want you to drench my face when you come."

"Holy hell, Owen," she whispers, her eyes as wide as saucers. "That was fucking hot."

I chuckle as I rise and climb onto the bed, pushing her shoulders back until she hits the pillows.

"Let me eat, baby. I'm starving," I whisper as I throw both thighs over my shoulders and take a long, luxurious lick from bottom to top. Harper immediately lets out a guttural moan as her hands find my hair, and she latches on, holding me in place. For someone who was self-conscious not even ten seconds ago, she's on board now.

"Holy shit, I'm gonna come …" she murmurs, and I immediately sit back to blow a stream of air onto her pussy. "What the fuck, Owen?"

"You come when I tell you to come, baby. And not a second earlier," I tell her as I lean forward and latch on her clit, suckling hard. Harper's eyes close as her head falls backward, and I stop. She whines and refuses to look at me. "Eyes on me, sweetheart. I need your eyes. Want to see you when you come on my face."

"Owen, please," she whispers as I begin a brutal assault with no pattern. Harper attempts to control my movements by holding my hair where she wants me, but I'm stronger than her. I add two fingers, thrusting them into her wet heat at a different interval than my tongue, and she's moaning incoherently and begging me to let her come. As soon as I feel her walls tightening, I back off.

"You ever been edged like this, baby? Ever been taken to the brink so many times you thought you'd never come? Anyone pay this much attention to what you like, what works for you? Had anyone worship this fucking amazing pussy? Because that's what I'm doing, baby. No one can ever match up to me, Red. No one *will* ever match up to me," I snarl as my fingers quicken the pace. Harper's eyes are open but unfocused as her hands drop from my head. I grab one and lace our fingers together. "You and me, baby. Us. And this little man. Our family. Forever."

"Forever," Harper whimpers.

"Come, Red," I demand as I take her clit in my mouth, sucking hard and flicking it incessantly with my tongue. Harper's entire body bows as every muscle tightens. She stops breathing as the orgasm overtakes her. I can't even remove my fingers because she has them gripped inside her so fucking hard. My dick is painfully trying to break through my pants. I'm so hard watching her come like this.

Harper's orgasm seems to go on for minutes as I slowly lick the remnants off her pussy and thighs. Aftershocks course through her body as her hand grips mine tightly.

"Owen," she whimpers, "What the hell was that?"

"Best orgasm of your life," I answer.

"No fucking kidding," she mumbles.

I chuckle against her incredibly sensitive pussy, which makes her body shake.

"Just don't touch it ... leave it alone. I need a minute," Harper says quietly. "I'll never second-guess you again about edging. Holy shit."

I slowly crawl up her body, stopping to press kisses along her baby bump. I pull her tits out of her bra and spend a few minutes lavishing her nipples. Harper has the best fucking tits.

And now that she's pregnant, they're even bigger. More sensitive, too. She moans as I suck and nibble on the diamond peaks before I slide further up and onto my side next to her. Can't lay on her directly due to the baby bump.

Harper turns her head toward mine and leans over to kiss me. I love that she will kiss me after going down on her. So many women hate to taste themselves, but Harper gets off on it. Her hand slides down and grips me through my pants, and it's my turn to groan.

"Should I return the favor?" she whispers against my lips, and I shake my head.

"No, baby. Not this time. I need to be inside you. Been dreaming about this for weeks. I need you," I say as she unhooks my belt and unzips my pants. I help her remove my pants before she straddles me and gives me a seductive smile before sliding down onto my length. I hiss as her heat envelops me. God, I've missed this. I grab ahold of her shirt and pull it over her shoulders, then pull both bra straps down, so I have better access to her tits. Fuck. I could play with her breasts all fucking day and never get tired of them. They're so perfect. She's so perfect.

Harper begins to slowly slide up and down as I lean forward and latch onto a nipple. I know I'm not going to last long. I need her to come again. Sliding one hand between us, I find her clit and begin strumming it at the same tempo as her movements. I can tell she's already close. I take my other hand and grip her hip, helping force her down onto me harder. Slamming her down as I'm thrusting up allows me to hit so deep inside her that she cries out each time.

"Owen! Oh my God, Owen ..." she cries. "Can I come? I need to come!"

"Come, Red. Come all over my cock. Mark me as yours," I roar as I feel my own orgasm starting. Once Harper tightens as her orgasm crests, her body naturally squeezing my cock sets me off. "Fuck!"

Harper falls onto my chest as we come down from our orgasms.

"That was something else," she mutters breathlessly.

"It was fucking perfect. You were perfect, baby. So fucking perfect for me," I murmur as I place a tender kiss on the top of her head.

"When can we do that again?" she jokes.

"Give me a minute," I respond, chuckling. Harper turns her head and rests her chin on my chest, giving me a wicked grin. I feel her tighten her walls around my half-hard cock, and I let out a groan.

"Really? A whole minute?" she teases as her walls flutter in rhythm. I stare at her incredulously.

"What the fuck ... how are you doing that?" I wonder.

"I can surprise you too, you know," she says. My dick is now fully hard. I could barely catch my breath two minutes ago, but now I need to fuck her again. I flip her, so she's on her back, and I'm on my knees.

"Let's see if I can surprise you into an orgasm or two," I say as I position her ass on my thighs and begin to pummel her. Harper immediately begins to cry and moan as I thrust as hard as possible.

"Fuck, Owen, fuck! Don't stop, don't stop, right there, right there, right there ..." her mouth opens in a silent scream as she comes.

"I think you can give me one more, Red," I tell her as I lean forward to pinch one nipple with my thumb and forefinger while flicking her clit with my other hand. She comes again in less than a minute, this time with a scream so loud the neighbors probably heard her. I follow her in my own loud release before falling to the side and pulling out of her. I know my two releases are seeping out of her onto the comforter, but

I don't care. I can't think about anything except the most phenomenal sex of my life with the woman I love.

"Jesus, that was mind-blowing. I didn't think that actually happened except in smut books," Harper giggles.

"Gonna happen every day for the rest of your life, Red. You ready for that?" I say as I turn my head toward her. Her eyes meet mine, and she beams.

"You're saying we're gonna have sex every day?" she asks.

"Yep. Probably more than once. I don't think I'm ever getting tired of your perfect pink pussy," I tell Harper as I lean forward and kiss the tip of her nose.

"Promise?" she asks hopefully.

"Promise. You and me forever, Red. This is it."

"I love you, Owen."

"Love you too, Harper."

CHAPTER TWENTY-EIGHT

Harper

Our new life together evolves quickly. Owen was right in his quest to make sure we have sex every day. Not that I'm complaining. Second-trimester hormones have taken over, and I'm basically always horny. Let's just say Owen hadn't complained when I showed up at his office in the middle of the day and demanded a quickie.

While our relationship is solid, our friendship with Liv and Liam is beyond rocky. While Liv initially showed me support after the blowup at their house, she has since turned on us and fully backed her husband.

"I really don't know what they're smoking to think so highly of themselves," I comment one afternoon as I pull on my maternity pants and a flowy top, watching Owen as he slowly buttons his shirt. We literally just got done having sex, and if he wanted to, I'd completely go again. He's so fucking sexy.

"Quit looking at me like that, Red. As much as I'd love round two, I have a client coming in fifteen minutes," he drawls with a smirk.

"It's not my fault you're so damn sexy. It is completely your fault. Also your fault that I've got your spawn inside me wreaking havoc on my hormones," I retort. Owen reaches over and pulls me to him, sliding his arms around me.

"My spawn?" he asks, his eyes full of mischief.

"At this moment, yes. He's definitely your spawn," I say.

Owen covers my lips with his and kisses me passionately. I moan into his mouth and immediately try to wrap a leg around his hips so I can get some friction. My girly bits are ridiculously greedy and want all the orgasms.

"Dammit, woman, I just can't get enough of you," he whispers as he drops to his knees and pulls my pants and undies down, then sucks my clit in between his lips. "How many times can you come in fifteen minutes, ya think?"

Turns out it's six. I can come six times in fifteen minutes. Who knew?

"Mr. Taylor, your one o'clock appointment is in the conference room," his administrative assistant, Nancy, announces over the phone speaker.

"Thanks, Nancy. Tell him I'll be there in five minutes," Owen answers as he finishes buttoning his shirt and straightens his tie. "You okay, baby?"

"I don't think I can walk just yet, sweetie," I murmur. I'm splayed across his desk and have lost feeling in my legs. My entire body is humming.

"Take your time, Red. We'll finish this at home. I think I can do better than six," he whispers against my ear. I shudder at the thought. "My meeting will be the rest of the afternoon, so head out whenever you want."

"Mmkay, love you," I mumble.

"Love you too, baby."

I hear the door softly open and close, then hear Owen murmuring to his assistant. I assume he's telling her to leave me alone. If I can listen to him talking to her...that means she could hear us when we were in here. Oh. Well. Surprisingly, that seems to turn me on.

I manage to slither off Owen's desk and into his chair, straightening my clothes as I do so. My legs are shaking horribly, so I take a few calming breaths and chug from a water bottle Owen left behind. Goodness. That was an unexpected lunch break. I'm thankful I don't have another hair appointment until three, giving me much-needed time to bask in that amazing orgasm palooza Owen just bestowed upon me.

I hear muffled voices outside that quickly begin to rise, but I don't hear Owen's voice.

"Miss, you can't go in there!" I hear Nancy shout as the door to Owen's office is thrown open with gusto, slamming into the opposing wall. Standing in the doorway is none other than Amelia McCallister. This woman is nothing but trouble.

"What are *you* doing in here?" she seethes.

"Visiting my boyfriend for lunch, obviously," I say dryly. Her eyes narrow as she stares at me. I'm pretty certain my face is red, my hair is probably askew, and I know if I had to stand right now, my knees would buckle.

"Is that what we're calling fuck buddies these days? Boyfriends?" she sneers.

I sigh and ignore her dig.

"What can I help you with, Amelia?" I ask.

"You can't help me with anything, Hope. I'm here to see my child's father," she says with disdain. She knows my name. She's doing this purposely to try and get a rise out of me.

"You know my name, Amelia. Stop acting like you don't.

And when is your husband supposed to be here?" I ask. She gives me a wicked grin.

"Oh, I'm not talking about my soon-to-be ex-husband, Harper. I'm talking about Owen. I'm three months along. Can you believe it? He's going to be an amazing daddy," she gushes with an evil glint in her eye.

"Is that so?" I say, standing up so she can see my protruding baby bump. I slowly walk toward her, cradling my stomach. "You're telling me that you somehow managed to get with Owen three months ago when he's been with me this entire time?"

Amelia balks at my statement for a moment and then sputters.

"Well, yeah, we ran into each other at a bar in Colorado Springs, and one thing led to another ..." she trails off as she squares her shoulders and attempts to stand taller than me.

"You know what's funny? He told me about running into you. I called him, and he came to me right after. So you're saying he literally fucked you at a bar and then came right to me and fucked me? I think I'd have noticed if he smelled like your God-awful perfume. What the hell is that, anyway? Smells like skunk-flavored fruit," I comment.

"It's Poison by Dior," she retorts, and I bark back a laugh.

"Wow, I think my grandmother still wears that. Didn't realize you had a thing for bad eighties perfume, Ames," I say dryly.

"Do *not* give me a nickname," she growls.

"Why not? You called me Hope."

"I forgot your name. I didn't give you a nickname."

"You didn't forget my name, Ames."

"Stop doing that!"

"No."

"Stop it!"

"Oh, am I upsetting you? Poor little rich girl. I don't just bow down and let you bulldoze over me like everyone else. Must be frustrating," I whine with a fake pout.

"You're nothing but trailer trash," she spits out.

"Can honestly say I've never been in a trailer, but I get the sentiment. I may be trash, honey, but at least I'm not a lying psychopath who fakes a pregnancy to try and land a man," I comment.

"I'm not faking anything, bitch," Amelia snarls.

"You're faking something, *bitch*," I respond. "I know Owen isn't the father of that baby."

"Oh yeah? How can you prove it?" she smiles evilly. "Owen gets around. I'm sure it's not the first time he fucked two women in the same night."

Throughout my life, I've had times when I've had to throw my trust implicitly into someone's corner without knowing if it's a good idea. Even six months ago, I don't know if I could trust Owen wholeheartedly. But right now? At this moment? I trust him completely. I know he hasn't been with her, and he certainly wouldn't fuck her and then come right to me and act like nothing happened.

"Amelia, I don't know what your relationship with your husband is like. However, I'm going to assume that the two of you have no trust. I'm sure you both fuck around, and then you can't believe anything the other says. And while that may work for you, it doesn't work for me. Owen and I are in a committed and monogamous relationship. That means the only pussy he gets is mine. And trust me, he gets it all the time. No time for him to be messing with you as well. And frankly, once you experience the Holy Grail of pussies, why on earth would you demote yourself to a revolving door snatch?"

Amelia stares at me, her mouth wide open as she tries to formulate a response. Finally, she growls at me right as I see movement behind her.

"She's right, Ames," Owen drawls, and I snicker when he

uses the same nickname I just used. No one has ever called her Ames. It's fucking brilliant.

"Don't fucking call me that!" she screeches.

"Don't fucking come in here and make up stories trying to start drama. You and I both know I'm not the dad. I bet you aren't even pregnant. But we could very easily issue a court-ordered paternity test. You know they do those on pregnant women, right? So let's just settle this once and for all," Owen says as he reaches into his pocket to retrieve his phone.

"What are you doing?" Amelia says quietly, her face draining of color.

"Calling a friend of mine at MSPD. Gotta make sure I do this completely by the book, so you don't find some fucked up loophole and drag us all through months of toxic drama. Plus, I figure we can do a background check on whether or not you've played this 'I'm pregnant with your baby' game with anyone else. Something tells me this isn't your first time trying to trap a man," Owen says with a bemused smile as he brings his phone to his ear.

"God dammit, no! Stop!" Amelia shouts. Owen raises his eyebrows at her as he returns his phone to his pocket. "Fine. It's not yours."

"And why is it not mine? For clarification purposes. I need you to say the words, Ames," Owen chuckles as she growls again.

"Because we've never had sex," she snarls.

"That's right. Everyone hear that?" Owen calls out, and I hear Nancy in the other room shouting affirmatively. "Get the fuck out of my office, Amelia. Don't even think about coming back here. And if I hear you've terrorized any of my friends, family, or my woman, I'm throwing a restraining order on you so fucking fast you won't know what happened."

Amelia whirls around, stomps toward the door, and slams it shut with a flourish. Owen turns to me.

"You okay?" he asks with a worried look.

"Yeah, I'm fine," I tell him with a smile. "I know you. I know your heart. You wouldn't do that to me."

He leans his forehead against mine and exhales.

"Thank fuck," he mumbles. "When Nancy came and got me, I didn't know what to think. But watching you take her on? Dammit, Red, that was so fucking hot. I love you so much."

I lean in and give him a soft kiss.

"I trust you, Owen. I know you wouldn't do that to me. And I love you too," I tell him. "Now go back to your meeting. I have to get to the salon."

"How late are you going to be tonight?" Owen asks.

"My last appointment is at five, so I should be home by six thirty," I tell him, and he gives me a wide smile.

"Love that."

"What?"

"That you call it 'home,'" he says tenderly as he gives me a quick kiss. "I'll order in. What is my man craving today?"

I giggle as I think about the little Owen growing in my tummy and what sounds good for dinner.

"Mexican," I blurt out. "I need queso and enchiladas."

"Alright, baby. I'll have it ready for you when you get home. Love you," he says as he walks back toward the conference room.

"Love you, too," I call as I stare at his suit-clad ass. His pants fit exceptionally well today. His perfect bubble butt is on display, and I can't say that I don't love the view.

As if he knows what I'm looking at, he slaps his own ass as he opens the conference door.

"Sorry about that, Stan. My girlfriend needed me," he says as he looks back at me and winks.

I shake my head, laughing. This version of Owen, this one is my favorite.

CHAPTER TWENTY-NINE

Owen

Two more weeks pass in bliss. It's now been over a month since I've spoken to Liam. I've kept incredibly busy with cases, including still putting together a case against Harper's asshole of a landlord, and the rest of the time I spend buried in Harper. Never knew it could be like this. I can feel my blood pressure lowering every time I'm near her, even if it's just sitting on the couch to watch her favorite Gilmore Girls episodes. She is my peace. My salvation. My home.

We're hit with a hell of a winter storm at the beginning of March. Ironically, the front range of the Rockies has the most snow in March. And it tends to be doozies of storms. This one shutters the town with almost three feet of snow. We lose electricity, but I have a wood-burning fireplace that keeps us warm. I can even cook some food in the fireplace to ensure Harper continues getting good nutrients. She's finally in the third trimester, and while I know she's feeling uncomfortable, she's never looked more breathtaking to me. My favorite thing is putting my head on her stomach and letting little man kick me. I whisper all my thoughts into her stomach as she slowly runs her fingers through my hair. No better place to be.

We're sitting by the fireplace in silence on the second night of the winter storm. Harper has a cordless book light attached to one of the romance books Liv got her obsessed with.

"What's this story about?" I ask her. She gives me a wicked grin.

"Oh, this one is a good one! I've never read her books before, but this is really good. Her name is Katie Rae. It's about two best friends who fall for the same girl. One guy is an NFL quarterback, and the other guy is a professional baseball player. They decide to share her," she tells me.

"Share? Like, *share* share?" I ask.

"Yep."

"How the fuck does that even work?"

"They take turns, obviously," Harper tells me.

"Do they ever ..." I clear my throat awkwardly.

Harper cackles.

"No, Owen. They don't ever."

Oh, thank fuck. Harper knew what I was asking without me having to be a complete buffoon.

"Want me to read a scene out loud?" she asks quietly and looks at me through her lashes. I nod. She begins reading a particularly salacious scene where they both 'paint' the girl with their cum. Holy shit. I'm now rock-hard.

"Damn, Red," I mutter, discreetly adjusting myself in my sweats. Harper closes the book and turns off the light before turning to me.

"Do you want to do that, Owen?" Harper asks quietly. "Come all over chest?"

Jesus.

"No, Red. I want to come deep inside you, feeling you clamp down on me," I tell her as I drag her onto my lap and split her legs, so she's straddling me and my rigid length pushes right against her core. Harper immediately grinds into me, and I moan. I wrap a handful of her waves around my fist and yank her head down to mine. Lust flashes in her eyes as she stares at me. "What do you need, baby?"

"I need you inside me, Owen. I need to come," she whimpers.

"How do you want it? Hard and fast where you'll feel me for days? Or so slow, so excruciatingly slow, that it's like fucking torture?" I've got her hips in a vice grip so she can't move, and I can tell she's getting frustrated. Pregnant Harper, when horny, is even more impatient than regular Harper. And boy, do I love riling her up like this. When she finally explodes around me, she sets me off every damn time.

"Sweetie, please," she moans.

"Which one? Answer."

"Hard and fast, Owen. Please."

"Stand up and take off your pants," I order. Harper clambers to her feet and quickly rids herself of her leggings before trying to jump back in my lap. "Uh uh. Stand there, and let me look at you."

I see a flash of irritation in her beautiful green eyes, and I give her a big smile in return. This is the game we play. She'll get hers, and she knows it, but there's always that one moment where she battles her inner brat and tries to defy me. But I always win.

I grab her maternity shirt by the hem and raise it slightly to see Harper isn't wearing underwear.

"Commando, baby? Really?" I ask, chuckling.

"Easier access," she responds breathily with a cheeky grin. I slide my hand between her thighs and find her soaked. She moans gutturally as I easily slide two fingers into her channel and locate her G-spot. I feel her clench and yank my hand away from her. She orgasms so quickly right now, but I want her on me when she comes.

"Don't you dare come until I tell you to," I threaten as I push my sweats down and onto the floor.

"Owen," she whimpers and actually stomps her foot in frustration.

"You know I'll make you feel good, Red," I remind her before standing up and pushing her toward the window. My living room has a massive window that looks out onto my backyard. Behind my property line is an open space with walking trails and many natural habitats. I know no one should be back there right now, as it's the middle of a winter storm and after dark, so I want to play with Harper and see how far she lets me push her.

"Put your hands on the window," I tell her huskily as my tongue slides out to drag along her neck.

"Owen, what are you doing?" she stammers. "There could be someone back there."

"That's kinda the point. Need to fuck you right here, baby. You gonna let me?" I murmur as I suck on her pulse point before sliding my hand around her thighs and finding her clit, flicking it hard before stroking through her wetness. Harper groans and pushes her ass into my groin, making me groan.

"Do it, Owen. Fuck me right here," Harper whispers. Well, hell. I didn't think she'd get on board *that* quickly, but I'm not letting her change her mind. I push down on her back, so she's tilted, and I can thrust into her. She cries out as I begin a harsh tempo. I promised hard, and I'm giving her hard.

Harper climaxes almost immediately, but I'm not done with her. "Told you not to come unless I said you could, woman!" I reach out and smack her ass. She cries out, but I feel her walls clamp down on me. Holy fuck. My woman likes to be spanked.

"Did you like that, baby?" I ask, and she nods, so I spank her again.

"Owen, please."

"Please, what?"

"Turn me around. I need to see you when you come," Harper tells me. Jesus. I almost lose my load right then and there. I pull out, turn her, and then grab one leg to put around my waist. Thrusting back inside, I let out a big exhale as I stare into her eyes.

"Jesus, I love you so fucking much," I mutter as I pummel her. Harper reaches up and grabs my neck, bringing my forehead to hers.

"Make me come again," she orders.

I push her back against the cold glass, and she gasps.

"I'm in control, baby. You'll come when I decide," I say clearly.

"Yes, sir," she responds, and I groan. Fucking hell. I'm two seconds away from coming, and I know she isn't there yet. I decide to try another new trick to see how she reacts. I slide my hand between her ass and the window, trailing down until I find her puckered rosebud. I hear her sharp intake of breath as my finger circles it slowly before I push the tip of my finger inside. Harper lets out one hell of a moan before her walls clamp down on me so tightly I can barely move. As she shudders through her orgasm, the shaking walls bring me to a mind-altering climax.

"This window is really cold, but I can't move my legs yet," Harper mumbles against my neck. I chuckle and manage to maneuver both of us to fall into a chair next to the window.

"That was ... wow," I say breathlessly.

"Yeah. Wow is what I was going to say, too," Harper replies. Then, as I'm about to suggest we head upstairs and cuddle under my massive down comforter, I hear a weird sound.

"What the hell was that?" I wonder out loud.

"Kinda sounded like an injured animal?" Harper replies.

I hear it again. Something is crying outside our back door. Screaming would be a more accurate word. Every few seconds, I hear a shriek. I wrap a blanket around me before opening the back door into heavy snow. Looking around as my eyes adjust to the darkness, I hear the sound again directly to my left. I look down and see a ball of black fur huddled up against the side of my house. I don't even think twice. I immediately grab it and get out of the snow.

"Oh my God! What is it?" Harper asks.

"I think it's a kitten," I say quietly as I dry it off with the blanket. The poor kitten is shivering and has its eyes squeezed shut. "I don't think it's more than eight weeks old."

"Oh, wow. Oh, it's so cute," Harper gushes. I look at Harper's face, knowing we're keeping this cat.

"Baby."

"What?" Harper asks before her eyes meet mine. "It's just … I always wanted a cat. Just never got one."

"Looks like this little guy decided it was time for you to have your first cat, huh."

Harper beams as she takes the bundle out of my arms.

"Can you google what we can give him? Obviously, we don't have cat food. Maybe boiled chicken? I wonder if they can eat any fruits or vegetables. Oh, no! We need litter!"

"Actually, I have that covered. I always keep a box in the garage in case my car gets stuck in the driveway," I say as I grab my sweats and throw them on. I quickly head into the garage to grab the box of litter, then find a small plastic container that can serve as a litter box until we can get to the store. The weather is supposed to clear up overnight, and knowing how Colorado weather tends to flip a switch after a winter storm, I bet we'll be able to leave tomorrow afternoon.

After warming up the kitten, I pull out some leftover chicken from the cooler. We've been without electricity for over twenty-four hours, so I moved a cooler inside for our most-used items to ensure we didn't have to open the fridge and ruin all the food. As soon as I dangle a small piece of chicken in front of the kitten's nose, he immediately perks up and attacks it voraciously.

After eating some chicken, Harper took it to the sink and bathed it in dish soap. Probably not ideal, but it had to be done. The kitten was incredibly aromatic. The amount of dirt and grime that came off this poor kitten was atrocious. I had thought it was a black cat, but it appears to be closer to a Siamese with a dark head, ears, and paws, with a lighter body.

Once dry, we place the kitten in the litter box, and he immediately goes. Harper croons and praises the cat, which makes me chuckle. I can already see how she will be when our kid potty trains.

"What?" she asks, and I shrug, bemused at the spectacle she's making over a kitten using the litter box.

"Nothing. Just enjoying watching you get all cute over cat poop," I tease her.

"Oh, stop. I'm thrilled she knows how to use it. I don't know how to teach that," she says.

"It's a 'he,' baby," I tell her.

"How do you possibly know that?" Harper retorts.

"Because *he* has balls," I say as I pick the kitten up and show her his behind. Her eyes widen.

"Oh. Yes. I'm so sorry, sir, for calling you a 'she'. My mistake," she gushes as she grabs the kitten and nestles him into her neck. "Are you okay with this? Do I really get to keep him?"

"You think I'd separate the two of you now? I value my life, Red," I drawl.

"You think I'd hurt you if you made me give up the kitten?"

"Yep."

"You'd be right."

I bark back a laugh and then give her a quick kiss.

Not how I expected the evening to go, but I'm not complaining. Life sure isn't dull with Harper.

CHAPTER THIRTY

Harper

Fuck this shit.

I'm the size of a whale. A house. The whole fucking planet.

I can no longer pull my chair up to the table because my massive stomach gets in the way. With how much little man seems to be maneuvering around my internal organs, I'm beginning to think three of four kids are in there, and they all use my bladder as a punching bag.

I'll never admit this to him, but Owen is a rock star for putting up with me and my hormones. I'm all over the place. I broke a nail the other day and blamed it on the kitten, then felt instant guilt and sobbed into his fur. Owen wants to call the kitten Lucky, because we had just gotten lucky when we found him. Owen is already enjoying doling out dad jokes. Ha-freak-ing-ha.

It's now the beginning of April, and I'm in the home stretch. I've begun taking on fewer clients the closer I get to my due date because I just can't stand for that long anymore. My ankles are already morphing into the dreaded 'cankles', and Owen spends twenty minutes each evening massaging my feet and calves every night. Not that I'm complaining about that part. It's bliss.

The absolute worst part about this pregnancy is the damn acid reflux. I can no longer lay on my side in bed. Instead, I have to have my head somehow elevated. For a side sleeper, this is fucking torture. Needless to say, I'm barely sleeping. A tired Harper is a mean Harper. Dammit. Now I'm talking in the third person. Owen is rubbing off on me in weird ways.

Owen is taking it all in stride. I have no doubt he rolls his eyes at my antics, but fortunately, he does that without me seeing. Because Lord knows I would rip him a new one if I saw him do it. I know he feels frustrated because he can only talk to Nathan about this kind of stuff. We still have had no contact with Liv and Liam.

My anger is mainly with Liam. What he said to Owen was rude and hurtful, and he has yet to apologize to either of us. But when Liv got involved, that broke my heart. She didn't have to involve herself. She could have tried to play peacemaker and organized an intervention. Instead, she dramatically called me and shouted how out of line Owen was, and that her husband was right. Owen and I were just jealous of everyone else being happy. She even took it a step further and said she didn't think we would last. My best friend of most of my life doesn't believe in my relationship. That was so incredibly insulting. I haven't gotten that conversation out of my head, and neither has Owen. We're pissed.

Because of this rift, we've barely seen Nate and Emily. While Nate still talks to Owen, I know he feels incredibly conflicted because Liv is his sister. And Emily just has her hands full. I feel like I lost all of my friends and my support system.

By the second week of April, Em texted me and asked if I wanted to grab lunch, and I immediately said yes. I love Owen, but I need female interaction outside my salon. Owen has been incredibly busy with his caseload. He assures me he's trying to work more now so he can take a good amount of paternity leave once the baby arrives.

Em asks if I can meet her at our favorite diner in town. I used to meet Em and Liv there fairly often, and I haven't been in a while. So I'm thrilled with the opportunity to see Em and go to one of my favorite places.

I grab a booth and wait. When Em doesn't show up after ten minutes, I text her, asking where she is. Suddenly someone slams into the bench across from me. I look up to find a frazzled Liv.

"Hi," she says quietly.

"Uh, hi?"

"You aren't meeting Emily. You're meeting me."

"Is that so."

"Yeah. I figured you wouldn't come if I asked, so Em played middleman."

"You'd be right," I answer, as I begin to put my coat back on and slide out of the booth.

"Harp, wait! Please. I need to apologize," Liv blurts out.

I stop and stare at her. "You're going to apologize?"

"Yeah. I handled things so poorly. I'm a hormonal bitch, and I took things out on you and said such awful things. I'm so sorry, Harper. I never should have said those things about your relationship with Owen," she says, her eyes pleading with mine.

"You said I was jealous of you and only got pregnant because of that," I tell her, and she winces.

"I know. I was awful. I swear, having all this extra testosterone in me has turned me into a raging lunatic," Liv mutters. My ears perk up.

"You're having a boy?" I ask, and she gives me a huge smile.

"We just found out last week. Liam is so excited," she gushes.

"Well, congratulations." I stand and turn to her. "You also said you didn't think my relationship with Owen would pan out. That's what I can't forget, Olivia. That's what hurts the most."

Liv stands and follows me out to the parking lot. I'm driving Owen's car today. As much as I hate when he's right, I'm much more comfortable in his SUV.

"I know. Partially it's because I know Owen's track record, and I'm scared for you. I want you to find true love and have an epic love story because you deserve it, Harp. But I think I was also jealous of you. You sort of fell into this relationship and pregnancy, and my journey with Liam was so rough."

"My relationship with Owen hasn't been a cakewalk, Liv. That's incredibly insulting of you to say that."

"Well, I mean, it's really only been going on for a few months."

"No, that's not true. Since we first had sex, neither of us has been with anyone else. That means I've been faithful to Owen longer than you've been with Liam. Did that ever occur to you?"

"Did he tell you that? And you believe him?"

"Why wouldn't I? Owen has always bragged about his conquests. He's never hidden his desire for sex or women. So when he told me he hadn't been with anyone else since we were together almost two years ago, of course, I believed him. I have no reason not to. We weren't *together* together, so he could have slept with a hundred women, and I'd have no right to be angry about it."

"I keep forgetting you guys hooked up that long ago," Liv says quietly.

"Obviously."

"I owe Owen an apology," she says.

"Yes, you do. Liam does, too."

"He's getting there. Possibly today, but who knows. Stubborn ass."

"I don't know how to possibly make that any easier for him. Owen is incredibly hurt that his best friend basically turned on him. He didn't see that coming. Nate basically has to side with you, so Owen has no one," I tell her.

"Nate hasn't sided with us. He's remained as diplomatic as possible. He keeps telling me he's Switzerland, the weirdo," she tells me with a small smile. I chuckle lightly. That sounds like something Nathan would say.

"I just never realized that you and Liam thought so little of me, Liv. That's what hurt the most. Realizing the people I viewed as my family would demean me horribly to my face. I'm not sure how to move past it."

"I know, Harp. I'm so sorry. There aren't enough words in the world for me to apologize enough. I was so out of line, and Liam was too. I'm so incredibly happy for you and Owen. I know you're going to be amazing parents."

"And do you still think my relationship with Owen is doomed?" I ask her dryly.

"No," she says. "God, my first trimester hormones were out of control. I have no idea why I said that. Just a moment of pregnancy rage, I guess. I see how he is with you. He's never been like this. Owen worships the ground you walk on. And maybe if I hadn't been so self-centered a few months ago, I would have seen it earlier. And I know you've had a thing for him for years."

"I wanted to fuck him, not live with him and have his

baby," I joke. "I just thought he was hot. He irritates the shit out of me all the damn time."

"That's why he's perfect for you."

"How on earth do you figure that?"

"Because you need a challenge. Someone who calls you out on your shit and allows you to call him out on his. If you had an introverted man like Nathan who wants to stay home with his family, always rocks a resting bitch face, and steers clear of as many public outings as possible, you'd become incredibly bored. You need the excitement. The tension. Owen is perfect for you from that standpoint. I can only assume the arguing is great foreplay for you as well."

"You'd be correct."

Liv chuckles.

"I'm sorry for everything, Harp. Really. I'm so sad that I've missed out on the last two and a half months of your life and that we haven't been able to experience our pregnancies together. I really hope we can move forward now," Liv says quietly.

My brain is demanding I zing her with something awful as a way to give her a dose of her own medicine, but my heart is pleading to forgive and forget. I've missed Liv. My bestie. She's been my ride-or-die for twenty-plus years. I'm a little over a month away from delivering this baby, and I need my person.

"Okay," I breathe. Liv's eyes whip to mine in disbelief.

"Really?" she blurts out. "Shit. I thought you'd make me grovel more."

"I thought about it. But honestly, I'm just too tired. I can't sleep, and I have acid reflux, and this kid is constantly standing on my bladder," I moan miserably as I place my hand over my stomach. He visibly kicks, moving my hand.

"Wow! Can I feel?" she asks, and I nod. She places her hand where mine is, and the baby immediately kicks it. "Oh my God! Harper, that's your baby!" Liv begins to cry.

"Why are you crying?"

"I don't know!" she wails, which makes me laugh.

"I've missed you, Liv," I tell her as she throws her arms around me and awkwardly hugs me. Difficult when we both have baby bumps. Or, in my case, a beluga whale.

"I've missed you, too," she says tearfully. "Now, let's go back in the diner and talk pregnancy and baby stuff. I'm starving."

CHAPTER THIRTY-ONE

Owen

Apparently, there was a coup in our group because while Harper was getting forced into talking to Liv, Nathan did the same thing to me and forced me to speak to Liam. Evidently, the animosity and anxiety were getting to everyone. Nate was bound and determined to end it all before Harper gave birth.

Nate asked me to hit up Top Golf with him. Honestly, golf isn't my thing. Even Top Golf, which is basically just an excuse to drink beer and whack a ball as hard as you can for no reason, isn't for me. I find no joy in golf. Boring, mundane, and frankly, any sport that requires me to be quiet is bullshit.

Nate offered to pick me up, as Top Golf is about an hour away. Nate likes golfing. I'd wonder why, but that's much more his speed. He's quiet and reserved, the exact opposite of me. Liam was always the middle ground for us. I like to refer to Liam as an introverted extrovert. He can be social and the life of the party when needed, but then he requires time to recover and will become a hermit. I think that's why it didn't surprise me he bought a massive house in the mountains that no one knew about for years. So he could escape there and recharge.

As I get into Nate's truck, he guns it out of my driveway.

"Damn, Nate, where's the fire? Why are you rushing?" I joke.

"Had to get going so you couldn't get out of the truck," he mutters. Wait, what?

"That makes me the fire," a muffled voice from behind me mumbles, making me jump. I whip around to find Liam hiding under a blanket.

"What the fuck?"

"Figured you wouldn't come if you knew I would be here."

"You're fucking correct, asshole."

"How am I supposed to apologize and make things right if you won't answer the damn phone or respond to my texts?" he asks.

"Didn't know you were trying to call me," I say nonchalantly. Liam cocks his brows at me. "I blocked you, dumbass."

"Well, that's mature," he mutters.

"You blocked Liv last year, so don't even give me crap about it."

"Oh, fuck. I forgot about that."

Silence fills the truck cab as Nathan gets on the interstate heading to Top Golf. No one talks for fifteen minutes. Nathan doesn't even have the radio on, so we all sit and stew silently.

"So," Nathan finally says, "What's new with you, Liam? Anything to share?"

"Oh!" Liam shouts from the backseat, jarring me. "Look!"

He thrusts an ultrasound picture into my face.

"Okay ..." I mutter.

"It's a boy!" he shouts with so much enthusiasm I can't help but smile.

"Congrats, man. That's great."

"Thanks. I can't believe I'm ... well, you and I ... are going to be dads to sons. So now all three of us will have sons," Liam muses. I hadn't even thought about that.

"Any words of wisdom, seasoned father?" I ask as I turn to Nathan.

"Never open a boy's diaper without something ready to cover him. Boys pee when cold air hits them. Every fucking time," he says with a wicked grin.

"Lovely," Liam mutters. "Anything else?"

"Soak it in. It goes by so fast. My girls are almost toddlers. I don't even know how the last year went as quickly as it did. The days are long, but the years are short, guys. Seriously."

I take a moment to let that sentiment sink in. It's true of life, really. I'm thirty-nine years old, and I really don't know where the last decade went. I can't believe Harper and I first got together almost two years ago, and now we're about to have a kid. Mind-boggling.

"With that being said, you two need to iron your shit out. I'll be damned if we invite y'all to birthday parties and other events, and we have to referee the two of you. Get it together. Apologize and move on," Nathan tells us.

"Did you just say 'y'all'?" I ask with a smile. "Your wife is rubbing off on you."

"Honestly, it wasn't until Monica moved here that it seemed to start sticking. Having both of them around me all the time, I'm picking up the southern mannerisms and crap," Nathan chuckles.

"Just as long as you don't use the word 'fixin.' I will troll you for that," Liam deadpans. I nod emphatically.

"Whatever. But you two need to talk. Hash it out. We've got a good half hour before we get there."

"Don't think that's enough time," I mutter. I refuse to start the conversation. Liam needs to. He was outrageously out of line.

"I'll start," Liam says as if he read my mind. "I said some really awful things to you, O. I have no excuse. It was reprehensible, and I sincerely apologize for hurting your feelings. I don't know what came over me."

"You called my woman 'easy pussy', man. You owe her an even bigger apology."

"I know." Liam sighs. "I'm a work in progress. I've been working with my therapist again. She thinks finding out Liv was pregnant brought up some more negative associations with my childhood. Somehow, I transferred that to you and Harper. We're still working on why I would do that."

I'm thrilled Liam is still seeing his therapist. He's come a long way in the last two years, and I'm incredibly proud of his progress. However, it's hard to understand how my pregnant girlfriend fits into his path to redemption.

"I just don't understand why you went after Harper like that. You know I've always been attracted to her, and you knew I had stopped sleeping around. So to call her 'easy pussy' in front of everyone was so hurtful."

"I know, man. I know. Sometimes I really put my foot in my own fucking mouth and have no explanation for why I've done it. I'm so sorry."

I sit for a few minutes, quietly contemplating his apology. I'm still frustrated that he doesn't really have a valid reason for why he attacked my relationship like that.

"Do you really think I did all this just because I was jealous?" I ask softly.

"No, Owen. I swear, I don't. It was just the heat of the moment. I made an incredibly uncouth joke that didn't go over well, you reacted, and then I reacted. So it was just a perfect storm of epic bad decisions on my part."

"You seemed somewhat excited when you found out about Harper, but you turned so quickly a few weeks later. That's why I'm confused."

"I don't know how to explain my reaction because I don't even understand it. I lost my head for a moment. Some of it is that I'm worried about you. I want you to be happy."

"What makes you think I wouldn't be happy with Harper? Furthermore, did you think I was incredibly happy and content with living the single life? Because newsflash, Liam, I thought I was. Until I had Harper. Until she was living with me, and I looked forward to coming home to her every evening. Waking up with her each morning has been an exquisite torture that I didn't know I craved. She's it for me, man," I tell him vehemently.

"I know that now, O. I know. I'm so sorry that I misjudged your relationship and missed out on the last three months of our friendship and Harper's pregnancy," Liam says quietly.

"Thank you. I accept your apology. But you need to apologize to Harper."

"Liv is with her now."

"What?" I bellow, whipping out my phone to text Harper.

"There may have been another staged intervention with the ladies," Nathan mutters.

> Me: Are you okay?

Harper: I'm fine. Are you?

> Me: Yes, surprisingly.

Harper: Did Liam apologize?

> Me: Yeah. Did Liv?

> Harper: Yeah.

> Me: Liam still needs to apologize to you, though.

> Harper: Eh. I don't really care. I was way more hurt by Liv siding with him and cutting me off. I wanted him to apologize to you, so I'm glad he did that.

> Me: He didn't know how I really felt about you.

> Harper: Oh, yeah? And how do you feel about me?

I grin. Harper is one hell of an independent woman, but she straight up preens when I compliment her and tell her how I feel. I don't think she realized how much she craved praise and validation.

> Me: You're my world, Red. You and little man. Never been this happy. Sun rises and sets in that sweet pussy.

> Harper: Well, that's nice, considering Liv just heard your car read that text to me.

I throw my head back in laughter. I forgot she's driving my car today. Finally made a little headway in her steadfast stubbornness about our cars, and we're planning to go shopping for an SUV for her soon.

> Me: Sorry, baby. Hi, Liv.

> Harper: She says hi.

> Me: Where are you going?

> Harper: We're going to walk around Target and look at all the baby things.

> Me: Did you pick out a crib yet?

> Harper: No.

> Me: Might want to get on that, Red.

> Harper: I have Em's old bassinet we can use at the beginning. I'll find a crib at some point.

> Me: Okay, baby, we're almost at Top Golf. Have fun with Liv. I love you.

> Harper: Love you, too, sweetie.

Fuck. I love when Harper calls me that.

"You ready to get your ass handed to you, Taylor?" Nathan calls out to me as we get out of the car at Top Golf.

"Yep."

"Not even gonna trash talk, man? That's unexpected."

"Dude, I suck at golf. We all know this. Not only do I suck, but I hate the fucking sport entirely."

"At least we can have some beers," Liam offers with a shrug.

"I can do that at home," I say dryly.

"Let's play a little bit, and then we can just hang out. The three of us haven't hung in a while, so this will be nice," Nathan says.

"Sounds good. But if either of you trolls me about my swing, I'm not liable for my reaction. So duck and cover, motherfuckers," I say with a wicked smile, and both guys chuckle.

All in all, it was a nice afternoon. I've missed hanging out with my two best friends. I'm glad we put the past behind us.

CHAPTER THIRTY-TWO

Harper

Owen was only slightly surprised when he came home from Top Golf, and his entire living room looked like Target exploded in it. I bought so much that I had to make two trips to fit it all in my car. I found the crib of my dreams. And I don't mean that figuratively: I literally dreamt of a specific grey crib. It had a matching changing table and dresser, and I picked out a dark grey glider with an ottoman for all those late-night feedings. Thank goodness Owen is handy because I'm not going to be able to put any of this together without me ending in a puddle of tears.

I also grabbed a ton of clothes, diapers, bottles, pacifiers ... basically any and all items I thought I might need. I may have opened a Target credit card to get an extra discount. It's gonna take me a few months to pay it all off, but it was all needed. The kid can't go without clothing or a bed.

As I'm slowly taking all the price tags off the clothes so I can wash everything, I hear the garage door go up, then the car door slamming.

"Honey, I'm home!" Owen calls out as he strides into the house, then abruptly stops when he sees the chaos. We both look down as some of the bags move. Our kitten, whom we've named Boots due to his darker-colored paws, appears to be attacking some of the Target bags. I refused to let Owen call the kitten Lucky. I have some standards, after all.

"Um, I may have gone a little overboard at Target," I whisper bashfully. His face spreads into a sweet grin as he takes it all in.

"It appears that way. Do you want to show me everything?"

"You're not mad?"

"Why would I be mad? Obviously, we needed everything. Did you find a crib?" he asks as he steps gingerly through all the bags.

"Yeah, it's in the car. It was too heavy for me to lift. Target is delivering a chair and ottoman tomorrow for the nursery. I couldn't fit that in the car."

"Alright, show me what you got," Owen says as he finally reaches the couch and sits next to me. He grabs Boots from under the bags and cuddles him on his shoulder. Boots immediately begins purring. Owen may say the cat was for me, but he's as attached to the furry little screamer as I am. He throws one arm across my shoulders and kisses my temple before devoting his attention to the bags in my hands.

"Well, I got a whole layette of clothes."

"What the hell is a layette?"

"It's like an entire set of clothes that a newborn needs. Onesies, sleepers, hats, mittens, and burp cloths. Then I grabbed a couple cute outfits. And there was this adorable 'baby's first' set of onesies for the summer holidays, so I had to get those. Then I fell in love with these little newborn sandals. And these sleep sacks for sleeping. Then I found this bouncer seat, and the gal working the baby area said it's great for right after feeding, so they aren't flat and don't spit up as much. Then I got this thing called a jumperoo, but I guess that's not until he's older. Oh, and lots of diapers. And wipes. And a mobile for the crib. Pacifiers, bottles, diaper cream, teething toys..." I trail off as Owen's amused chuckle reaches my ears.

"I love you, baby," he says with a smile.

"I love you too, but why are you looking at me like that?"

Owen has a weird expression of amusement, tenderness, and confusion on his face. He shakes his head softly before responding. "You're gonna be the best mom to this kid. You know that, right?"

I feel my cheeks heat as a blush rises up my neck and spreads across my face. I look down, slightly embarrassed. There are times when Owen doesn't even know he's saying the right thing exactly when I need it. I've spent the last three nights up worrying about anything and everything. I didn't have the best role model for a mom. I'm not close to any family, and I don't have a lot of close friends. Emily wanted to throw me a baby shower, and I said it was pointless because it would just end up being a couple people anyway. My anxiety has increased the closer I get to my due date, so for Owen to quickly hone in on that and tell me he believes I'm going to be a great mom is incredibly poignant.

"Why are you blushing?" he asks softly, using his thumb and forefinger to nudge my chin up so I can look at him.

"I'm nervous," I blurt out. "I don't know what I'm doing."

"You're gonna be a natural, Red. Look around you. You basically bought out the damn store to ensure your baby has everything he could possibly need. You're not letting any stone go unturned with researching things. Hell, I bet you have that

'What to Expect' book memorized at this point," he says with a crooked smile.

He's right. I do have sections memorized.

"I guess there are so many unknowns that it's making me feel crazy," I tell him. "I've never been incredibly spontaneous, and this feels like I have absolutely no control over anything."

"Well, I think you're probably right. You don't have control over how labor is when you deliver him or what happens after. But you *do* have control over how you react and what kind of support system you have. You have me, babe. And together, we're gonna rock this parenting thing."

IT TAKES us a week to get the entire nursery set up and ready for baby Taylor to make his arrival. First, Em and Liv surprised us with gifts, including five freezer meals, a Costco box of diapers, and four cute three-to-six-month outfits. Em explained that babies go through clothing quickly, so she wanted us to have some later outfits ready should the baby have a big growth spurt.

Then Liam stopped by with his own gift and an apology for me. He was incredibly heartfelt in his apology, and he took full ownership of the rift. He purchased another bouncing seat. When I told him I already had one, he explained this way, we could have one on the first floor and one upstairs. That's kinda brilliant.

As we head into May, I'm becoming more and more uncomfortable, both physically and emotionally. My skin is stretched so tautly there is no extra give in my abdomen. Baby boy just sort of maneuvers around and pushes any organ he touches off in tight spots. I'm peeing seven hundred thousand times a day. Okay, maybe that's an exaggeration, but not by much. I've started having Braxton-Hicks contractions, which according to my pregnancy books, are the body's way of getting ready for labor. They feel weird but not painful. Yet. Em assures me that they're going to get worse. While I appreciate her willingness to be honest with me, I sure would like it if she'd lie to me about the pain. My pain tolerance is zilch.

As I'm nearing my due date, I've stopped working completely because it hurts to stand for that long. So when Owen busts into the house in the middle of the day one afternoon, he finds me sprawled out on the couch, a container of queso sitting on my massive stomach, a bag of tortilla chips sitting precariously on the edge of the couch, and an episode of Gilmore Girls is on the television. Comfort food and comfort show.

"I did it! I finally figured out a way ... baby, are you crying?" Owen asks as the smile on his face drops.

"Luke and Lorelei broke up ..." I sob through a mouthful of queso and chips. Owen chuckles, removes the queso from my bump, and then grabs the remote to pause the television.

"I'm sorry to interrupt your Gilmore time, Red, but we need to talk."

"Is everything okay?"

"I finally figured out how to nail your landlord. Not only is he in violation of raising your rent more than once in twelve months, but I also reached out to other tenants, and he's done the same thing to them. Did you know he only rents to single women? Then, after one or two years, he begins raising the rent. He's doing this all over the county, babe. I've convinced five other tenants to sue."

"Holy shit," I breathe. "Does that mean I can get my apartment back?"

"What?"

"I could get the apartment back. You'd have your space back," I say, thinking out loud.

"What the fuck?"

"I just figured you'd want your space back. It's not like you chose for me to get evicted and move in here. It all happened so fast. Thought you'd want to be you again."

"Are you fucking kidding me, Harper?"

"I don't know why you're getting mad at me, Owen, but please lower your voice," I say, my voice trembling as tears fill my eyes. God, I'm such an emotional basket case right now. These hormones are fucking *killing* me.

Owen slides his arms around me and hefts me into his lap. I'm a whale at this point. I'm probably going to break some of his bones by sitting on his legs, but he latches his arms around me, so I can't move.

"Baby. You're not moving out," he says quietly, his eyes drilling into mine. "I'm shy of forty. I'm not about to hide my feelings or act like something makes me happy if it doesn't. You? Living here? It fucking makes my day, Red. Waking up next to you, finding your hair all over my stuff, seeing your coffee cup next to mine? It's extraordinary. I'm fucking giddy driving home from work every day because I know you're going to be here. I've never been this happy or content. This relationship, this house, and this baby? All ours, Red. Forever. I'm not losing you."

"Owen," I whisper as tears cascade down my cheeks.

"I love you, baby. Forever. You don't like this house? We can find another one. You want different furniture? Done. You want to redo the backyard? Sign me up. You're not moving out. Ever. We're in this together, you hear me?" he says deeply.

"Yes, sweetie. I hear you."

"Good. Now give me those lips. I have to go back to the office for a couple hours, then we can get dinner. What's little man craving today?" he asks as he drags my head toward his for a kiss.

"Chinese," I murmur against his lips as he deepens the

kiss. How I can go from crying one moment to incredibly horny the next, I'm not sure. But suddenly, I'm squirming in Owen's lap, trying to get friction to quell the urge in my girlie bits. I swear I hear my pussy mewling for Owen to take me to pound-town.

"Feels like mama is craving something a little different," Owen muses as his hand finds a nipple and pinches. I moan.

"Owen, I need you. I need to come," I whisper against his lips.

"Stand up, baby," Owen commands, and I automatically follow instructions.

"Yes, sir," I say saucily, and he groans.

"Fuck, I love when you say that."

I'm well aware.

"Go put your hands on the kitchen counter."

I walk to the counter, face it, and place my hands on it. Owen stands behind me, and his hands find my hair before moving it all to one side. He licks a path from my shoulder blade up to my ear.

"I don't have much time today, Red. Gonna have to be hard and fast. You okay with that?" he whispers against my ear before nipping the lobe with his teeth.

"Fuck, yes," I moan. Owen grabs my pants and undies, pulling them down and sliding his hand between my legs.

"Fuck, baby, you're soaked! You been thinking about this all day?" he asks as he finds my clit and strokes me furiously. I respond, but it's all gibberish. Owen lines up his cock and thrusts in hard, and I let out a guttural moan of delight. He starts a punishing pace as I brace against the counter. I love that we're only a few inches apart in height. It makes sex so much easier. We can basically go at it anywhere.

"Owen, I'm coming!" I scream as a powerful orgasm topples over me. That was a doozy.

"Fuck, woman, fuck! I can't ..." he roars as he finds his

own release. "Jesus. You gripped me so tightly I couldn't move. I wanted to keep fucking you. Damn."

I've got my head on the counter as the final aftershocks of my orgasm wane, but Owen hasn't moved from inside me.

"Are you okay?" I say quietly.

"Just memorizing this. Everything about this."

Oh, my heart.

"Owen ..." I trail off.

"I love you, Red."

"I love you, too, Owen."

Needless to say, I don't need my Gilmore Girls episodes anymore today. Instead, I'm blissfully content and satiated for the remainder of the day.

CHAPTER THIRTY-THREE

Owen

To say that Harper was pissed when her due date came and went is a massive understatement. Somewhere along the line, she convinced herself that a due date was set in stone. She didn't take too kindly to me pointing out that her son, well, our son, would be just as stubborn as she is, so it was to be expected that he'd arrive at any time that he deemed acceptable. She threw a plate at me.

At three days past her due date, everyone is avoiding Harper. Well, everyone but me. I got her into this mess, so I have to take the brunt of her demonic ministrations. Seriously, are all nine-month-pregnant women like this? Harper sounds like she's morphed into all nine circles of hell, and she's showing me that personality. The rage that can come out of this woman is mind-boggling. When she growls at me, it's not sexy. Nope. Sounds like a dog in heat somehow got eaten up by a demon and spat out in a pit of despair.

I know she's uncomfortable. I get it. Really, I do. I just wish she wouldn't take it out on everyone. At the forty-one week mark, she dragged me to the obstetrician and demanded to be seen without an appointment. They acquiesced because they had an open time slot, which probably didn't help my cause at all. Harper has become a little too comfortable with everyone fawning over her.

"Dr. Thomason, smoke this little fucker *out*," she shouts as soon as the obstetrician walks into the exam room.

"Jesus, Harper!" I hiss. Dr. Thomason just chuckles, like he gets this every day.

"Not the first woman to ask to be induced today, but that certainly was the most colorful way I've ever heard someone ask for it," he says as he washes his hands.

"I'm miserable. He's too happy in there. He's too content. He needs to be evicted. O-U-T *out*."

"Let's examine you and see if you're at least showing some signs of labor," he says as he puts on gloves.

I always stay next to Harper's head. Trust me, I've seen everything down there. It's imprinted on my brain for eternity. It's my favorite location in the world. Best pussy on the planet. But I'd prefer not to watch another man elbows-deep in my woman, no matter the reason.

"Well, the good news is, you're two centimeters dilated," Dr. Thomason says. Before he can continue, Harper lets out a growl.

"What the fuck? Only two?" she yells.

"Woman, I will muzzle you," I mutter with my teeth clenched. Listen. I've been as calm and patient as I can with Harper. I've been at her beck and call. But this morning, she muttered that she could smell me fifteen feet away, then asked me to fuck her while wearing a trash bag so she wouldn't be *forced* to smell me. I'm done with this. Smoke the baby out, doc.

"*But*," the doctor continues, "you are about fifty percent effaced, which is the thinning of the cervix. This is a great sign. If you want to do an induction, we can get that going as soon as tomorrow."

"YES!" Harper and I both shout in unison. Harper turns to me with a murderous expression.

"Oh, has this been difficult for you?" she sneers.

"You're damn right it has been, woman. I want *my* Harper back. This she-devil bitch act running the show right now is on my last damn nerve," I retort.

"Okay, I think I'm going to step out. I'll send a nurse in with an instructional packet, and we'll get you all set up at the hospital. See you both tomorrow," Dr. Thomason says as he sheepishly exits the room.

"Could you be any more embarrassing, Owen?" Harper taunts me.

"Me? Are you serious? You asked him to *smoke* out our child, woman! Where did you even learn that saying? Is that a real thing?"

"Heard it in a 'Friends' episode," she says nonchalantly as she gets dressed.

"Lovely. Well, at least it wasn't a fucking Lorelei saying. Nice to know you're branching out," I retort.

"Oh, you just *shut up*. Mr. 'I can watch every episode of Law and Order'. You got a hard-on for Stabler, don't you?" she says.

"You know that's the guy character, right?"

"Yeah, I know." Harper stares at me. "You heard me correctly."

Oh, that's how she's gonna play this today? Game fucking *on*.

Our fight continues out into the parking lot.

"What do you want for dinner? Or do you want me to hit fifteen different places so I can bring every single option off every menu just in case you change your mind?" God, I'm being awful. But she started it, and I'm all for arguing with Harper. Generally, it makes her incredibly horny, even more so now that she's this pregnant, and the sex is off the charts.

"I'm going to murder you in your sleep," she growls.

"You'd have to be able to reach me, and with that stomach?" I say, pointing at her beautiful, perfect, oh-so-kissable tummy, "Ain't no way you're getting to my important parts."

"You fucking asshole!" she shouts as we go to my car. After my accident in January, I replaced my car with a newer version of the same Infiniti. I love it and know it'll be the safest car for us. But best of all, it has a lot of room for ... things.

"Get your ass in the backseat," I growl.

"Oh, I'm relegated to the backseat now? You gonna treat me like a kid?" Harper taunts as she slides into the backseat. Well, not slides. She sort of collapsed and then flung the rest of her body into the car. I don't fucking care. She's in. Now down to business.

"Take off your fucking pants," I snarl.

"What?" Harper stares at me incredulously.

"You fucking heard me, woman. Take off your pants."

It's twilight, so a slight glimmer of light still comes into the car. I see Harper's eyes widen, then become hooded as her pupils dilate.

"I'm too angry at you. You won't be able to get me off," she taunts.

"I'll get you off just fine. Multiple times. Bet I can get you off twice in the next five minutes," I gloat. She pulls out her phone. Of course, Harper pulls out her fucking phone.

"Hold on. I'm timing this."

"Fine."

"Fine."

She slides her pants off, and I help because her ability to reach her feet is basically nonexistent.

"Ready ... set ... go!"

I reach over, slide the seat all the way back, and recline the seat. Fucking power reclining seats. Wasting time here. Harper gives me an amused grin as she can see I'm frustrated.

"Worried, stud?" she asks.

"Nope. This is just giving you a little extra time to think about what I'm going to do to you."

"You're down to four minutes now."

Fuck. I grab her by her hips and shift her toward me, throwing her legs over my shoulders as I bury my face in her pussy. She shrieks as soon as I latch onto her clit. Harper has been weird about me going down on her lately. Waxes have become too painful, and she can't see to navigate shaving. I volunteered to shave her, and she adamantly refused.

I don't fucking care if she has hair. I'm all for a walk in the jungle. Don't care. My goal is to make her come as often as I can.

Harper attempts to kick my shoulder to get me off of her, and I refuse to move. I have one arm around her, holding a tit, and the other gripping her hip.

Harper comes for the first time with a silent scream. As she shakes through the orgasm, I slide my hand down from her breasts and immediately slide three fingers into her sopping wet channel. Fuck, she's soaked. As I lick, suck, and nibble on her clit, she comes a second time. But I don't let up. I send her up a third and fourth time before the timer on her phone finally goes off.

I sit back, letting her see the evidence of her desire all over my face. God, I could do that all fucking day. Never get tired of eating her pussy.

"Holy fuck," she mutters.

"Yeah. I'd say I won," I gloat.

"Pretty sure I won in that whole game," she says with a breathy giggle. Her eyes slowly open, somewhat unfocused, until she turns slightly to see me. "I'm sorry I've been such a bitch."

"I'm sorry I let it get to me today."

"You really have been great about letting me run you over."

"Well, you're birthing a whale, apparently, so I have to give you some credit," I joke before fucking as she chucks her shoe at me.

"Owen!" she shrieks, but with a smile on her face.

"It's okay, baby. The hate sex and makeup sex are always worth it," I tell her, and her cute little grin morphs into a wicked smile.

"You are right about that. Your turn now?" Harper whispers as she struggles to get herself into a seated position.

"I don't think there's enough space for any sex shenanigans in here, Red. Not where you'd be comfortable," I say as I look around, trying to figure out some logistics. I don't even realize she's somehow dropped to her knees between the seats and unhooked my belt.

"I can certainly do this," Harper says before yanking my dick out and sucking it into the back of her throat.

"Holy fuck, Jesus, Harper," I mutter as white spots dance in my vision. Harper gives amazing head. It's like I'm the best damn lollipop in the world, and she's just lapping me up.

"How fast you think you can come, baby?" she whispers. God damn. She doesn't call me baby really often.

"Less than a minute," I say with a strangled voice. Harper licks me from my balls to the tip, then circles the head a few times before bobbing back down and sucking hard. "Fuck woman, do that again."

She grabs my hand and puts it on the back of her head. Then, looking up at me, she nods.

"You want me to fuck your face?"

"Mmmhmm."

"As you wish."

I grab a handful of her curls and start a rhythm. Not even thirty seconds later, I'm coming down the back of her throat. Not a drop was missed as Harper slowly licked me down from my high.

Not even one minute later, there's a loud rap against the driver's window.

"Step out of the vehicle with your hands up," a deep voice commands.

"Oh my God!" Harper whispers, horrified. She grabs her pants and slips them back on as carefully as she can while I open my door and step out. I turn around and burst out laughing.

"What the fuck, man. Seriously? A parking lot?" An amused Liam stands in his deputy uniform with a shit-eating grin.

"Liam! You scared the shit out of me!" Harper screeches as she waddles around the car.

"Baby, where are your shoes?" I ask.

"I can't get those on by myself anymore, you know that."

Liam laughs and turns to me. "Seriously, though, someone in there did call and ask for a welfare check because you two were screaming at each other. So I guess I can report that you're fine."

"Yeah, we're fine. She's gonna be induced tomorrow," I say proudly.

"No way! That's amazing. Do you need anything?" Liam asks with a huge smile.

"Unless you have a way for me to avoid all pain, I don't think I need anything else," Harper deadpans. She's scared about the pain. Unfortunately, my girl doesn't have the highest pain tolerance.

"It'll be worth it when you have that screaming bundle that will undoubtedly look like Owen in your arms," Liam says jokingly.

"Aww, I'd love a little Owen," Harper gushes, and I slide my arms around her.

"I love you, baby," I murmur into her hair. We might fight, and sometimes they are pretty damn intense fights, but there's nothing I wouldn't do for this woman. Love her more than life itself.

"Alright, lovebirds. I'll let you get back to your makeup sex, and I'll let the reporting party know that all is well in the Taylor/Williams household," Liam says. "Oh, quick question. Are you hyphenating the baby's last name? Or will it only be Taylor?"

"Hyphenating," Harper says simultaneously as I say, "Taylor."

We look at each other.

"Well, shit. Guess I started your next fight. Bye!" Liam takes off for his squad car and peels out of the parking lot while Harper and I stare at each other.

"Harper, please."

"Please, what? Why wouldn't I hyphenate it? The baby will be both yours and mine," she says.

"But what happens when we get married, and you become a Taylor?"

"Who says I want to change my name?" she asks with a slight cock of her head.

"You ... you don't want to take my last name?" I ask quietly.

"You haven't even asked me to marry you, Owen. So I don't see why we have to talk about this now."

"Because we are filling out paperwork tomorrow for a baby, Harp. And for a birth certificate. I want you both to have my last name, Red. I didn't realize how important it was to me until just now. I need you both to be Taylor's. I need this," I tell her vehemently. My hands find her cheeks as I rest my forehead against hers. "I need this, baby."

"Owen," she whispers. "Okay. I didn't know you felt like this. We won't hyphenate. His last name will be Taylor."

"Yours too."

"You need to propose first."

"Already in the works."

"What the hell does that mean?"

"Don't worry about it. I've got it all figured out. Oh, yeah, it's all coming together," I tell Harper in my best Kronk from Emperor's New Groove voice. It's her favorite animated movie, so I know she'll get the reference.

"Okay, sweetie. Can we really go get food now? I am hungry, and I know they're gonna cut me off in the morning. Gotta enjoy my last few hours of a food coma," she says as she pats her stomach.

"What my wife wants, my wife gets," I tell her, and she stops as her breath hitches.

"That sounded really nice," she whispers.

"Felt really nice saying it, baby."

I already have the ring. I've had it for a couple months. I've been waiting for this exact time to give it to her. I need the missing piece of our puzzle to arrive. I need our son to witness the proposal.

I'm proposing tomorrow.

CHAPTER THIRTY-FOUR

Harper

───❀───

It should come as no surprise that I didn't sleep a wink last night. In fact, it was just the opposite. I was so wired I rearranged the baby's closet, deep-cleaned the fridge, and finally finished a book that has been on my TBR for well over a year.

I began texting Monica because I knew she'd be up. That tiny little chaotic ball of energy can operate on one hour of sleep and a red bull.

> Me: I asked the doc to smoke the baby out today, but he said no.

> Monica: Ahh, I love a good Friends reference.

Me: Well, obviously, this stubborn bugger ain't budging, so desperate times call for desperate measures.

Monica: I just googled 'can you smoke a baby out,' and all it did was bring up every fucking website that talks about how bad smoking is during pregnancy. Like, duh. I know. Jeez.

Me: Even Google doesn't understand good television.

Monica: Ain't that the truth.

Me: What are you even doing up right now?

Monica: Girl, you know I don't sleep. Plus, I'm horny as hell and was about to text Marcus for a booty call.

Me: Do they still refer to them as booty calls?

Monica: IDK. Who cares. He'd get the reference, and then I'd get mine. Ya know? Wink Wink.

Me: I thought you weren't seeing Marcus anymore.

Monica: I'm not. Just use him to scratch an itch every now and again. It's been slim-pickins in the men's department as of late.

Me: I could totally see you just hanging out in an actual men's department, trolling for penis.

> Monica: I have no shame.

> Me: When's the last time you went on an actual date?

> Monica: Fuck. Months ago! I don't even think Marcus ever took me out on a date. He was the king of the 'Netflix and chill.'

> Me: You need someone to woo you, my friend.

> Monica: Nah. I'm not interested in wooing.

> Me: Didn't think I was either until Owen started doing it. He kinda blew my mind.

> Monica: Among other things that he blew.

> Me: Yep. Jealous?

> Monica: Little bit.

I toss my phone to the side and look around at my clean house. Cleanest it's ever been, I'd say. Well, clean by my standards. Owen is more of a minimalist, so I bet he had a housekeeper before I moved in.

Owen attempted to sleep, but I kept waking him up to ask him stuff. Because really, I needed to know at three o'clock in the morning whether or not Alzheimer's ran in his family or if he thought I needed to add a fourth baby outfit to the hospital bag.

"Baby, you need to get some sleep," Owen muttered as he attempted to drag me into bed at four.

"I can't sleep! I'm too jittery. Nervous. Anxious. Excited. I don't understand how you're sleeping, honestly. Are you not excited? What the fuck, Owen? How can you sleep right now?" Somehow I went from excited to pissed in the span of five seconds.

"Harp, I don't have enough brainpower to handle the crazy right now. I'm a man. I compartmentalize. You know this," he says, his voice all husky and deep from sleep. "I'm excited, Red. Of course, I am. But if one of us doesn't get some sleep, we'll likely burn the hospital down with an epic fight tomorrow. Fuck, I mean today. Whatever. Woman, please let me sleep."

My eyes fill with tears as I realize I'm being such a bitch, and I begin blabbering all over Owen. "I'm so sorry, sweetie, I'm a mess! I don't know why you put up with me when you could have someone so much more put together and someone who doesn't treat you like this ..."

"Shhh," Owen croons as he yanks my arm, so I fall onto the bed next to him. His arms circle around me as he forces my head under his chin. I reflexively throw my leg over his legs to get comfortable. "I love you, baby, just as you are. Yeah, you have some batshit crazy moments, but life is never dull with you, and it's exactly how I like it."

"Okay," I murmur against his chest as I sniffle. His heartbeat calms me as he slowly strokes up and down my spine. I don't even realize I've fallen asleep until he jars me awake hours later.

"Baby."
"Hmm."
"Harp."
"What."
"Red!"
"What, Owen?"
"You wanna go have this baby or what?"

My eyes pop open as I realize what today is. It's my baby's birthday! I get to be a mom today!

"Oh my God, Owen! We're going to be parents today!" I shriek as Owen's wide grin grows.

"Only if we get to the hospital, baby. You ready?"

"I just want to take a shower first. If something happens and I'm in there longer than I want, it'll be a few days before I shower."

"I was just about to get in the shower, too. How about we shower together and enjoy our last few moments of being a family of two?" Owen asks as he reaches down and grasps my hand, helping me to sit up.

"You're planning some funny business in there, aren't you," I say, my eyes narrowing. Owen gives me an innocent and angelic smile.

"Why Harper Williams. I can't believe you would suggest such a thing!" Owen says mockingly as I stand up before quickly slapping me hard on the ass. I gasp and look over my shoulder at Owen, giving him a saucy grin. I enjoyed that slap. I give him a wink, and he barks out a laugh. "Again with the spanking? Thought that was a one-time thing, woman."

"I don't know. Maybe that's something we can revisit in six weeks when we're allowed to do the deed again," I tell him as I saunter into the bathroom.

"Fuck. Six weeks. Well, I went close to a year in between our bouts, so six weeks is nothing, I guess. Although having you next to me in bed is gonna be brutal."

"I may have read that oral is allowed."

"Where the hell did you read that?"

"In an online baby forum."

"Yours or mine?"

"Both, I think."

"Duly noted."

We both get undressed as the shower warms up and step into the steam. Owen's bathroom is somewhat small, but the shower is huge. I've barely wet my hair before Owen drops to his knees and buries his head in my pussy. My stomach is so big I can't even see him. He has me on edge within minutes before pulling away and standing up.

"Owen!" I whine.

"You're coming when I tell you to, and it'll be with me inside you. Gotta feel this if it's gonna be six weeks before I get it again," he tells me as he turns me and moves my hands to the wall. Pushing against my back until I'm in a more suitable position, Owen rubs the head of his cock up and down my wetness before sliding snugly inside. "Fuck, woman. This pussy was made for me."

"Enjoy because it's gonna feel quite a bit different the next time," I moan. I don't even want to tell him what I've read online. Suffice it to say childbirth is actually quite disgusting. I'm just hoping I don't rip my entire hoohah.

Owen doesn't respond as he concentrates on the tempo. As soon as he can feel me getting close, he slows down. He's edged me three times before I feel he's getting close. Owen always loses a little focus the closer he gets to his own orgasm, and the thrusts become erratic. He reaches around and finds my clit, pinching it between his thumb and forefinger. I have my face plastered to the shower wall as every muscle tightens, and a wave of pleasure crashes over me. As my body shudders, I hear Owen gutturally groan as he pulses inside me. He rests his head against my spine as we both pant.

"You know, I didn't tell you to come," he teases breathlessly.

"Too bad."

"Gonna punish you for that, Red."

"Oh yeah? How so?"

"I'm not gonna let you touch me at all for six weeks. But I can touch myself all I want."

"Umm, that's not really a punishment."

"Watching me come won't be a punishment? Watching

me, knowing I'm thinking of you and thinking of all the things I want to do to you?"

"Oh, that's just mean."

"Told ya." Owen pulls out, and I immediately feel a gush.

"Jesus, how much cum did you have in there? I feel like I'm peeing." I stand off to the side of the water so I can see down around my feet. Well, in the general vicinity of my feet. It's been months since I've actually seen my feet.

"Holy shit. Baby, I think your water broke. That's definitely not me coming out of you right now," Owen blurts out.

"No fucking way!" I shout.

"Hurry up, we need to get to the hospital!"

"Oh, don't be silly. It'll still be hours. Maybe now they won't have to give me the Pitocin. I've heard horrible things about that," I say, shuddering.

"Oh, yeah. What I've read online makes it sound pretty bad."

"Wait," I say as I'm shampooing my hair. "You've read about it online?"

"Yeah?"

"Why were you reading about Pitocin?"

"Baby, I read everything I could on pregnancy and childbirth."

"But ... why?"

"Because the two most important people to me are involved. Harper ... don't cry again."

"I can't help it! You're so sweet, and I'm a fucking disaster!"

Owen begins massaging my head to wash the shampoo out. It makes me remember him massaging my scalp after finding out my rent had been raised. And I'm pretty sure that's the night he knocked me up. I feel a smile come to my face, and Owen leans down to kiss my lips softly.

"You're remembering one of the times I did this, aren't you?" he says quietly, and I nod.

"When you found out about my landlord raising the rent."

"That was in August, right?"

"Yeah."

"So it was the night we got pregnant?"

"We?" I ask, amused. He shrugs.

"I get that I'm not physically doing anything. But emotionally, I'm so fucking invested in this, Harp. We both participated in the sex. So, therefore, we both are pregnant. But trust me, I know you absolutely got the short end of the stick with what you're about to go through. Like I said, I've done the research."

"You look kinda horrified right now, O."

"I made the mistake of watching a full delivery video. Do not recommend." He shudders, and I giggle.

After finishing the shower, I dry my hair when my first contraction hits.

"Oh!" I cry out.

"What? What happened?" Owen shouts as he comes running in.

"I'm having an actual contraction," I tell him as I pull up my contraction timing app. Owen stands at attention like he's ready to go into battle, a worried expression on his face. "You need to leave if you're going to hover like that. I'll let you know when hovering is acceptable."

"Uh, okay. Shout if you need me, I guess," Owen murmurs with his brows furrowed in confusion.

I've finished drying my hair when the second contraction hits, and it's much more painful. I try and focus on my breathing, trying the techniques Owen and I learned in a mostly pointless parenting class where the two of us were the oldest by over a decade.

The third contraction hits almost on top of the second one, and I drop to the floor. My legs feel weirdly warm and wet.

"Owen? I need you!" I cry out.

"I'm right here, baby, oh my God ..." Owen trails off as he looks at me, horrified. "You're bleeding, Harp."

"What?" I gasp before another pain takes hold.

"I'm calling 911."

I'm trying to focus as the pain overtakes me. I can only see Owen's face, which is white as a sheet. I've never seen him look like this. He looks terrified as he talks to the dispatcher.

"Please be okay, little man," I whisper to my stomach. I can't lose him. Never thought I'd be this connected to someone I've never met, but I feel like my entire life led up to this moment, and I need him to be okay. We haven't even picked out a name yet. My eyes fill with tears as I try to remember our top names.

"Harp, you need to breathe. Focus on the breathing techniques we learned, okay? Ambulance is almost here."

Owen kneels down to brush a quick kiss on my forehead before dashing downstairs to open the door and let the paramedics in.

"Ms. Williams, I hear we're having a baby," a smiling paramedic calls out as he walks into the bathroom.

"I sure hope so," I say tearfully. "If not, something is definitely wrong with my periods."

He chuckles as Owen looks on from the doorway.

"We're gonna get you loaded up on a stretcher and take you to the hospital, okay? I want to get you there as quickly as possible."

"Do you know what this is?"

"I have my suspicions, but I'm just a lowly paramedic, ma'am. I'll let the doctors make the big decisions. I just get to drive fast and honk my horn a bunch," he says with a wink.

I'm loaded onto the stretcher quickly, and Owen follows us down the stairs. He climbs into the back of the ambulance with me.

"Do you want to drive separately?" I ask him. Clearly, I'm not thinking well right now.

"No. Liam or Nathan can come to get me if I need to go home." Owen's face is rigid with emotion as he stares at me. He leans down and puts his forehead against mine. "Please be okay, Red. I can't lose you."

"I'm sure it's fine, Owen. Must be just some weird age-related complication or something," I tell him. "This is what happens when thirty twelve and pregnant boys do make."

"Uh, what?" Owen looks at me weirdly, and the paramedic cocks an eyebrow.

"Can you repeat that, ma'am?"

"Sure nope dis whatcha ambo smidgeon baby boop snoot," I say as my eyes close.

"What the fuck is happening right now?" I hear Owen shout.

"Sir, sit back while I work on your wife."

I'm not his wife, I say in my head. *Boy, I'd sure love to be, though. Am I flying? Why do I feel like this? It's weird.*

"Baby! Red, don't you dare leave me!"

Huh. Did someone say something?

I'm tired.

Gonna take a nap.

CHAPTER THIRTY-FIVE

Owen

They say there are moments when your life flashes before your eyes. But I've never experienced that firsthand until this moment. Until I watched the love of my life die in front of me.

My Harper, my spitfire with the gorgeous red locks, the green eyes that sizzle when she's fired up, and that amazing porcelain skin that I dream about ... I watched her die. I watched the blood drain from her face and the life disappear from her eyes.

Seeing your future cease to exist in front of you when there's nothing you can do about it is an acute pain I wouldn't wish on my worst enemy.

All I can do is pray. Pray to whatever God is listening.

Please, God. Please. I'll do whatever you want. Just don't take her. I need her here with me. Please.

I don't even realize we've arrived at the hospital until the ambulance doors are thrown open, and I'm ordered to get out. So many voices, but they're all muted as I stare at Harper. Someone is kneeling on the gurney while pushing on her chest. I vaguely hear someone calling out numbers, but I can't figure out why. Another is shouting gibberish about medication. I try to grab her hand, but I'm pushed away as they run into the emergency entrance.

Sir.

Sir.

"Sir?" I finally turn my head to see a nurse has been trying to talk to me. "Sir, I need you to follow me and give me some information about your wife."

"She's not my wife yet," I mumble. Fuck do I wish she was, though. My mind is reeling with all the regrets I have. Should have proposed. Should have locked her down ages ago. Should have told her I couldn't live without her. Does she know how much I need her? I really don't even know.

"Please follow me, Mr. Taylor. Her name is Harper Williams? Do you know her blood type?" I shake my head. I don't even know mine. How the fuck would I know hers? Who the hell knows their love's blood type? Fuck. I bet Nathan knows Emily's. That would be something he'd know.

"How far along is she?"

"Forty-one weeks. We were getting induced today," I say quietly.

"What happened before she began bleeding?"

"We had sex, and then her water broke. She started having contractions, and then she just gushed blood," I whisper. Seeing her on the floor in a pool of blood is something I'll never forget. Seared into my memory for eternity. Fuck. If that's the last memory I have of Harper in our house, I'm never stepping foot in there again.

"They've taken her right to surgery. If you wait here, I'll go find out some information. Is there anyone you'd like to call?"

"Yeah, I'll call my best friends." I slide my hands into my pockets and realize I must have left my phone at home. Shit, I don't even know Nathan's phone number. "I don't have a phone and don't know their numbers."

"Okay, Mr. Taylor. This is a small town. I'm sure we can track down the numbers. Are you trying to reach Liam and Nathan?"

"How do you know that?"

"You're in a daze right now, but we went to high school together. My name is Lacey. I graduated with Harper and Olivia. I bet I can track down Olivia's number, which will get you into contact with Liam, okay?" Lacey says gently. I nod. She steps to the desk for a moment and immediately returns with a number.

"Here you go. Use my phone," Lacey says as she hands me her cell. I shakily dial Liv's number.

"Hello?" Liv answers uncertainly.

"Liv," I blurt out, my voice trembling. "It's Owen."

"Oh my God! Owen! What happened?" she shouts.

"Can you come to the hospital? It's Harper. I don't know what was happening, she was bleeding, and I had to call 911. Please come …" I trail off as I begin to weep. Lacey puts her arm around me and gently pats my back.

"Oh my God, we're on our way. Oh, Owen. Oh my God," Liv just keeps repeating. I hear her shout for Liam and then a flurry of sounds. "We're coming, okay? We'll be there in ten minutes."

"Five minutes. We'll be there in five minutes," I hear Liam say as car doors slam and he guns the engine.

"Can you call Nathan? I forgot my phone, and I don't know his number," I mumble.

"We've got it, Owen. We'll be there in a couple minutes,"

Liv says. I end the call because I'm crying and can't focus. I hand the phone back to Lacey.

"Do you want to wait here for your friends, and then I can take you to a waiting room near the operating room?"

I nod. I need my family here. I can't do this alone.

Not even a minute later, Liam and Liv come flying through the doors. Liam's arms come tightly around me as Liv sobs next to us.

"I can't do this without her, man," I sob.

"I know, buddy. I know."

Liv settles herself against me on the other side and hugs me tightly. I feel our circle grow when Nathan crushes his arms around us.

"Em will be here as soon as my mom can get to our house. We're here for you. She's gonna be fine. Your boy is gonna be fine. I just know it," Nathan says quietly into my ear.

"I hope you're right," I whisper brokenly.

Lacey directs us to a small waiting room near the operating rooms. Emily joins us a few minutes later, her eyes puffy from crying. She immediately comes to me and gives me a hug.

"I don't know what this means, but Jack wanted me to tell you everything will be fine. He said your son is fine. He was adamant that I tell you this," she says with a hesitant smile.

"The little clairvoyant at it again, huh," Liam says with a chuckle.

"Did he say that Harper was fine, too?" I ask, and everyone stops. "He said the baby is fine, but what about Harper? I can't do this without her, Em. She needs to be fine. I can't parent without her. Fuck, I can't even live without her. She's the air that I breathe! How am I supposed to go on without her now?"

I collapse into the chair and openly sob.

"Let's not get ahead of ourselves just yet, okay? We don't

know anything. Harper could be fine, too," Liv says as her voice trembles.

"You don't know that."

"Well, neither do you. So let's just sit here and be positive. Harper is the strongest woman I know. She's a fighter. She wouldn't leave you," Liv says confidently.

"I saw her die in front of me. Her heart stopped. I saw the life drain from her eyes. I'll never be able to get that image out of my head. We had sex this morning. Did I do this? Was this my fault? Fuck, it's all my fault. Everything is my fault," I mutter as my head falls into my hands.

"You're spiraling, man. There's no way this was your fault. Something else must have happened. You are not responsible for this, okay?" Liam says gently.

"She was getting induced in a couple hours. We were just enjoying our final few hours together. I didn't know ... I didn't think anything like this would happen ..." Emotion clogs my throat as I think back to the last twenty-four hours. Our fight in the doctor's office. Our fun in the backseat of my SUV. Fuck, is that what did it? She was on her knees, all scrunched up in the car. Did that somehow mess with the baby? And then I fucked her in the shower this morning ... was that the problem?

Everyone is silent for a few minutes. Or maybe it's an hour, I really don't know. Time ceases to exist as I flashback to every single interaction I've had with Harper since high school. I knew her back then, although we didn't interact much. I just knew her as my best friend's sister's best friend. I always thought she was hot, but I figured she was off-limits. Then, once we were both adults, I didn't want to complicate things if we ran in the same circles. But I always wondered what it would be like to be with her. And now I know. It's amazing. Life-changing. Immaculate. Exquisite. Happiness I never knew I could experience.

I'm overcome with emotion as I realize how much Harper has changed my life. She's made me a better man. She helped me realize I can have a successful relationship and how I want to be in one with her. I want to be the person Harper needs. She's one hell of an independent and strong woman. But she needs me as much as I need her. We both were only half content until we joined. Now we are whole. She makes me whole.

"Oh my God, Owen," Liv whispers. I look up to see her staring across the waiting room toward the door as tears stream down her cheeks. I follow her line of vision to see someone covered in OR scrubs, holding a bundle.

"Mr. Taylor, would you like to meet your son?" the man says.

"What?" I breathe, actually shaking my head to see if this is a vision I'm creating in my head.

"Your son, Owen. Do you want to meet him?"

"He's okay?" I ask, my voice trembling.

"He's absolutely perfect."

I sit, unable to move, staring at the bundle. All I can see is a hat on the top of his head until one little hand flies up as if he is beckoning me to come to him.

"Daddy, go get him," Liam whispers as he pushes me off the chair.

I slowly walk to the man holding my son.

"Put some hand sanitizer on, then I can hand him to you," the man says as he motions to the wall where a sanitizer station is mounted. I fill my palm with sanitizer and scrub both arms. "I'm Dr. Mitchell. Dr. Thomason is still working on your wife. But this little guy wanted to get out of there and meet you."

Dr. Mitchell slowly puts my son in my arms, and I finally get a look at his face. Dark eyes are wide open, peering up at me. I'm completely overcome. A wave of peace crashes over me as I look down at my son. I've never known this kind of love.

"Hello, my boy," I whisper.

"He passed every test we give newborns with flying colors, even the oxygen saturation test. Lots of babies here need oxygen after birth because of the altitude, but your guy is doing just fine so far. All things considered, this is an absolute miracle," Dr. Mitchell explains.

"What's going on with Harper?" Emily calls out from the couch. No one has approached me yet, which I am thankful for. I needed this moment, just my son and me.

"I don't know much, as I'm on the pediatric side of childbirth. I do know that Harper had what's called placenta previa, which is where the placenta completely covers the cervix. Sometimes the problem corrects itself during pregnancy, and other times it doesn't. I'm not entirely sure why it wasn't detected on an ultrasound at all during Harper's pregnancy. Could just be that the baby was blocking the view, so Dr. Thomason couldn't see it correctly. In any case, he's working on Harper now, and someone should be out to update you shortly. Congratulations, Mr. Taylor," Dr. Mitchell says, slapping me on the shoulder lightly before vacating the waiting room.

I stand in the same spot, staring wistfully down at my son.

"He doesn't even have a name," I murmur.

"Did you and Harper have any favorites?" Liv asks quietly as she comes to stand next to me.

"Hudson, Greyson, and Kingston were our top three. But I don't think he looks like any of those," I whisper. My son blinks at me like he agrees.

"Any other names that you remember?" Liv asks.

"Braxton," I say with clarity. My son throws his hand up toward my face as he stretches. "His name is Braxton."

"Braxton Taylor. It's nice to meet you, sweet boy. Happy birthday," Liv whispers.

"Holy shit. It's his birthday," I muse.

"It is. And you're a daddy."

"I'm a daddy."

"Mr. Taylor?" A voice calls from the doorway.

I look over and see Dr. Thomason removing his mask and smiling.

"Would you like to see Harper?"

"She's okay?" I breathe.

"She's okay. I'll be honest with you, it was touch-and-go for a little bit, but I got the bleeding under control. She's going to be fine," Dr. Thomason says with a smile.

"Did you have to remove her uterus?" Emily asks. Shit. I didn't even think about that. Harper and I haven't discussed if we want more kids, but I don't want that decision taken away from her.

"No, I saved it. Having any more children will be high risk, but we'll cross that bridge if and when we come to it. No use worrying about it now," Dr. Thomason says. "Come with me so I can take you to Harper. She should be waking up from anesthesia any minute now, and I know she'll want to meet her son."

"Stay here, okay? I'll come back as soon as I can," I tell my friends. My family.

"We'll be here, buddy. Give Harper our love," Liam calls out.

I follow Dr. Thomason down a few hallways before he leads me into a recovery room. Harper lays in the bed, her beautiful red hair in waves around her head and her hands placed serenely on her still-plump belly. Harper's eyes are still closed, but her skin is pink and beautiful, not like it was when we arrived at the hospital.

"You can go over and sit by her," Dr. Thomason says. "She'll wake up any minute now."

"You ready to meet your mom, buddy?" I whisper to Braxton. He stares at me and blinks. I swear he's talking to me with his eyes.

I pull a chair next to Harper's bed and wait. I can't believe I get to introduce our son to his mom for the first time.

CHAPTER THIRTY-SIX

Harper

Everything is fuzzy.

My body feels like it's humming, though, which is kind of weirding me out. A distant beeping noise is beginning to bug me, but I can't figure out what it is.

Do I hear a cat meowing?

Wait.

No.

That's not a cat. What the hell is that noise? Something mewling. I try hard to concentrate on the sound but can't place it. It's something I've never heard before.

Then a sudden high-pitched screech and I jolt.

A baby!

Is that my baby?

Did I have him? Where is he? Why can't I see him?

I struggle to open my eyes as I can hear a muffled voice. Is that Owen? I swear, if this is some fucked up version of hell, I'm gonna raise some ... well, that doesn't make sense.

Dammit, Harper. Focus. Open your eyes. You can do this.

One eyelid cracks open to bright white light. I blink a few times to try and focus, then manage to pry open the other eyelid.

I blink a bunch as I hear that weird mewling again.

My eyes hone in on the sound.

It's the most beautiful thing I've ever seen. Owen is holding my baby. Our baby. Is this real? Am I dreaming? If this isn't real, I never want to wake up. I could watch him holding our son forever.

"Mommy's gonna wake up soon, little man, I promise. I know you want to meet her. Patience, Braxton," Owen whispers.

Braxton?

"Braxton?" I hear myself croak. Owen's head whips up with his eyes wide.

"Red, thank God," he breathes as he walks toward me.

"Is this real?" I whisper, unsure if I'm still dreaming. Owen chuckles quietly.

"Yeah, baby. It's real."

"Is he ..." I stammer. I'm scared to ask about the baby. "Is he okay?"

"He's perfect, Harp. He's absolutely perfect," Owen says quietly as he leans down and places the baby in my arms. "Meet your son. I've been calling him Braxton, but it's totally fine if you want to change it. I just think he looks like a Braxton. The three names we had picked out don't fit."

I stare down incredulously at the most beautiful boy I've ever seen. He has a perfect button nose, lips that look exactly like Owen's that I can already imagine will pop out in an adorable pout, and huge round eyes. His head is covered in dark brown hair that sticks up in every direction. He's perfect. And he's definitely a Braxton.

"Owen, he's beautiful."

"I know, baby. He's so fucking perfect."

"Shhh! You can't say the f-word anymore. We're parents now."

Owen chuckles.

"I don't think he's got a grasp of profanity just yet, Red. We have time before we have to worry about that."

"Braxton," I whisper as Owen perches on the side of the bed and leans down to press a tender kiss against my temple. "It's perfect, sweetie. He's definitely a Braxton."

"Knock knock," a voice says from the doorway. I look up to see Dr. Thomason. "How's my favorite family doing?"

"I hardly believe we're your favorite," Owen says with a mischievous smile.

"Well, you're definitely the most exciting family. Never had to call and ask for a welfare check on a couple in a car that appeared to be rocking in the parking lot right after an appointment."

I pretend to hide my head behind Braxton.

"We weren't having sex," Owen declares loudly.

"Owen!" I hiss.

"Well, we weren't. We were making up in a different way," he says with a saucy wink. So now I'm really hiding behind Braxton.

"In any case, I'm glad everything worked out. Harper, I'd like to see you in my office in one week, then again two weeks after that. You call me if you have any problems, okay? Take it easy this week. No lifting anything heavier than your son. Let Owen take care of you," Dr. Thomason says.

"I will take the best care of her," Owen says confidently as his hand slides into my hair and massages my neck.

"I know you will," Dr. Thomason replies as he waves

goodbye and steps out of the room. Owen and I are quiet as we both stare down at our son.

"I can't believe he's ours," I whisper reverently. "We made this. It's surreal."

"I know. God, Harp. I thought I lost both of you, and now I'm just so fucking grateful. I don't know what I would have done ..." Owen's voice catches as he buries his head in my hair. "I love you both so much. I can't do this without you. You're everything to me, baby. This right here? It's my world. Can't do life without you."

"Love you too, sweetie," I murmur as I turn to kiss him. He holds my head to his with just our lips touching for a few moments.

"They kept calling you my wife," he mumbles against my mouth.

"I thought that was a dream," I respond.

"I don't want it to be a dream. I want it to be a reality."

I pull my head away to look at him. His eyes are clear, determined, and full of love, adoration, and tenderness.

"I want you to be my wife, Harper. I want everyone to know that I'm yours. I want you to wear my ring and have my last name. I want to cook dinner with you, sit by the fire with you, and have you force me to watch Gilmore Girls reruns that I'll inevitably get sucked into. I want to wake up with you in my arms every morning and make love to you every night. Please marry me, baby. Spend the rest of your life letting me love you how you deserve."

Tears are falling rapidly as I nod.

"Say the words, baby."

"Yes, Owen. Yes, I'll marry you."

"Thank fuck," he whispers as he kisses me hard. Braxton lets out a little cry as if he wants to be involved. I let out a teary giggle as Owen ends our kiss. "I guess someone wanted to be involved in the proposal, huh."

Owen slides away and stands up as he reaches into his pocket. "I forgot my phone in all the chaos this morning, but this was already in my pocket. I had every intention of proposing today, Red. I wanted to do it once Braxton was here. I guess I thought he needed to be part of it, ya know?"

Owen takes Braxton's tiny hands and pretends to have him open the small box. Inside is a breathtaking emerald surrounded by tiny diamonds.

"Couldn't get just any old diamond for you, my little ginger spitfire. I needed something that screamed 'Harper.' Something that is a showpiece, full of fire, sass, and love. And I wanted it to match the earrings I gave you in January. Plus, it's Braxton's birthstone. There's nothing normal or ordinary about our relationship, Red. A typical diamond wouldn't suit you or our story. This ring is a symbol of our history and the unconditional love I have for you," Owen says as he removes the ring from the box and grabs my left hand. Only then do I notice that I'm shaking.

"Owen, it's gorgeous," I whisper.

"Nowhere near as gorgeous as you are, my love."

Owen takes a moment, staring at the ring before he slides it onto my ring finger.

"I love you so much, baby," he says passionately.

"I love you too," I say. "Now kiss me."

Owen chuckles as he leans down and gives me a searing kiss. Braxton again cries out.

"Already cockblocking, I see," Owen muses.

"Maybe he's hungry?" I ask.

At that moment, a nurse comes in.

"Oh good, you're awake! Want to try breastfeeding?" she asks.

"Uh, sure?"

"Baby, I'm gonna go update everyone, okay? I'll be back in a few minutes," Owen says, leaning down to kiss my forehead before doing the same to Braxton. Oh, my heart. Seeing him kiss our son's forehead just made my ovaries sing.

Owen leaves, and the nurse begins explaining the do's and do not's of breastfeeding. I'll be honest. I wasn't too sure about breastfeeding. It seemed incredibly daunting as I watched Emily tackle it. But possibly it was just overwhelming for her because she had two mouths to feed. I'm thankful I'm only handling one.

After a few moments of uncertainty, Braxton latches on perfectly and settles in. It's an odd sensation. It doesn't hurt exactly, but there's definite discomfort.

"Oh, he's latching perfectly. Try to remember this exactly as he is. How his lips are positioned. If you ever feel pain, it could be because his lips are not in the correct place," the nurse tells me.

"Is he supposed to have his mouth so wide open like that?" I ask quietly.

"Yep. They suck in the whole areola. That's exactly how he should be."

Huh. Chalk that up to what I didn't know. Guess I've never watched a woman breastfeed before. Emily always discreetly covered herself if she had to breastfeed one of the twins in front of us.

I stare down at Braxton, almost mystified that he's here and okay. That I'm okay. The last thing I really remember is drying my hair. Everything is blurry after that.

"Damn, woman. That's the most breathtaking thing I've ever seen," Owen says from the doorway. I look up to see him leaning against the frame with a look of adoration.

"Can you tell me what happened this morning? I remember drying my hair, and then it gets fuzzy," I ask, and the smile on his face drops. "Owen, are you okay?"

He shakes his head.

"Do we have to talk about it? I'd kinda like to block that from my memory, baby."

"I just don't understand how I got here. What happened?"

Owen sighs before crossing the room to sit beside me on the bed.

"They said you had something called placenta previa. It's where the placenta covers the cervix. They don't think either of us did anything to cause it. It just happens."

"How would you have caused anything?"

"I didn't know if the sex this morning did something. Or when you were crouching in the car yesterday. I was worried that it was my fault," he admits.

"Oh, Owen. I hate that you thought you were to blame. I remember reading about placenta previa, and yeah. It just happens. I'm really lucky you were right there and got me to the hospital so quickly. Many cases don't end that way, sweetie."

"I know that now. But all morning while you were in surgery, fuck. I felt so much guilt because I didn't know anything. The doctors didn't tell me about the placenta until they brought Braxton to me."

I'm quiet as I think about this morning. How excited we were to get induced and meet our son. I had no idea about the course of events that were already in place.

"Do you think we can get married quickly? I really want to be married to you as soon as possible," Owen whispers against my neck.

"Can we get married at the courthouse and then have a massive wedding where we have an insane party afterward once I lose the baby weight? I want to get a dress and look amazing," I tell him with a huge smile. He chuckles.

"You'd look amazing in a paper bag, but whatever you want, Red. Whatever makes you happy. I'll do anything," he says before leaning in to give me a quick kiss.

A nurse pops back in and reminds me to burp the baby. Crap, I completely forgot about that. I take a very unhappy Braxton off my boob and place him on my shoulder, lightly tapping his back.

"You can be rougher than that. Trust me. Light taps won't bring up the gas," the nurse says with a smile. I whack Braxton harder, and he lets out a massive belch. My eyes widen in disbelief.

"That's the Taylor side coming out, I think," I hear an amused voice say from the doorway. I look up to see Nathan, Emily, Monica, Liam, and Liv all standing there. I immediately check to make sure my boobs aren't hanging out, and with a relieved exhale, I give them a smile.

"Come meet my son," I gush.

The girls swarm the bed and coo over Braxton.

"I bet he's going to have your green eyes, Harper," Emily says.

"How can you tell?" I ask.

"I just really want him to have Owen's brown hair and your green eyes. I think that would be adorable," Emily tells me.

"He's definitely got your nose and Owen's mouth," Liv comments. I had already noticed that. I honestly don't care who he ends up looking like. I'm just so thankful he's here, and we're going to be okay.

"He actually is really cute," Monica blurts out before a light blush covers her beautiful olive-toned Italian skin.

"Actually?" I ask, amused.

"Well, some kids come outta there looking like they were stuck in a vacuum tube. Conehead and all that shit," Monica says sheepishly. Owen barks back a laugh as I reflexively take my left hand and hold Braxton's beautiful head.

"Hold *up*," Liv shouts, startling Braxton and making him cry. "Crap. Dang it, I'm sorry, little man. But, Braxton, can you help me understand the rock sitting on your mommy's ring finger?"

Owen chuckles as I beam.

"Owen asked me to marry him."

The girls quietly shriek, and the guys give Owen the standard man hug before everyone switches to congratulate us.

"So happy for you, sweetheart. You deserve the best," Liam whispers in my ear. I give him a smile. Liam and I are still awkward around each other after our tumultuous few months, but we're getting there.

"Can Uncle Nathan hold Braxton, please? I need a baby fix," Nathan says before winking at Emily.

"Goodness. Our girls just turned one. Can you relax on trying to knock me up already?" Emily says with her hand on her hip.

"Nope. Need more sunshine in my life, baby girl," he replies as he takes Braxton from my arms. He turns to Monica and motions for her to look closer at Braxton. Monica scrunches her nose in derision and shakes her head.

"I prefer to hold them when they're older or only when I'm forced to because I'm related to them," she says.

"You hold the twins all the time," Em says, and Monica shrugs.

"Sometimes you're related by blood. You and I are sisters by choice, my girl. Them babies are my nieces. Plus, they're girls. That one," she says as she points to Braxton, "has a pee-pee, and I don't want to be marked."

"Jesus, Mon, he's wearing a diaper," I say, rolling my eyes.

"And when he has a little better control over it, maybe I'll hold him then. Wait. They really never get good control of it, do they? Fuck. I don't know. Ask me again in a month. I'm not good when they're this breakable," she mutters.

Good lord. Whoever ends up with Monica is in for one hell of a ride.

Owen comes back and sits beside me as I attempt to shift into a more comfortable position.

"You okay?" he asks quietly.

"I'm uncomfortable, but I don't know what to do to find a better position," I admit. C-sections are no joke. My midsection throbs as I try to shift.

"Let me call the nurse and see if you're due for another dose of pain meds, baby," he says as he pushes the call button. A nurse immediately walks in. "Is she due for more pain meds? She's not feeling the best."

Gotta admit, I'm loving this caretaker side of Owen. He's been great about getting me food and whatnot throughout pregnancy, but this is a new side to him. I think Owen is relishing this new role, and I'm happy to let him do it. I didn't realize how much I craved someone who could and would take care of me.

"I love you," I whisper to him.

"I love you too, but what's that for?" he asks, looking over at me.

"For everything you do, baby. For everything," I tell him. His eyes soften as he gives me a quick kiss.

"Told you, baby, I'll do anything for you. And please, keep calling me baby. Does all kinds of things to my insides," he says with a cheeky grin. I giggle.

"Uh, I guess I'm boring. Braxton is asleep," Nathan says sheepishly.

"Well, that's good timing. Visiting hours are over, and it's time for momma and baby to rest," the nurse says as she returns with my medication.

Everyone says goodbye to Owen and me. I take the medication and settle in as Owen places Braxton in the hospital bassinet, then comes back to sit next to me. He wraps his arm around me and slowly strokes my arm and hair.

"How long do you think we'll need to stay here?" I mumble.

"They said a couple days."

"Gimme a kiss before you go," I murmur.

"Not leaving, baby. Sleeping here."

"Mmmkay."

"Love you, Harp."

"Love you too."

CHAPTER THIRTY-SEVEN

Owen

Harper and Braxton are both released from the hospital three days later. Braxton passed every possible test, including a CT Scan, to ensure he had no adverse effects from his birth. The hospital requested we complete an infant screening between four and six months to check on development at that time as a precaution. Everyone is thrilled with his progress so far. Even the doctors are surprised at his attentiveness and alertness. I have a feeling he's going to be an incredibly curious baby.

Harper's recovery has been slower going. Abdominal surgery is intense. She's in a lot of pain but handling it like the fucking rock star that she is. Upon arriving home, we find a balloon arch inside and big balloons spelling 'Braxton' by the fireplace. Nathan's mom, Kathryn, cooked up a storm this week and supplied us with five meals. Nathan and Liam dropped off DoorDash gift cards as well. We're set for food for the first couple of weeks at home.

I've given myself the next four weeks off to help Harper and settle into being a family of three. The only pressing matter I have is the case against Harper's landlord, Michael Jensen. It's looking like a slam dunk case. With the first few other tenants agreeing to sue, other tenants are coming out of the woodwork to be part of the case. I've got plaintiffs going back fifteen years. Jensen won't be able to lease anything for the rest of his life ... if he ever makes it out of jail.

The first week at home is rough. Not even gonna sugarcoat it. Harper is in pain, and Braxton has nights mixed with days. So we're just trying to survive with zero hours of sleep. But I look at them, and I'm overcome with emotion. I've never been this happy, this content, and this at peace with my life. I wouldn't change a fucking minute.

By the second week, we're starting to get our act together, and I decide to take action.

"Hey, Red?" I call out one morning as Braxton has his morning boob. That's what I've been referring to it as. The morning boob. The lunch boob. Midday boob. Harper stopped correcting me eventually. I refused to call it a feeding. It's a boob.

"Yeah?"

"Let's go get married."

Her head whips around to stare at me.

"Today?"

"Yeah, baby. Today. I may have already made an appointment for one o'clock. It's in between feedings and gives us enough time to shower. Liam and Liv are meeting us there as witnesses," I tell her tenderly, reaching over to cup her cheek. "I want to marry you today, Harp."

Her eyes fill with tears. "I want to marry you, too, Owen. So much."

I reach for her and gingerly pull her toward me to give her a deep kiss. My tongue slides into her mouth, gliding against hers perfectly. I break off the kiss and sigh.

"Let's get Brax down for his nap, and then I can help you shower," I tell her.

"No funny business in the shower, Owen Michael!" she warns. I chuckle. I know. That's a no-passing zone for four more weeks.

"Got it, babe. I can still help you, though. I'll wash your hair. I know you love it when I massage your scalp," I say.

"I do," she says wistfully.

"Then let's get going, future Mrs. Taylor," I tell her as I jump up and take Braxton from her, then give her my hand to help her get up. Every day her pain level diminishes, which I'm incredibly thankful for. There's nothing worse than watching your woman wince in pain, and there's nothing you can do about it. I'd take it all away if I could.

Braxton is already asleep, peacefully sucking on his pacifier as I place him in his bassinet. I meet Harper in the bathroom and leave the door open so we can hear if he cries. Harper carefully removes her clothing and checks her incision in the mirror. It's a vicious-looking mark by her bikini line. Dr. Thomason explained if he'd had more time, he would have made the incision a little more uniform. But his goal was to open Harper as quickly as possible to get Braxton out and stop the bleeding, so the incision is jagged and wonky. He had to staple it closed, and she had the staples removed two days ago. We both wish the healing process would hurry up.

I don't care about a scar. Harper is the most beautiful human on the planet, with or without that scar. It just shows she's a fucking warrior to live through what she did. I'm so proud of my girl. Still boggles my mind that I get to call her mine.

"You coming in?" she calls from the shower. I was so in my

head that I didn't even realize she was in the shower already. She's washing her body, obviously waiting on her hair for me to do it. Secretly, I love washing her hair. I don't know what it is about that, but it's my favorite thing to do. Her hair is my kryptonite.

I take the loofah from her and bend down to wash her legs. It's difficult for Harper to bend over still, and I'm more than happy to help out in any way I can. I place a bunch of kisses all over her abdomen. She sighs and runs her fingers through my hair. I silently stand back up and hug her so I can wash her back. We stand under the water for a moment, just soaking each other in.

"Let's get your hair done so we can get dressed," I say huskily. Harper looks down and sees I'm hard. "Don't worry about that. I'm naked against you. Of course, I'm going to get turned on, baby."

"We can't do much, but I can do this," she whispers as she takes a soapy hand and slides it over my cock. I hiss. It's been two weeks since we were last together. In the grand scheme of things, that's a blip on the radar. Chump change. I went almost a year between our sexual excursions, and I know I can go the whole six weeks. But if she *wants* to jack me off, I'm not gonna turn it down. "Kiss me, Owen."

I lean down and crush my lips against hers as Harper quickens the pace on my cock. The slippery soap makes her hand glide against me quickly, and I'm immediately on the cusp of an orgasm. I grab her other hand and grip her fingers tightly while my other hand clutches a fistful of her glorious hair. Right as I'm about to come, she stops altogether.

"What? What the fuck, woman?" I hiss. She giggles against my lips.

"Figured it was about time I showed you how it feels to be edged," she whispers back. Her grip slackens so much that she's almost not touching me. It's like her fingers are hovering as they slide along my flesh. It's painful and exhilarating all at the same time.

"Baby, please," I whimper. Yeah. I'm whining now.

"You wanna come, Owen?"

"Desperately."

"You come when I tell you that you can come."

"Fuck. Is that how I sound?" I ask painfully as I rest my forehead against hers. She gives me one hard stroke and then stops again.

"Yep."

"Jesus. Controlling bastard."

Harper giggles before setting a pattern of quick-quick-slow. My knees shake as she licks my lips and parts them with her tongue.

"Woman, if you don't finish me off, I'm liable to collapse right here, and we won't get to the damn courthouse," I mutter.

"Now you know how it feels."

Her pace quickens dramatically, and I feel the orgasm, but it's somehow holding off. What the fuck?

I open my eyes and look at Harper. She's smiling devilishly at me.

"Baby, please. Can I come?" I whisper. Boy, what a change of roles.

"Come, Owen," Harper demands, and I immediately let go. My body was waiting for her to let it happen, and damn, what a release. I lean back against the wall, panting.

"Holy fuck," I say breathlessly. "That's what it feels like after edging? Damn. We're adding that to the repertoire."

"We have a repertoire?" Harper asks as she chuckles.

"Yep. That's going in the rotation. Now turn around so I can rinse your hair. We gotta get dressed before Brax wakes up for the late morning boob."

"I'm fine with you referring to that in front of me, but can you quit calling it that in front of other people?"

"Nah."

"Meet me halfway here, Owen."

"Alright. I love a good bargaining. I'll refrain from calling a feeding 'the boob' in front of people we don't know, but I still get to call it that in front of Nate, Liam, and the girls," I tell her.

"Fine," she says, sighing.

THREE HOURS LATER, a well-nourished Braxton accompanies Harper and me to our marriage ceremony. Of course, I'm refusing to call it a wedding because that'll come whenever Harper is ready. But the marriage? Damn, I'm excited to start that right now.

Liv and Liam meet us at the courthouse. Liv is eight months pregnant and looks just as miserable as Harper did, but she gives Harper a huge smile and a gentle hug.

"I'm so happy for you, Harp. And honored to be here as your witness," she gushes, her eyes tearing up. "Damn these hormones!"

Liam looks sheepishly at me and shrugs. I nod in acknowledgment. Just went through it. I know exactly what he's going through. Fucking hormones at the end of pregnancy are brutal. Hell, they're brutal all the way through.

We head inside and find the judge's chambers, where the ceremony will be held. I'm wearing one of my favorite suits, and Harper is wearing a simple light peach maternity sheath dress. At only two weeks postpartum, she still has a tiny baby bump. In all my research during Harper's pregnancy, I found out that the body doesn't just 'bounce' back to normal after giving birth. Who knew? In any case, I tell her she's gorgeous every fucking opportunity I get. Because she is. Most breathtaking woman ever.

Within thirty minutes, Harper and I are married. We chose to do a civil ceremony with simple vows. We will write our own vows for our wedding down the line. A quick kiss and signing a document, and bam. Married.

"Well, Mrs. Taylor, where would you like to have lunch to celebrate?" I ask her as I bring her left hand up to my mouth, kissing her ringed finger first and then the front of her hand, and finally kissing the inside of her wrist. She sighs blissfully.

"Well, husband," I smile widely at that, "I would really love if we could get some Mexican to go so I can eat it sprawled out on the couch if that's okay with you. Sitting at a restaurant might be a little painful for me."

"Are you in pain now?" I ask, worried I've made her do too much today.

"No, just tired. Eating at home might be a better option. Just trying to be proactive so I don't accidentally overdo it."

"Do you want me to tell Liv and Liam to go home?"

"Oh, no! I want them to come and eat with us, too. Is that okay?"

"Sure, baby. Whatever you want. Wife," I add, and Harper gives me a tremendous smile.

"Love how that sounds," she whispers, giving me a quick kiss.

I let Liam know the plan, and he volunteers to grab the food. Harper and I head home with Braxton, and thirty minutes later, Liv and Liam bring the food.

I organize tv trays throughout the living room so we can all eat together and be comfortable. I think Olivia was secretly pleased Harper suggested we eat at home so both women could be comfortable. As soon as she walked in, she kicked off her sandals and collapsed into a recliner with a satisfied moan of relief.

I've taken the first bite of my food when Braxton starts to cry.

"I've got him, baby," I say quietly, immediately standing to grab the baby. I look at Harper and see a distressed look on her face. I realize her body isn't cooperating, and her boobs are telling her to feed the baby.

"Just give him to me, but sit here and shovel the queso into my mouth, please," Harper blurts, and everyone laughs. Harper looks confused. "I don't joke about queso, people."

"We know," I say, chuckling.

I don't even think anything of it as Harper pulls the maternity dress down enough to pop a boob out, and Braxton latches on. I hear a throat clearing as Liv looks at Harper and me.

"What?"

"You're in mixed company, baby. Liam isn't supposed to see the girls like this," I say deadpan.

"Oh, fuck. I'm sorry, Liam, I didn't even think," Harper stammers.

"It's okay, really. It's fine. This is your house. Your baby. I'm just gonna stare at the wall, so don't take it personally, okay?" he replies.

"Uh, okay?" Harper answers, chuckling quietly.

We continue eating in silence as I dutifully shovel food into my new wife's while Braxton noisily eats. I swear, this child, so far, isn't quiet about much. He's loud when he eats, shits, cries and sings. He will just bellow out a note for a minute straight, then take a breath and do it again. I had no idea newborns could be this loud. I've even caught him crying in his sleep like he's having a nightmare.

Liam is getting more and more uncomfortable. It's comical to watch the blush creep up his neck and ears, then onto his face. Liv and I have both been watching him, and before long, we're both giggling.

"What's so funny?" Liam asks Liv. He still refuses to look at Harper.

"You. You avoiding even looking in that direction," Liv says, giggling.

"Seriously, dude, what are you afraid is gonna happen? You think a laser beam will come out of her nipple and zap you or something?" I ask amusingly.

"Look, I don't know how to act right now, so I'm facing the fucking wall and ignoring whatever is going on over there because he sounds like he's chugging a damn beer, and I'm just waiting for the corresponding belch," Liam says. And on cue, Braxton belches. "See? Vindicated!"

"You can look now, Liam. I'm completely covered," Harper tells him. He hesitates, which makes me bark back laughter. "I swear! I'm not lying."

Liam turns to Harper and exhales. "Good. Sorry, Harp. Only boobs I want to see belong to my wife."

"And I appreciate that, truly. But you can look at my *face* instead of the wall next time, okay?"

"I'll try. Not making any promises, though."

"That's fair."

Liv and Liam leave not too soon after that. Liv wanted to take a nap, and Liam was, unfortunately, working a night shift that night. So, after settling Braxton down for his second nap of the day, Harper and I cuddled in our bed.

"Are you planning to hyphenate your name now? We've never talked about your name, only Braxton's," I ask softly.

"No, I'm not going to hyphenate," She answers. I stiffen rigidly next to Harper. "What's wrong?"

"You're not going to take my name?" I know I must look absolutely crestfallen and rejected, but I can't help it. I'm feeling devastated she doesn't want to take my name. Take our son's name. It's a moment before she sighs and lets out a light giggle.

"Oh, sweetie, no. I meant I'm just going to change it to Taylor. I don't want to be Williams-Taylor. I want to be a Taylor because my husband and son are both Taylors," she tells me tenderly. I let out a relieved exhale as my entire body relaxes.

"Thank you, baby. That means so much to me," I whisper before giving her a sweet kiss. I hold her against my side as close as possible without hurting her. She falls asleep with her head on my chest, and I know she's listening to my heart. My last thought before falling asleep is that my heart beats to the same rhythm as hers. Our hearts beat together in a beautiful symphony of love and laughter, and I cherish this little family we've created.

CHAPTER THIRTY-EIGHT

Owen

Three months later

It's my wedding day.

Well, my second wedding day. I guess the first one does technically count. But this is the day we get all dressed up and promise to love each other in front of our friends and family. To me, this is just as important as our first ceremony. Harper tells me I'm nuts. She says our first ceremony was the big one, and this is just a party. Well, it's going to one big-ass party where I shout from the rooftops that I actually managed to lock down the girl of my dreams.

I don't have a tremendous amount of money, but I do okay. I have a nice little nest egg socked away. I'm not Liam rich, but I can spend a lot of money on making this wedding whatever Harper desires. Ironically, she doesn't actually expect that much. She told me she just wanted a simple backyard wedding like what both Emily and Liv had. I had to put my foot down and say no. Owen Taylor doesn't do backyard weddings. Owen Taylor does glamour and ritzy weddings. Harper then told me she wouldn't marry me again if I continued to talk in the third person. Noted.

We're having the wedding at a country club in Garden of the Gods, a beautiful park in Colorado Springs with these massive red rock formations. The ceremony will be outside, overlooking the rocks, with Pikes Peak in the background. It gives Harper the outside wedding she wanted and the glamorous side I needed. Yeah, I know. I sound pretty high-maintenance. But I only plan on getting married once. Well, twice. Damn semantics.

It's the beginning of September, which can always be a dicey time for outdoor events. Typically it's still quite warm, but we've had a few freak winter snowstorms even this early. So I am relieved when the day comes, and it's supposed to be sunny and beautiful all day.

I stayed in a hotel last night, which was incredibly odd. Harper and Braxton were at home, but we wanted to at least do one bridal tradition correctly and not see each other until she walked down the aisle. I chose not to stay with Liam because their baby Archer is only about seven weeks old. Nathan has his hands full at his house, so I didn't want to intrude on their family either. Staying at a hotel just made the most sense. But, man, I missed my wife and son something fierce.

By lunchtime, I'm going bonkers. I begged Liam to go and get Braxton so I could at least spend some time with him. Not even twenty-four hours since I've seen him, and I'm losing my mind. I don't know how people choose to not see their kids.

"Alright, man, here you go. Now you can calm down a

little bit," Liam says jokingly as he plops a smiling Braxton into my lap.

"There's my main man! I missed you," I gush as I lean in and take a big inhale of his infant awesomeness. The damn detergent Harper uses on Braxton's clothes, plus the lotion she puts on him makes him a drug. I need a hit. Gimme the baby, so I can sit here and sniff him all day.

"God, don't they smell the best?" Liam sighs. I nod in acknowledgment.

"Do you want a sniff?" I ask, holding out Braxton.

"Nah, man, I'm fine," Liam says, chuckling, but then looks over at me again. "Fuck it. Yes. Gimme the kid."

He takes Braxton from me and buries his nose in Braxton's neck to inhale sharply. Braxton just giggles, which is the most precious sound in the world.

"Fuck, this is addictive," Liam mutters as he goes in for another sniff.

"I know," I respond, itching to grab my son back to resume sniffing.

"Are you two passing a baby around to smell him?" Emily asks from behind us.

"Yes," we both respond. Liam leans halfway so I can smell Braxton, too. Emily sighs loudly.

"Men."

"What do you need, Em?" I ask as Braxton grabs my face with his hands, and Liam reluctantly lets go of him. I pepper kisses along his cheeks and rub my scruffy beard against his face. I get tons of giggles in response.

"Harper wanted me to give this to you." She hands me a package and a card.

"Oh, wait. I have something for her. Can you take it back?" I ask, and Emily nods. As she's about to leave, she turns to me.

"I forgot to tell you. Harp said to open the gift first and then read the letter." She gives me a wink before leaving.

"Okay, that's odd, but whatever," I mumble. I hand Braxton to Liam and then open the gift. Inside I find the watch I'd been ogling for months. It has a marble clock face and a see-through case back and automatic movement, meaning it continues to work as long as I continue to move. The band is made of maple wood and antique silver stainless steel. I'm shocked because I never once mentioned to her, let alone anyone, that I was thinking about buying this watch. I'm also shocked because I know how much this cost.

As I turn the watch over so I can see the see-through case back, which allows me to see the interior of the watch and how it works, I see three sets of coordinates etched into the metal. I have absolutely no idea what they are. They are all very similar in numbers. I open Harper's note to see if she's explained the coordinates.

Hello, my husband. I'm sure you're already confused, trying to figure out what this gift means and what the coordinates stand for. First of all, I know you've never mentioned this watch. But you aren't very good at hiding your perusal of the company website. I knew which one you wanted and ordered it a month ago. And the coordinates? They're for the three places that mean the most to me. The first set of coordinates is for this exact location, where we are celebrating our love in front of our chosen family. The second set of coordinates is where you told me you were in love with me for the first time: at your house. And the third set, and quite possibly the most important set, is the coordinates for where we made our son: my apartment. I'm so incredibly thankful for you, my love. You've given me everything my heart desires, and I can't wait to spend the rest of my life cherishing you. Love always, your wife.

"Fucking hell, that's deep," Liam says over my shoulder. I jolt, as I didn't even know he was behind me. "What?"

"Fuck, man, warn a guy," I mutter as my heart rate lowers back to normal. Jesus. Who knew Harper was such a romantic? Well, I did. She's fucking perfect. I take off my current watch and excitedly put my new watch on. It's going to go perfectly with my suit for today. Harper doesn't know it, but I got Braxton a matching suit. We will be one hell of a dapper duo when she walks down the aisle.

I feel kinda bad, though. The gift I got Harper is nowhere near as romantic as this. I hope she likes it. I got her a matching emerald necklace to go with her engagement ring and the earrings I gave her months ago. The letter I wrote her is just as sentimental, though.

"Hey, Owen? Umm, we need you. Bring Braxton," Liv says from the doorway. She's holding Archer, but she has a worried look on her face.

"Is everything okay? Did something happen?"

"Well, no. Maybe. I don't know. Jack said something to Harper, and Harper kinda got hysterical. I don't even know what Jack said. But either you or the baby needs to settle her down before she hyperventilates," Liv explains. I take off jogging to the room where Harper is getting ready. Fuck this. I'm not letting my wife become hysterical and not helping out.

I burst into the room and find her sitting in a chair with her head between her knees, breathing into a bag. Monica stands at the window guzzling a glass of champagne, and Kathryn hovers over Em and Harper while wringing her hands. I don't even have time to take in how fucking beautiful and exquisite she looks in her wedding dress. I just want to get to her and help soothe her.

"Harp, it's okay, just tell us what Jack said," Emily says soothingly as Harper tries to take deep breaths.

"Red."

Harper's head pops up when she hears me call to her, and she launches herself at me. I catch her as she burrows into me.

"Woman, what's wrong?" I say quietly into her ear.

"Jack said I'm pregnant, and I'm freaking the fuck out!" she replies loudly enough that both Liv and Em gasp. "I can't be pregnant, right? I thought breastfeeding was supposed to stop you from getting pregnant! But he's always right! He knows before any of us do ..."

I hear Monica straight cackling from the window, and I shoot her a death glare. She attempts to hold in her giggles as she mutters something that sounds like "fucking crazy people and their ability to procreate."

My heart rate has eclipsed Liam scaring me, and has gone straight into tachycardia. Holy shit. Another baby? Woah.

"Did he, um," I stammer, "Did he say what it was?"

Please be another boy. Please. I love Harper, but I can only handle one of her. A mini-Harper running around ... Jesus. Pray for everyone.

"He said it's a boy," she murmurs against my neck, and I exhale in relief.

"Thank fuck," I mutter. Harper's head pops up.

"What?" she asks, confused.

"I can handle another boy. I can't do another Harper, baby. You're a lot," I confess.

"You're not … upset?" she asks incredulously.

"No. Why would I be? I'd love to have another baby with you. A little time between kids would have been nice, but it is what it is. Do you want to get a test to confirm before we start talking hypotheticals?"

"Here!" Emily shouts, running forward with her handbag. She shoves a test in my hand.

"Why do you have a test with you?" Harper asks, her eyes narrowing.

"Nathan and I aren't exactly trying for a baby, but we aren't exactly *not* trying for one either. So I always have a test with me. Just in case," she says. "And this is a prime example of 'in case,' I think."

"Go pee on the stick, Red. Let's get this settled so we can celebrate with our family," I tell her, nudging her toward the suite bathroom.

One minute later, she returns and sets the test on the table.

"He could be wrong, yeah? I mean, he's been right all this time, but the dang kid isn't even double digits yet. How clairvoyant can you be at nine years old?" Harper muses.

"Clairvoyant enough to predict this, considering the test just showed 'pregnant' after a minute," Emily says as she looks at the test.

"What?" Harper shrieks.

"You're pregnant, Harp."

Harper turns to me as her eyes fill with tears.

"We didn't plan this," she mumbles.

"We didn't plan Braxton, either, baby. I don't care what you think we should plan. I'm happy as fuck for this. Fuck, woman, I love you so goddamn much," I say as I wrap my arms around her and kiss her deeply.

"Hey hey hey! Save that for when you're pronounced married!" Emily screeches.

"We're already married. It's a damn technicality. I'm

kissing my pregnant wife, so deal with it," I tell Emily before kissing Harper again. She hums into my mouth happily.

"I love you too, husband," Harper finally says when I break off the kiss. "Now go back to your side of the resort so we can get ready. Oh, I need Braxton. It's dinner boob time."

Yep. She started calling it boob time, too.

We're fucking perfect for each other.

EPILOGUE

Harper

Two years later

"Ha-ee Bird Day, Daddy!" Braxton whispers as we take Owen breakfast in bed. It's Owen's forty-second birthday. Besides a few grey whiskers that sneak into his scruff when he foregoes shaving and the smattering of grey hairs on his head he's had since we first slept together, he doesn't look a day over thirty-five. He's still the beautiful man I fell in love with.

"Hey, Brax! Thank you. What did you make?" Owen says groggily as he scoots up to put his back against the bed headboard. Owen has been working a ton on a really awful child custody and divorce case. I've met the mom, and she's an angel. Three kids under the age of five and the husband was caught stepping out on her with his secretary. My heart just breaks for her.

"Pa-cakes, daddy," Braxton says happily. My little man is the most cheerful two-year-old I've ever met. His favorite thing to do is just hang with Owen. His second favorite thing to do is play with Archer, Liv and Liam's son. They are two peas in a pod.

"And what about Ashton? Did he help?" Owen gives me a wink.

"Oh, he helped. Pretty sure he licked the batter when he stuck his entire face in the bowl," I tell him dryly. Our one-year-old, Ashton, is an absolute terror. He was crawling at six months and walking by ten months. He already mastered how to climb out of his crib, and I've had to add child locks to the upper cabinets in our kitchen because the little daredevil scales the counters to reach stuff. I want to wrap him in bubble wrap to protect him. Every day that goes by without him breaking a bone, I consider a blessing.

While Braxton is the spitting image of Owen, with dark brown hair and chocolate brown eyes, Ashton is my mirror image. His hair is a deeper auburn color, but he has my green eyes. Our personalities also match. Ashton and I are quick to temper, whereas Braxton and Owen are calmer and more likely to logically rationalize something.

I was incredibly lucky in my second pregnancy. It very closely mirrored that of my pregnancy with Braxton. I hardly had any morning sickness in the first trimester, but I was a hormonal nightmare the entire time. I don't know how Owen put up with me. Dr. Thomason monitored me incredibly closely throughout. I had tons of extra ultrasounds to check the location of the placenta to ensure I didn't have a repeat of the placenta previa, and then a scheduled c-section at thirty-nine weeks. Ashton came out screaming and hasn't stopped since. We thought Braxton was loud, but we didn't really know what loud was. Ashton enjoys using his lungs. A lot.

"Oh, that's, umm, really nice," Owen says as Ashton clambers onto the bed and manages to nail Owen right in the groin. He groans and clutches himself while Ashton looks on mischievously as if he knows what he is doing. Probably did. Again I say, he's a fucking terror. I absolutely love him. He's wonderful. But still, he's a terror.

I walk to the side of the bed and lean down to kiss my husband. "Happy birthday, baby," I whisper against his lips, and I feel him smile. He loves it when I call him baby. This strong man, this dominant alpha, loves it when I call him a somewhat feminine pet name.

"Where's my present, Mrs. Taylor?" he asks quietly as his right-hand slides up the back of my leg until he can grab my ass. "Oh, there it is!"

"Ha ha," I say. Owen's all about the ass these days. He'd love to take me there. I know Liv loves it. Em won't tell us, but I think Nathan has gotten her to do it as well. Maybe someday for me, but it's not today. Right now, that's a no-fly zone. Exit only.

"I'm teasing. You know that, right?" Owen looks concerned like I'm angry with him for grabbing my butt.

"You can grab all you want, Owen. Nothing more than that back there right now, though," I caution him. He gives me a wicked grin.

"You said 'right now,' so that means there's a chance," he leers.

I roll my eyes.

"Not today."

"I know, baby. It's fun to tease you."

"I promise we can do other fun stuff after the boys go to bed."

"Naptime?"

"Maybe."

"Score."

I laugh as he makes a touchdown motion.

Never a dull day in the Taylor household, and I wouldn't change a thing.

———

MUCH TO HIS CHAGRIN, nap time passed with no fun stuff. Braxton fell asleep, but Ashton wouldn't. Then Ashton fell asleep right as Brax woke up. Just a typical day.

We decided to divide and conquer after dinner. After the boys had a joint bath, we each took a kid and did story time in their respective rooms. I have more success getting Ashton to sleep, so we figured that was a good place for me to go. After his short nap today, Ashton fell asleep with relative ease, and I was in our bedroom before Owen got Braxton to sleep.

I had barely removed my shirt before Owen's arms came around me and gripped my boobs. Two pregnancies in quick succession made them pretty huge, but I could do without the sagging afterward. Gravity is a bitch. Owen never complains, though. He lavishes attention on them as much as the first time we were together so many years ago.

"How much time do you think we have before one of them ends up in here?" Owen whispers as he finds my nipples and pinches them through my shirt. I whimper softly.

"An hour, maybe? I don't know. Lock the damn door, so we at least know they're trying to get in," I order.

"Already done. I put a child lock on the outside so they can't even open the door if they figure out the lock," he replies deviously.

"Ooooh, good thinking!" I say with a smile. We actually high-five. We are that couple now.

"On the bed, baby. It's been a while since I've had that sweet pussy," he tells me.

"What, like two days?" I ask, rolling my eyes as I get onto

the bed. I'm not complaining. Owen loves to eat me out, and I love him to do it. He'd do it for hours at a time if I let him.

"Hey, that's an eternity in Owen hours."

"Oh, for the love. I swear, Owen, if you go back to talking in the third person again, I'm closing these thighs off. You won't be tasting this sweet pussy for a while," I warn. He has the audacity to laugh.

"You can't resist Owen. Or Owen's tongue. Don't be acting like you don't enjoy yourself, Red. Let Owen do what Owen wants to do," he whispers as he situates himself between my legs and blows against my core. His tongue snakes out to lightly touch my clit, making me moan.

"Just shut up and make me come," I demand, and he laughs against me. The vibration of his laugh is felt all the way into my channel, and I clench in response.

"Liked that, did ya?" he says cheekily as he slides one finger inside. My walls immediately clamp down on him. "Ahh. My girl did like it."

"Fucking hell, Owen, just get with it before we get interrupted by our little hellions!" I say harshly. I'm too turned on to deal with edging tonight. Owen's been basically edging me all day. I think it's one of his favorite things to do. A full day of foreplay, essentially.

Owen licks me from bottom to top, circles my clit, and then begins the dance again. I groan in frustration.

"Patience, baby," he mumbles against me.

"If you want me to suck you off, you better make me come right fucking now!" I snarl.

"God, I love when you get all scrappy like this, woman," he says, and I can hear the grin in his voice. Before I can respond, he latches onto my clit and sucks hard as his tongue flicks repetitively. An orgasm crashes over me with no warning. As I'm shaking through the aftershocks, Owen jams three fingers inside and curls his fingers just right to hit my G-spot, making me come again. Then, before I can even realize what's happening, he wets another finger and slips it past my forbidden ridge of muscle, rotating it at the same pace as the fingers in my pussy. Another harsh suck on my clit, and I have the most powerful orgasm of my life.

"What the fuck was that?" I pant breathlessly as Owen removes himself from me and goes to wash his hands.

"Just a sneak preview of what could happen if you let me do what I want to do," he teases from the bathroom.

"Not tonight," I mutter. After that orgasm and that amazing onslaught of sensation and pleasure, I'm half tempted to let him. But one of the reasons Owen and I work is the give-and-take of our relationship. I know I'll eventually give in. He knows it, too. But this battle of wills is as important to us as our love for one another. We'll get to the same conclusion when it's exactly the right time for us. And I wouldn't change that for anything. But for the first time, I'm actually looking forward to giving that last piece of myself to Owen.

"I know, baby," he says as he returns to the bedroom and climbs onto the bed, settling himself on top of me. The tip of his cock rests against my trembling pussy, and I shudder involuntarily at the contact.

"Have you ever ..." I trail off. For some reason, I just can't verbally say the word 'anal.' It's so gross to me. But now that he's shown me that there are good sensations back there, I'm intrigued.

"Done anal? No. I haven't, Red. I'd like to do it with you. But it's not expected. Our sex life is amazing, so I don't feel like I'm missing out on anything," Owen tells me honestly. I smile up at him. He's so fucking refreshing. He's completely honest with anything I ask him. He doesn't sugarcoat anything. In some ways, that can be brutal. But I know he's never trying to hurt me with what he says.

"Okay, I'll think about it," I tell him. His eyes widen.

"Seriously?"

"Yeah. Just not tonight. I think I need to be mentally prepared for that."

"I probably do, too. I mentally prepared for doing what I did, so if you had said I could fully take your ass tonight, I don't know what I would do," Owen says, chuckling. He leans down and kisses me, and I wrap my arms around his neck to hold him to me. He turns his head, his lips slanting over mine in a deep and intense kiss.

My hips automatically begin to push upward as if my pussy is seeking him out, knowing it'll give me the friction I need. I just came three fucking times, and I'm craving more. Owen makes me insatiable.

"Owen, please," I whimper. He laughs lightly into my mouth as he continues kissing me. I spread my legs wider, wrap them around his waist, and then use my feet to push down while my hips thrust upward. He's inside me immediately.

"Damn, woman, couldn't let me do it myself?" he chuckles as he begins to thrust.

"Every now and again, I like to control things," I respond.

"Don't I fucking know it."

Owen's right-hand grips my hair, and his left forearm rests beside my head as he raises himself slightly so he can peer down at me.

"Need to see you come again, baby. Need to see that glorious rush of blush cover your entire body as you find your pleasure. Gonna feel you clamp down on me and make me come, aren't you? God, you're so fucking perfect, Red. So fucking perfect," Owen mutters. I'm not even sure he knows he's talking out loud.

His thrusts become more erratic as he nears his orgasm, and he thrusts into me harder. As I come, I scream, but Owen covers my mouth with his to drown out the noise. He swallows every sound I make, so we don't wake our boys. His subsequent orgasm is roared into my mouth. He collapses on top of me as we both try to regain our breath.

"How does it always seem to get better?" I wonder aloud.

"I don't know, baby. But it sure as fuck does seem to get better every time," Owen replies. He slides off me and pulls me, so I'm against his side. Grabbing my hand, Owen brings it to his mouth and kisses the palm and then my wrist before finally kissing my ring finger. "I love you, Harper."

"I love you too, Owen."

Five years ago, I never could have imagined this would be my life. How an innocent crush on Owen would end up with my happily ever after and two beautiful boys who are as different as night and day. I'm one lucky bitch, that's for damn sure.

THE END

READY FOR MORE IN the Forever Series? Check out Monica's preview on the next page!

FOREVER MINE SNEAK PEEK

Monica

─ ✧ ─

Present Day

The only thing I can think right now is that if my grandmother could see me at this point in my life, she'd be so fucking disappointed. Never in a million years would she think that I'd end up here. I'm her little spitfire. The one who never lets anyone get the best of her.

Yet, here I am, cowering in the back of a hole-in-the-wall bar in Colorado Springs because my occasional fuck buddy decided to beat the crap out of me.

I don't even know how I got here. How this happened. Did I ignore all the signs? Never thought I'd be someone who would end up in this situation.

"This is all your fucking fault, Monica. All your fucking fault," Marcus mutters.

I was never serious about Marcus. For a few months, I thought maybe I could make it work with him. That I could ignore the red flags and just enjoy the sex. But honestly, the fact that none of my friends liked him should have been a *huge* red flag. They made it blatantly clear any time Marcus came to a social event. Em not so discreetly told me I shouldn't bring him to her house anymore, that she didn't trust him around her kids.

And while I completely agree with her on many things, I took that comment personally. To me, it meant she didn't trust my judgment. Which, in hindsight, is absolutely fucking correct. I evidently can't trust my own damn judgment. If I could, I wouldn't be here right now. I'd be anywhere else.

"Marcus, I don't know what I did to make you so angry," I stammer. I don't even see his hand as it whips across my face. I only feel the excruciating sting against my cheek and lips as I cry out in agony.

"Of course you don't, you fucking stupid bitch! Jesus! I had you exactly where I wanted you, Monica. It was fucking perfect, and you had to go fuck it all up and go after that other guy," Marcus snarls.

I'm confused.

There's no other guy.

Other than Marcus, I haven't gotten laid since I left Oklahoma.

"There's no other guy, I swear," I whimper. My voice doesn't even sound like my own. I've never been so scared.

Marcus stands over me, leering at me with disgust in his eyes.

"Your asshole boss, Mon. I know you're fucking him," he growls. My eyes widen in shock.

"The hell I am!" I shout.

"Oh, come on. All the late working hours? The business

trips to real estate conferences? That shit doesn't even exist. I'm not that fucking stupid," Marcus says, rolling his eyes.

"I swear to you, Marcus. I'm not sleeping with my boss," I tell him clearly.

"I can also confirm she is not sleeping with me, Marcus. Not for lack of hoping on my part, though," a deep voice announces from the doorway. I cringe. It's him. My boss.

Gabriel Campos.

The most beautiful man in the history of the world.

Also, my boss. And also an asshole.

Well, maybe not an asshole. He's been perfectly nice to me and respected my wishes ... most of the time.

But God, he's so damn pretty. A foot taller than me with dark blonde hair and a smattering of grey hairs throughout. Crystal clear blue eyes that unnerve me every time his studious gaze lands on me. He has a habit of studying me with his head cocked slightly to the side as if he's trying to read my mind and learn all my secrets.

"So, Marcus. You gonna explain why my employee looks like she's had her face smashed in a bunch of times?" Gabriel asks wryly from the door as he calmly crosses his arms across his chest and stares unblinking at Marcus.

"She needs to learn that I'm in charge," Marcus explains. "I've got this under control, man. You need to leave. She's mine."

"Ahh. That's an interesting explanation. Considering I know she's not your woman, as I watched her block your number when you wouldn't stop calling her," Gabriel says as he cocks his head to the side and smirks at Marcus.

"It was just a fight. We'll be fine. Will you excuse us, please?" Marcus says before turning his back on Gabriel and facing me. His eyes are wild as he stares at me, and I know he's going to make me pay for Gabriel turning up here.

I don't even see Gabriel move. He's like a fucking stealth

ninja. One minute he's at the door, and the next minute he's got Marcus pinned up against the wall.

"See, that's the thing. You won't be fine. Because Monica is my responsibility. And I'll be damned if your bonehead ass is gonna touch her beautiful skin once more. Ya feel me, *Piço*?" Gabriel asks.

"What the fuck does that mean?" Marcus stutters.

"It means dick, jackass," Gabriel mutters as he twists Marcus's arm hard. Gabriel turns to look at me, his eyes burning with intensity. "You alright, *anjinho*?"

I nod, unable to speak. I wonder what *anjinho* means. I know Gabriel's parents emigrated from Brazil, and he usually calls me *querida*, so I assume he's calling me something. I'm just not sure if it's good or bad.

Two police walk into the back room and take Marcus from Gabriel. He immediately comes to me, crouching so he's at eye level. He gingerly reaches to gently pull my hair away from my face and sighs.

"Oh, *querida*. Let's get you to the hospital," Gabriel says quietly. I attempt to stand, but he grabs me and slides his arms under my legs, picking me up and holding me against his chest. "She needs medical attention. Can we go to the police station tomorrow?"

"We'll have an officer accompany you to the hospital, ma'am, so you can give your statement while it's still fresh in your mind," the officer tells us. I nod silently. My face is throbbing, and I'm pretty sure I sprained my wrist when I landed on the ground after the first hit.

Gabriel takes me directly to his car and carefully deposits me in the passenger seat before putting my seatbelt on. I love his car. It's a Mercedes sedan with every damn bell and whistle imaginable. But what I love most is it smells like Gabriel. Woodsy with leather and amber. It's a scent I'll never be able to think of without thinking of Gabriel now. It's a smell that permeates my dreams.

I expect Gabriel to take me to the hospital, but he doesn't start the engine once he's in the car.

"What the fuck were you thinking," he states quietly.

"What do you mean?" I stammer. He turns to me, and I can see the anger simmering in his gaze.

"I heard you tell your friend that he had gotten more angry. More volatile. Why would you agree to meet him? Why would you put yourself in that situation? If I hadn't seen your car at this bar ..." he trails off and wipes a hand across his face in frustration.

"How did you know it was my car?" I whisper.

"I know everything about you, *anjinho*," he responds.

"What does that mean?"

He sighs, struggling with his response.

"It means my angel."

I inhale quickly as I stare at Gabriel. He's been my boss for over six months. I never believed his words that he wanted more with me. I always knew ... or thought ... that it was just a fun game. That he didn't feel anything and knew he wouldn't cross that line because of our working relationship. Granted, we've had a few moments together. Ones that live in my mind rent-free. Times where I almost let my attraction to him overcome the realistic part of my brain that reminds me I'm not cut out for relationships. Happily ever after isn't meant for broken girls like me.

Gabriel is the managing and designated broker at my relatively small real estate firm. I'm a real estate agent. He's in charge of all the day-to-day administrative tasks for our office and oversees all the agents. With only fifteen agents on staff, Gabriel takes a more hands-on approach to interacting with the realtors. Up until recently, I assumed he joked around with all the agents and flirted with all the women.

I just never thought he'd be interested in me. I'm a decade younger than him. Gabriel is around forty-five. I just never thought his antics had any meaning. I figured he just found me amusing and wanted to see how far he could push me. I knew he was attracted to me, but I figured I was a conquest he was trying to conquer. The thrill of the chase.

"Let's get you to the hospital, *anjinho*," he says quietly.

I don't respond. My mind is moving a million miles per minute. Is he joking? Why is he calling me that? How did he find me tonight? Should I be worried? Ugh. My head is pounding now. I close my eyes as the car headlights approaching us are grating on my senses.

"Gonna rest my eyes," I mumble.

"Stay awake, okay? You might have a concussion if he hit you hard enough. So you need to stay awake, Monica," Gabriel orders.

"Okay, daddy," I mutter.

I hear his intake of breath.

"*Puta merda*," Gabriel says under his breath.

"What does that mean?"

"It means holy shit."

"Why did you say that?" I ask.

"Because I liked it, *anjinho*."

"You liked me calling you daddy?"

"Yes."

Oh. *Puta merda* indeed.

ACKNOWLEDGMENTS

I'm going to clue you in to a little known fact about me. I actually *love* surprise pregnancy books. I know I'm definitely in the minority here, but I find them especially amazing when a book chronicles the entire pregnancy, not just flash-forwarding to the birth or afterward. It gave me an opportunity to re-live how I felt during my two pregnancies, as well as both emergency c-sections I required. In fact, Harper's story is somewhat close to my own, as I suffered a uterine rupture after twenty-five hours of labor at forty-one weeks pregnant. My son and I both almost died. Eight years later, and I'm able to write a book about it. The epilogue detail of Ashton scaling the counters to open upper cabinets? Yeah. That detail is courtesy of my eight-year-old son.

Forever Ours is my favorite of the three in this series so far. The banter, the chemistry, and the storyline were just so perfect to me (patting myself on the back). I knew from the moment I wrote both their characters in the first book that they'd have a tumultuous relationship with arguments and hate sex. I was unprepared for where their arguments would lead, though. I can't even tell you how many times I laughed out loud at the retorts between the two of them, especially at the OB office when Harper asked the doctor to "smoke the kid out".

To my amazing beta and arc readers, thank you so much for listening to me, giving me feedback, and sending me so many TikTok and Instagram thirst traps that I have ideas for about twenty new stories. To all the wonderful people I've met on social media, as well as great new author friends, I'm so appreciative of all of you. This is a dream come true, and I'm so thankful.

Monica is coming soon! Who's excited to read about her and Daddy Gabriel?

ABOUT THE AUTHOR

Jennifer was born and raised in Ohio but has lived all across the country and even across the pond in England. Currently calling Colorado home, Jennifer spends most of her free time within her zoo: two kids, two dogs, and two cats...all of which are male! When not containing the chaos, Jen can be found lounging on her covered porch devouring books on her Kindle.

ALSO BY JENNIFER J WILLIAMS

Forever Sunshine

Forever Yours

Forever Ours

Forever Mine

Printed in Great Britain
by Amazon